D1130574

# IMPRESSIONS OF AFRICA

# IMPRESSIONS
# OF AFRICA

*a novel*

By RAYMOND ROUSSEL

Translated by
Lindy Foord and Rayner Heppenstall

UNIVERSITY OF CALIFORNIA PRESS
Berkeley and Los Angeles - 1967

University of California Press
Berkeley and Los Angeles, California

Originally published as *Impressions d'Afrique* by
Alphonse Lemerie, Paris 1910 (4th impression
1932) Re-issued by Jean-Jacques Pauvert, 1963;
© Jean-Jacques Pauvert
© This translation, Rayner Heppenstall, 1966

Library of Congress Catalog Card Number: 67-13139

Printed in Great Britain

# I

A T about four o'clock on that 25th June, everything appeared to be ready for the coronation of Talu VII, Emperor of Ponukele and King of Drelshkaf.

Although the sun was low in the sky, the heat was still overpowering in that part of Africa, near the equator, and the thundery atmosphere, untempered by the slightest breeze, weighed oppressively on every one of us.

Before me lay the vast expanse of Trophies Square, situated in the very heart of Ejur, a noble capital consisting of countless dwellings and washed by the Atlantic Ocean, whose distant roar I could hear away to the left.

The perfect square formed by the esplanade was outlined, on each side, by a row of sycamores planted some hundred years earlier. Thrust deep into the bark of each trunk were weapons, on which hung severed heads, tinsel and trappings of every kind, piled up there by Talu VII or his ancestors, returning from their many victorious campaigns.

On my right, in front of the trees, at a point in the middle of the row, stood a kind of red theatre, like a gigantic Punch-and-Judy show, whose façade bore the words *The Incomparables Club* arranged in three lines of silver lettering in a glittering surround of broad golden rays, spreading in every direction like those around a sun.

On the stage at present a table and chair were to be seen, apparently intended for a lecturer. Several unframed portraits

5

were pinned to the backcloth and underneath was an explanatory label, worded thus: *Electors of Brandenburg.*

Nearer to me, in line with the red theatre, was a broad wooden pedestal on which stood Naïr, a young negro, barely twenty years old, bent over the absorbing task to which he applied himself. To the right of him were two stakes, each fixed to one corner of the platform and joined by a long slack string which sagged under the weight of three objects, hanging in a row and clearly displayed like lottery prizes. The first of these objects was nothing more nor less than a bowler hat with the French word ' PINCÉE ' printed in white capitals on its black crown; the next one was a dark grey suede glove with the palm turned outwards and a large 'C' lightly marked on it with chalk; lastly there dangled from the string a fine sheet of parchment, covered with strange hieroglyphs and bearing as a heading a rather crude drawing of five figures, deliberately made to look absurd by their general posture and exaggerated features.

Naïr was a prisoner on his pedestal, his right foot held in a mesh of thick cords which formed an effective noose, firmly anchored to the solid platform; like a living statue he performed slow, regular motions, rapidly murmuring strings of words he had learnt by heart. All his attention was concentrated on a fragile pyramid, constructed from three sheets of bark, fastened together, which rested on a specially shaped stand in front of him; the base, which was turned towards him and tilted perceptibly, served as a loom; within his reach, on an extension to the stand, lay a supply of fruit husks, coated with a greyish vegetable substance, similar in appearance to the cocoons of larvae on the point of hatching into chrysalises. Taking a fragment of one of these delicate shells between two fingers, the young man slowly drew his hand towards him, to create an elastic thread, similar to the gossamer which drapes itself about the woods in spring. With these invisible filaments he wove a fabric, as fine and intricate as the work of a fairy, for his hands moved with unrivalled dexterity, crossing, knotting, intertwining the dream-like threads a thousand different ways to merge in a graceful design. The phrases he recited to himself helped to regulate his precise delicate movements; the slightest mistake would have hopelessly endangered the whole work and, without the automatic guidance of certain formulae, memorised word for word, Naïr could never have accomplished his task.

Below him, to the right, other pyramids stood near the edge of the pedestal, with their apices pointing backwards so that it was possible to appreciate the full effect of the completed work; the base, placed upright and clearly visible, was delicately indicated by an almost non-existent tissue, finer than a spider's web. At the back of each pyramid a red flower, attached by the stem, drew the attention irresistibly beyond the scarcely perceptible veil of the fairy fabric.

Not far from the stage of the Incomparables, to the right of the actor, two posts, four or five feet apart, supported an apparatus in motion; from the nearer of the two jutted a pivot, around which a strip of yellowish parchment was tightly wound; nailed firmly to the further post to form a platform, a small square board served as a base for a vertical cylinder, which was being turned slowly by a clockwork motor.

The yellowish band, unfurling in a single coil which stretched, unbroken, across the space between, wrapped itself round the cylinder, so that as it rotated on its axis, it drew the parchment continuously towards itself and away from the distant pivot, which was thereby forced to participate in the gyratory motion.

A succession of crude drawings of groups of savage warriors, in various poses, followed each other across the parchment: one column appeared to run at break-neck speed in pursuit of a retreating enemy; another lay in ambush, behind a bank, patiently awaiting the right moment to appear; here, two armies, equal in number, fought fiercely man to man; there, fresh troops charged forward with great strides to fling themselves into the distant fray. As the reel continued to unwind, countless new and amazing strategies appeared, thanks to the infinite multiplicity of the effects obtained.

Opposite me, at the other end of the esplanade, extended a sort of altar, with several steps leading up to it, covered with a soft carpet; a coat of white paint, veined with bluish lines, gave the whole structure from a distance the appearance of marble.

On the sacred table, which consisted of a long board, fitted half-way up the erection and hidden under a white cloth, could be seen a rectangle of parchment, dotted with hieroglyphics, standing next to a massive cruet, filled with oil. Beside it, a larger sheet bore this title in careful gothic script: *Reigning House of Ponukele-Drelshkaf*; beneath the heading a round portrait, a delicately coloured miniature, represented two Spanish girls of thirteen or fourteen, wearing on their heads the national *mantilla*—twin sisters, to judge by the close resemblance between their faces; at first glance, the picture seemed to be an integral part of the document; but closer scrutiny revealed a narrow strip of transparent muslin which, adhering both to the periphery of the painted disc and

8

to the surface of the stiff vellum, joined as perfectly as possible the two objects, which were in fact independent of each other; on the left hand side of the double effigy, the name 'SUAN' was written in widely spaced capitals; underneath, the paper was covered with a genealogical table comprised of two distinct branches, issuing in parallel descent from the two beautiful Spaniards who formed the top of the tree; one branch ended in the word *Extinction*, in letters almost as prominent as those of the heading and clearly meant for brutal effect; the other, on the contrary, a little shorter than its companion, seemed to defy the future by the absence of any final line.

Near the altar, to the right of it, grew a gigantic palm of remarkable foliage which testified to its great age; a board, fastened to its trunk, bore the commemorative phrase: *Restoration of the Emperor Talu VII to the Throne of his Fathers.* In the shelter of the palm, on one side, a stake had been driven into the earth and on its square top had been placed a soft-boiled egg.

To the left, at an equal distance from the altar, a tall plant, old and withering, offered a sad contrast to the splendid palm; it was a rubber tree which had no more sap and was almost rotten. A stretcher, made of branches, lay in its shade, bearing the recumbent corpse of the negro king Yaour IX, wearing the traditional costume of Marguerite in *Faust*, a pink woollen gown from which hung a short alms purse and a thick golden wig with long plaits which fell over his shoulders and came half-way down to his knees.

On my left, with its back to the row of sycamores, and facing the red theatre, stood a stone-coloured building which looked like a model in miniature of the Paris *Bourse*.

9

Between this building and the north-west angle of the esplanade stood a row of life-size statues.

The first of these represented a man, mortally wounded by a weapon plunged into his heart. His two hands clutched instinctively at the wound, while his knees buckled under the weight of his body as it was flung backwards, on the point of collapse. The statue was black, and at first glance looked as though it had been carved out of a single block; but closer study gradually distinguished thousands of grooves, running in every direction, though generally forming groups of parallel lines. The work was in fact constructed entirely from innumerable corset whalebones, cut and bent to suit the shape of the moulding. Flat-headed nails, presumably with the points bent inwards, joined these pliant slats which were arranged side by side with such skill that not the slightest gap was left between them. The face itself, with all the details of its sad and agonised expression, was made simply out of broken fragments, carefully adjusted to reproduce faithfully the line of the nose, the lips, the arched eyebrows and the eyeballs. The shaft of the weapon, thrust deep into the heart of the dying man, gave some idea of the difficulty overcome, thanks to the elegant handle, in which could be detected the outline of two or three whalebones, cut into short lengths and bent into rings. The muscular body, the clenched arms, the sinewy legs half bent, all seemed to throb and suffer, as a result of the striking and realistic contours into which the uniform dark strips had been moulded.

The feet of the statue rested on a very simple conveyance, consisting of a low platform and four wheels, fashioned from more black whalebones ingeniously put together. Two narrow rails, made out of some coarse, reddish, gelatinous substance, which was in fact calves' marrow, ran across a surface of blackened wood and, by their shape if not by their colour, gave an accurate impression of a railway line; on these the four immobile wheels fitted without crushing them.

The floor, thus equipped for carriages, formed the upper surface of a wooden pedestal, black all over, on whose facing side the following inscription might be read in white : *Death of Saridakis, the Helot.* Underneath, in the same snow-white letters, could be seen this diagram, half in Greek, half in French, with a slender bracket :

$$\text{DUEL} \left\{ \begin{array}{l} \text{ἥδτον} \\ \text{ἥδτην} \end{array} \right.$$

Next to the helot was the bust of a thinker with puckered brow, who wore an expression of intense and fruitful meditation. On the plinth was the name :

## IMMANUEL KANT

Then came a sculptured group, which featured a stirring scene. A man on horseback, with the fierce face of a myrmidon of the law, appeared to be questioning a nun, who was standing before the door of her convent. In the background, in low relief, other men at arms, mounted on fiery horses, awaited an order from their leader. On the base, the title, engraved in hollow letters : *Sister Perpetua's Lie*, was followed by the question : ' Is this where the prisoners are hiding?'

Further along, a strange figuration, accompanied by these words of explanation : *The Regent Bowing before Louis XV*, showed Philip of Orleans respectfully stooping in front of the child-king, while he, about ten years of age, maintained an attitude full of natural and unconscious majesty.

In contrast with the helot, the bust and the two larger groups looked as though they were made of terracotta.

Norbert Montalescot, calm and watchful, walked among his works, keeping a specially close eye on the helot, whose fragility made it particularly vulnerable to a careless knock from some passer-by.

Beyond the last statue stood a small cabin without a door; its four walls, all of the same dimensions, were made of thick black canvas, which no doubt produced total darkness inside. The roof, which sloped gently on one side, was oddly made from book pages, yellow with age and cut into the shape of tiles; the text, in quite large print, and wholly in English, was faded, and sometimes quite effaced, but the top of certain pages remained legible and bore the title: *The Fair Maid of Perth*, still distinct. In the middle of the roof could be seen the outline of a judas window, tightly closed, which, instead of glass, was made of the same pages, discoloured by age and use. The whole of this thin covering must have diffused below a dim, yellowish light, full of softness and repose.

A chord, recalling the tone of brass, but very much fainter, sounded at regular intervals from the cabin, giving the exact sensation of a musical breathing.

Directly opposite Naïr, a tombstone, placed in line with the stock exchange, served as a stand for the various parts of a Zouave uniform. A gun and cartridge-pouches had been placed with these military effects, to all appearances with the pious intention of perpetuating the dead man's memory.

Standing upright behind the funeral slab was a hoarding covered in black material, which presented to the viewer a series of twelve water colours, arranged symmetrically, in four rows of three. The resemblance between the characters suggested that the pictures were concerned with some dramatic narrative. Above each image, by way of a title, one could read certain words, traced with a brush.

In the first painting a non-commissioned officer and a fair-haired woman in flashy clothes were lounging in the back of a luxurious victoria; the words *Flora and Sergeant-Major Lécurou*, summarily identified the couple.

Next came *The Performance of* Daedalus, represented by a large stage on which a singer in Grecian draperies appeared to be singing at the top of his voice; in the front of a box the sergeant-major could be seen, sitting beside Flora, who was gazing through her opera glasses at the performer.

In *The Consultation*, an old woman, clad in a loose cloak, was drawing Flora's attention to a celestial planisphere, pinned to the wall, and pointing imperiously with her index finger to the constellation of Cancer.

*The Secret Correspondence*, which began a new row of sketches, showed the woman in the cloak offering Flora one of those special grids which are necessary to decipher certain cryptograms and which consist of a single card with oddly placed perforations.

The setting of *The Signal*, was the terrace of an almost empty café, in front of which a dark-haired Zouave, sitting at a table on his own, was indicating to the waiter a great bell, being rung in a near-by church; underneath was written this brief dialogue: ' Waiter, what is that bell ringing for?'—' It's for Benediction '—' Right, bring me a plate of meat scraps '.

*The Sergeant-Major's Jealousy* depicted a barracks yard, where Lécurou, with four fingers of his right hand raised, seemed to be furiously scolding the Zouave who had appeared in the previous picture; with the scene went this brutal piece of military jargon: ' Four days' jankers!'

At the top of the third row was *The Rebellious Bravo*, which introduced into the plot a Zouave with very fair hair, who was refusing to obey some command of Lécurou's, and whose simple reply 'No!' was written underneath the water colour.

*The Guilty Man Dies*, which was underlined by the order 'Fire!' showed a firing squad, who, at the sergeant-major's command, were aiming at the heart of the fair-haired Zouave.

In *The Moneylender*, the woman in the cloak reappeared holding out several bank notes to Flora, who sat at a desk, apparently signing some sort of receipt.

The last row began with *Police at the Gambling Den*. This time Flora was throwing herself into space from a large balcony, behind which, through an open window, could be seen a large gaming table, surrounded by players in great dismay at the untimely arrival of a number of men in black.

The last picture but one, entitled *The Morgue*, showed in the foreground the corpse of a woman, lying on a slab, behind glass. Behind, a silver châtelaine hung conspicuously, weighed down by a valuable watch.

Finally, *The Fatal Blow* terminated the series with a nocturnal scene; in the shadows, the dark-complexioned Zouave could be seen slapping Sergeant-Major Lécurou's face, while in the distance, outlined against a forest of masts, a notice board, lit by a powerful street lamp, bore these two words: *Bougie Harbour*.

Behind me, making a pair with the altar, stood a dark rectangular shed of small dimensions, whose front wall consisted of a fine grating of thin wooden bars, painted black; four prisoners, two men and two women of native origin, wandered silently round this tiny prison; above the bars, the words *Cells* was set out in letters of a reddish colour.

14

By my side stood the large group of passengers from the *Lynceus,* who stood waiting for the appearance of the promised procession.

15

# II

PRESENTLY, the sound of feet was heard; all heads turned to the left, and from the south-east corner of the esplanade a strange and stately procession could be seen approaching.

At its head, the thirty-six sons of the Emperor, arranged in six columns according to height, formed a black phalanx, representing all ages from three to fifteen. Fogar, the oldest of them all, who was among the tallest in the rear, carried in his arms an immense wooden cube which had been turned into a gaming dice by being white-washed all over and marked with round hollows, painted black. At a sign from Rao, a native responsible for supervising the formation of the procession, the troop of children began to walk, with slow steps, along the side of the esplanade on which the stock exchange stood.

After them, in a captivating group, came the sovereign's ten wives, graceful Ponukelian women, distinguished for charm and beauty.

Finally, the Emperor Talu VII appeared, curiously dressed as a music-hall singer, in a blue dress with a low neckline, falling at the back into a long train, on which the number 472 was clearly printed in black figures. His black face, full of savage energy, was not without a certain character, contrasting as it did with his feminine wig of magnificent golden hair, which had been carefully waved. He led by the hand his daughter Sirdah, a slender child of eighteen, whose squint-

16

ing eyes were veiled by white specks of albugo, and on whose
brow showed a red birthmark in the shape of a tiny corset,
circled with yellow rays.

Behind him marched the Ponukelian troops, splendid
warriors with ebony skins, heavily armed beneath their trappings of feathers and amulets.

The column advanced slowly, in the same direction as
the children.

As they passed in front of the Zouave's tomb, Sirdah, who
had doubtless been counting her steps, suddenly went up
to the gravestone and, with her lips, gently impressed on it
a long kiss of the purest tenderness. This pious duty accomplished, the blind girl affectionately took her father's hand
again.


As they drew near to the extremity of the esplanade, the
Emperor's sons, directed by Rao, turned right to proceed
along the north side of the vast quadrangle. When they
reached the opposite corner, they changed course a second
time and came back towards us, while the procession, constantly fed at its source by numerous cohorts, followed close
in their tracks.

Finally, the last black warriors having made their entry at
the same time as the advance guard of children reached the
south end, Rao had a space cleared in front of the altar,
and all the newcomers massed in good order along the two
sides, their faces turned towards the centre of the square.

On all sides, a negro crowd, composed of the population of
Ejur, had assembled behind the sycamores to participate in
this exciting spectacle.

Still keeping in their six lines, the Emperor's sons reached the centre of the esplanade and came to a halt opposite the altar.

Rao took the huge dice from Fogar's arms and swung it several times before throwing it into the air with all his might; the enormous cube, almost two feet square, went spinning up into the air, a white mass flecked with black, then described a sharp curve and, rolling along the ground, came to a standstill. At a glance, Rao read the number *two* on the upper face, then, going up to the submissive phalanx, pointed with his finger to the second row, who alone remained where they were; the rest of the group picked up the dice and ran to join the crowd of warriors.

Talu, with slow strides, then joined the elect whom chance had chosen to serve as his pages. Soon, amidst a profound silence, the Emperor advanced majestically towards the altar, escorted by the privileged children, willingly bearing the train of his dress.

After mounting the steps which led to the sparsely furnished table, Talu signed to Rao to approach with the heavy coronation robe, which he was holding in both hands, inside out. Bending down, the Emperor slipped his head and arms through three openings cut in the centre of the cloth and, as the large folds fell into place, they presently enveloped him down to his feet.

Thus arrayed, the monarch turned proudly to the assembly as if to enable everyone to look at his new costume.

The rich, silky material was decorated with a large map of Africa, showing the principal lakes, rivers and mountains.

The pale yellow of the land stood out clearly against the graduated blue of the sea, which extended in every direction as far as the general shape of the garment required.

Fine silver lines streaked the ocean's surface, in graceful

zig-zag curves to suggest, schematically, the rise and fall of the waves.

Only the southern half of the continent was visible between the Emperor's neck and his ankles.

On the west side, a black spot, with the name ' Ejur ' beside it, was situated near the mouth of a river whose source, some distance to the east, issued from a mountain mass.

On both sides of the vast watercourse, a huge red area represented the states belonging to the all-powerful Talu.

As a form of flattery, the designer of the garment had indefinitely extended this impressive territory, which submitted to the rule of a single sceptre and whose boundaries were, in any case, largely undetermined; the brilliant carmine stretched to the southernmost point, where the words, ' Cape of Good Hope ', were set out in large black letters.

After a moment, Talu turned back to the altar. On his back, the other side of the stole showed the northern half of Africa, upside down against the same maritime background.


The solemn moment was drawing near.

In a loud voice, the monarch began to read the native text, written in hieroglyphics on the sheet of parchment which stood in the middle of the narrow table.

It was a kind of bull, whereby Talu, already Emperor of Ponukele, by virtue of his religious powers consecrated himself King of Drelshkaf.

Having delivered the proclamation, the sovereign took the cruet which was intended to represent the holy *ampulla* and, turning sideways, spread the oil over the top part of his hand in order to smear it on his forehead with his fingertips.

He replaced the bottle immediately and, descending the altar steps, with a few strides reached the litter of leaves which lay in the shade of the rubber tree. There, placing his foot on Yaour's corpse, he let out a long sigh of joy and raised his head with a triumphant air, as if to humiliate the remains of the dead king before us all.

He returned after this proud gesture, and, quickly taking off the heavy cloak, returned it to Rao.

Escorted by his six sons, who were again bearing his train, he walked slowly in our direction, then turned towards the Incomparables theatre to take up his position in front of the crowd.


At this point the Emperor's wives advanced to the middle of the esplanade.

Rao joined them soon after, carrying a heavy earthenware pot, which he placed on the ground in their midst.

The ten young women fell to the ground together, around the container, which was full of thick, black foodstuff; they ate hungrily using their hands to convey it to their lips.

In a few minutes, the earthenware pot, completely empty, was removed by Rao. The negro women, thus fortified, took their places for the *Luen' Shetuz*, a religious dance which was held in great respect in the country and was specially reserved for great ceremonial occasions.

They began with a few slow steps, mingled with lithe, sinuous movements.

From time to time they emitted from their wide-open mouths terrifying belches, which soon increased at an extraordinary rate. Instead of stifling these revolting sounds, they forced them out, as if competing with each other to see who could produce the loudest noise with the most ostentation.

This general chorus, providing a kind of musical accompaniment to the slow, graceful dance, exhibited the peculiar virtues of the unknown substance they had just eaten.

Little by little, the dance grew more lively and assumed a fantastic quality, while the frequency and volume of the noises increased in a powerful crescendo.

There was a moment of impressive climax, during which the harsh, deafening sounds marked the rhythm of a diabolic sarabande; the feverish ballerinas, dishevelled and racked by their terrible belching as if by blows, crossed and followed one another, and twisted themselves in every sort of contortion, as if overcome by a vertiginous delirium.

Then gradually everything grew calm and, after a long diminuendo, the ballet ended in an apotheosis, accompanied by a sustained final chord which gradually faded into silence.

Soon the young women, still shaken by delayed hiccups, returned with slow steps to their original places.


During the performance of the *Luen' Shetuz*, Rao had gone over to the southern corner of the esplanade to release from their prison a group consisting of a woman and two men of negro origin.

Now only one recluse still wandered about behind the heavy grating.

Rao, pushing his way through our midst, led the three newcomers, with their hands tied in front of them, to the spot where the ground had been trampled by the dance.

An anguished silence weighed on the whole assembly, who were moved to pity by the prospect of the tortures the trio in fetters were about to undergo.

Rao took from his belt a huge axe, whose blade, well sharpened, was fashioned out of a strange wood, as hard as iron.

21

A number of slaves had joined him to assist him in his role of executioner.

Supported by them, the traitor Gaïz Duh was ordered to kneel, with his head bent, while the other two condemned persons remained motionless.

Rao brandished his axe with both hands and struck the traitor's neck three times. With the last blow, his head rolled to the ground.

The spot remained unstained by any crimson splashes, on account of the curious wooden blade which, as it cut through the flesh, had the effect of immediately congealing the blood, and absorbed even the first drops whose loss could not be avoided.

Where they had been severed, the head and trunk presented the solid, scarlet appearance characteristic of butchers' meat.

One was reminded, in spite of oneself, of those dummies used by conjurers, which, having been cleverly substituted for the live assistant by means of some piece of furniture with a false bottom, are neatly cut up on the stage into slabs, prepared in advance with simulated blood-stains. Here, the fact that the corpse was real made the compact redness, usually due to the art of the brush, uncommonly disturbing.

The slaves bore Gaïz Duh's remains away, together with the faintly stained axe.

They soon returned, to place before Rao a burning brazier, in which were being heated the points of two long iron rods, fitted into heavy wooden hafts.

Rao took from the hands of a slave a parchment scroll which he spread open; it was the false certificate of Sirdah's death, drawn up by Mossem some time previously.

With the aid of an enormous palm branch, one of the negroes kept on stirring the fire, which burned fierce and bright.

Putting one knee to the ground behind the condemned

man, and holding the parchment in his left hand, Rao snatched one of the glowing rods from the brazier and applied the point of it to one heel of the man in front of him.

The flesh sizzled and Mossem, gripped by the slaves, writhed with pain.

The inexorable Rao continued his task. It was the actual text of the parchment that he copied painstakingly on the forger's foot.

From time to time, he returned the rod he was using to the fire and took out its fellow, glowing from the live coals.

When the left sole was completely covered with hiero-glyphs, Rao continued the operation on the right foot, still using alternately the two points of red-hot iron, which were quick to cool.

Mossem, stifling his muffled howls, made violent efforts to escape the torture.

When, at last, the false act had been copied down to the last sign, Rao, getting to his feet, ordered the slaves to release Mossem, who was seized with dreadful convulsions and expired before our eyes, overcome by his long agony.

The corpse was removed, together with the parchment and the brazier.


Returning to their posts, the slaves seized hold of Rul, a Ponukelian woman of remarkable beauty, and the only survivor of the wretched trio. The condemned woman, in whose hair could be seen long gold pins, arranged in a star, wore, over her loin-cloth, a red velvet corset, slightly torn; the garment offered a striking resemblance to the queer mark on Sirdah's forehead.

Kneeling to face in the same direction as Mossem, the proud Rul made vain attempts at desperate resistance.

Rao took one of the gold pins from her hair and applied the point at right angles to his victim's back, choosing a circle of skin, on her right side, which was visible through the first eyelet of her corset, whose lacing was knotted and frayed; then, with a slow, steady thrust, he drove the slender shaft deep into her flesh.

At the sound of the cries provoked by this terrible injection, Sirdah, recognising the voice of her mother, threw herself at Talu's feet to implore his sovereign mercy.

Immediately, as if to receive new commands, Rao turned to the Emperor, who with a gesture of confirmation, ordered him to continue the torture.

Another pin, taken from the black tresses, was planted in the second eyelet, and, little by little, the entire row bristled with glittering gold spikes. The operation was repeated on the left side until, finally, all the hair tumbled down and the round lace-holes had been filled, one after another.

A moment before, the unfortunate woman had ceased to cry out; one of the points piercing her heart, had brought about her death. The body was swiftly seized, and disappeared like the two others.

Raising the speechless and agonised Sirdah to her feet, Talu made his way towards the line of statues near the stock exchange. The warriors stood back to make room, and our group immediately joined the emperor; he then made a sign to Norbert, who, going up to the little cabin, called to his sister in a loud voice.

Soon the judas window in the roof was slowly raised to open outwards, pushed by the slender hand of Louise Montalescot, and as she appeared through the gaping aperture she seemed to be mounting step by step up a ladder.

Suddenly she stopped, with the upper part of her body emerging through the window, and turned to face us. She was very beautiful in her officer's costume, with her long fair curls escaping freely from a close-fitting forage cap, tilted over one ear.

Her blue dolman, which clung tightly to her splendid figure, was decorated on the right side with a shining gold shoulder-knot; it was from the aglets of this that proceeded the discreet chord which we had heard until then through the walls of the cabin and which was actually produced by the young woman's breathing, by means of a surgical connection, linking the base of the lung and the arrangement of coiled braids, which served to camouflage a number of separate sounding-tubes. The gilt tags, hanging from the shoulder-knot like graceful, elongated weights, were hollow and fitted inside with vibrating plates. At each contraction of the lung, a part of the air expelled passed through the multiple pipes and, setting the plates in motion, produced a harmonious resonance.

A tame magpie perched, motionless, on the charming prisoner's shoulder.

Suddenly, Louise noticed the corpse of Yaour, still stretched out in his Grecian costume, under the shade of the decaying rubber tree. A violent emotion was portrayed on her features and, covering her eyes with her hands, she wept hysterically, her bosom shaken with terrible sobs which set in motion the chords of her shoulder-tags and increased their sound.

Talu, growing impatient, uttered a few unintelligible words in a severe tone which brought the unhappy girl to her senses.

Curbing her sorrow and distress, she held out her right hand to the magpie, whose two feet landed with alacrity on the index finger she hastily extended.

With a sweeping gesture, Louise stretched out her arm to hurl the bird into the air, and, taking flight, it swooped down, to land on the sand in front of the statue of the helot.

25

Two openings, scarcely perceptible, and more than a yard apart, were cut in the side of the pedestal facing the audience, at ground level.

The magpie approached the further opening and thrust his beak into it sharply, to release some internal spring.

Immediately the carriageable platform started to tip slowly, at the left sinking down upon the pedestal to rise on the right above its habitual level.

Its equilibrium thus disturbed, the vehicle bearing the tragic statue moved gently along the gelatinous rails, which now lay at a considerable slope. Each of the four wheels of black whalebone was protected against any chance of derailment by an inner rim, which projected slightly below the frame, thus maintaining it firmly on the line.

Reaching the bottom of the short incline, the trolley was stopped short by the side of the pedestal.

In the few seconds which the ride had taken, the magpie hopped across to the other opening into the depths of which its beak vanished sharply.

After another release action, the see-saw motion was effected in reverse. The vehicle was gradually raised, then, pulled by its own weight, rolled to the right without any motor, on the silent line, and struck against the opposite side of the pedestal, the edge of which now in turn acted as a buffer.

These backward and forward motions were repeated several times, thanks to the manoeuvres of the magpie, which came and went ceaselessly from one opening to the other. The helot's statue remained fixed to the vehicle and followed all its movements. The whole contraption was of such lightness that the rails, in spite of their insubstantiality, showed no signs of flattening or breaking.

Talu watched with wonder the success of the hazardous experiment which he had conceived himself, without believing it to be workable.

26

The magpie ended this performance of its own accord and, with a few flaps of its wings, reached the bust of Immanuel Kant; on top of the stand, to the left, was a little perch on which the bird landed.

Immediately, a strong light illuminated the skull from within, and the casing, which was excessively thin, became completely transparent from the line of the eyebrows upwards.

One divined the presence of countless reflectors, placed facing in every direction inside the head. So great was the violence with which the bright rays, representing the fires of genius, escaped from their incandescent source.

Repeatedly the magpie took flight, to return immediately to its perch, thus constantly extinguishing and relighting the cranial dome, which alone burned with a thousand lights, while the face, the ears and the nape of the neck remained in darkness. Each time the bird's weight was applied to the lever, it seemed as though some transcendent idea was born in the thinker's brain, as it blazed suddenly with light.

Abandoning the bust, the bird swooped down upon the large pedestal devoted to the group of myrmidons of the law; here again the ferreting beak, introduced this time into a narrow, vertical pipe, set in action some invisible and delicate mechanism.

To the question: ' Is this where the fugitives are hiding?' the nun, posted before her convent, persistently replied : ' No ', shaking her head from right to left after each deep peck of the winged creature, who looked as though he was scratching for food.

Finally, the magpie touched the platform, smooth as a wooden floor, on which stood the last two statues; the place

27

chosen by the intelligent creature was a small disc, which gave half an inch beneath its light pressure.

At the same moment, the Regent bowed lower before Louis XV, whom that courtesy left impassive.

Hopping on the spot, the bird provided a succession of ceremonious greetings, then fluttered back to its mistress's shoulder.

After casting a long glance towards Yaour, Louise went back down into the interior of her cabin and closed the skylight at once, as if in a hurry to return to some mysterious task.

# III

THE first part of the performance had come to an end, and the festivities of the Incomparables could now begin.

First, however, the stock exchange was to open for the last time.

The black warriors stood back further to clear the entrance to the miniature *Bourse*, around which the passengers of the *Lynceus* gathered in groups.

Five stockbrokers, namely the associate bankers Hounsfield and Cerjat assisted by their three clerks, took their places at five tables under the colonnade of the building, and began repeating aloud endless rhymed orders which the passengers placed with them.

The stocks were designated by the actual names of the Incomparables, each one represented by a hundred shares, which rose or fell according to the personal forecasts of the gamblers on the outcome of the competition. All transactions were settled with ready money, in the form of bank notes or hard cash.

For a quarter of an hour without respite, the five agents shouted out deplorable alexandrines which the speculators hastily improvised, with a copious use of tags, according to the fluctuations of the market prices.

At length Hounsfield and Cerjat rose to indicate the close of business, then, followed by their three clerks, came down to mingle, as we did, with the crowd of speculators, who reassembled in their original position, with their backs to the prison.

The black warriors fell back into their first formation, still leaving the immediate surroundings of the *Bourse* clear, at Rao's injunction, in order to afford us a passage.

The gala performance then began.

First the four Bucharessas brothers made their appearance, each wearing an acrobat's costume of pink jersey and black velvet shorts.

The two eldest brothers, Hector and Tommy, both adolescents full of supple strength, each carried six dark rubber balls in a strong drum; they walked away in opposite directions, then, turning round to face each other, halted at two points a considerable distance apart.

Suddenly, uttering a little cry by way of a signal, Hector, who was standing in front of our group, used his drum to bat his six balls high into the air, one after the other.

At that same moment, Tommy, who was standing at the foot of the altar, had launched all his rubber projectiles in succession with the help of the taut circle of parchment he held in his left hand, so that they crossed his brother's in mid-air.

Having accomplished this first move, each of the jugglers began to return one by one the balls his partner had thrown, effecting an exchange which was then prolonged without interruption. The drums vibrated simultaneously and the twelve projectiles formed a sort of wide arch, in constant motion.

Thanks to the exact similarity of their actions, as well as to a close physical resemblance, the two brothers, one of whom was left-handed, gave the illusion of a single image reflected in a mirror.

30

For several minutes, the feat was performed with mathematical precision. Finally, at another signal, each player caught half the projectiles in the hollow underside of his drum and the two-way play ceased abruptly.

Immediately, Marius Bucharessas, a lively-looking lad of ten, ran forward, and his brothers, meanwhile, withdrew into the background.

The child was carrying in his arms, on his shoulders, and even on his head, a collection of small cats, all wearing red or green ribbons.

With the point of his heel he drew two lines in the sand, twelve or fifteen yards apart, parallel with the side where the *Bourse* stood, and the cats, jumping to the ground of their own accord, took up their positions in two teams of equal numbers behind these allotted boundaries. Thus, with the *green* ribbons on one side, and the *red* ribbons on the other, they lined up, facing each other, without any confusion.

At a sign from Marius, the graceful felines began a lively game of Prisoner's Base.

To engage, one of the *greens* went up to the *reds'* camp and with the tip of his claws slightly bared, touched the paw which one of his adversaries held out, three times; the last time he ran away fast, hotly pursued by the *red*, in an effort to catch him.

Just then, another *green* rushed at the pursuer, who, having been forced to turn back, was soon supported by one of his own side, who caught up with the second *green* and compelled him to flee in turn.

The same move was repeated several times, until the moment when one of the *reds*, having managed to hit a *green* with his paw, gave a triumphant miaow.

The game stopped and the *green* who had been captured went over to enemy territory and, taking three steps towards his own camp, stood quite still.

The cat to whom credit for the capture was due went up to the *greens* and opened again, by giving three sharp taps to the extended paw which one of the enemy eagerly proffered.

This lively and enthralling game continued without any infringement of the rules. From time to time, the prisoners who gathered in symmetrical rows, saw their numbers reduced when one of them was rescued by a deft partner who managed to touch him. Any member who was agile enough to reach the opposite camp without hindrance became impregnable for as long as he remained beyond the line he had succeeded in crossing.

Finally, the crowd of *greens* taken prisoner grew so numerous that Marius, in imperious tones, declared the *red* team the winners.

The cats ran back to the boy without delay and climbed up his body to resume the places they had occupied on entering.


As Marius retired, he was replaced by Bob, the last of the brothers, a delightful, golden-haired boy of four, with big blue eyes and long curls.

With extraordinary accomplishment and talent, a miracle of precociousness, the charming infant began a series of imitations which he accompanied with expressive gestures; the different sounds of a train getting up speed, the cries of domestic animals, a saw grating on a free-stone, the sharp pop of a champagne cork, the gurgling of liquid as it is poured out of a bottle, the fanfare of hunting horns, a violin solo and the plaintive notes of a 'cello, all these comprised an astounding repertoire which, to anyone who shut his eyes for a moment, afforded a complete illusion of reality.

The infant prodigy took his leave of the crowd to go and join Marius, Hector and Tommy.

Shortly after, the four brothers stood aside to make room for their sister Stella, a beautiful girl of fourteen, who appeared, dressed as Fortune, standing upright upon a wheel which revolved continuously beneath her feet.

The girl began to turn in every direction, spinning the narrow hoop with the soles of her feet, by skipping up and down without interruption.

In her hand she held an enormous cornet, deep and coiled, from which, like a shower of gold coins, there suddenly tumbled light, bright paper money, which produced no metallic sound as it floated slowly down to earth.

The louis, double louis and large hundred-franc pieces left a glittering trail behind the pretty cyclist who, with a smile on her lips, achieved wonders of balance and velocity without ever setting foot to the ground.

Like some conjurer's cornucopia, from which flowers of every species pour in an endless stream, the stock of coins seemed inexhaustible. Stella had only to shake the cornet gently to sow her riches, which lay scattered thick and uneven on the ground, and were crushed in places by the wheel as it revolved in its wandering course.

After much twisting and turning this way and that, the young girl vanished like a fairy, shedding her pseudo-metal coins up to the last moment.

All eyes then turned towards Balbet, the marksman, who had just taken from the Zouave's tomb the cartridge pouches, which were now strung about his hips, and the weapon, which was in fact a Gras rifle of a very old make.

Walking rapidly to the right, the famous champion, the object of everyone's attention, stopped in front of our group and carefully selected his position, facing the north side of the square.

Directly opposite him, a long way off, under the commemorative palm tree, stood the square post with the soft-boiled egg on top of it.

Further away still, the natives who were watching curiously from behind the row of sycamores, at a sign from Rao, stood back to leave a wide space.

Balbet loaded his gun, then, raising it to his shoulder with care, slowly took aim and fired.

The bullet, grazing the top of the egg, removed part of the white so that the yellow was exposed.

Several shots fired in quick succession completed the task thus begun, little by little the albuminous coating was shot away to uncover the inner content, which still remained intact.

Sometimes, between two reports, Hector Bucharessas ran to turn the egg round so that, as a result of this adjustment, the egg successively presented every part of its surface to the fire.

In the background, one of the sycamores formed a barrier for the bullets, all of which buried themselves in the trunk which had been partially flattened in order to prevent ricochets.

The twenty-four cartridges which formed Balbet's supply of ammunition were just enough to complete the experiment.

When the last puff of smoke had curled from the barrel of

the gun, Hector took the egg in the hollow of his hand to display it.

No trace of white remained on the delicate interior membrane which, although completely exposed, still covered the yellow without showing a single scratch.

Soon, at the request of Balbet, who was anxious to show that over-cooking had not facilitated the exercise, Hector closed his hand for a moment so that the yolk, which was quite liquid ran through his fingers.

Punctually at the appointed hour, La Billaudière-Maisonnial, the builder, had just appeared, carting before him, like a knife-grinder, an apparatus embodying some oddly complicated crank-shaft mechanism.

Stopping in the middle of the square, he placed the bulky machine in a line with the altar, where it rested, perfectly balanced, on two wheels and two legs.

The contraption consisted of a sort of large grindstone, which was worked by a pedal and which set in motion a whole system of wheels, rods, levers and springs, forming an inextricable tangle of metal; from one side extended an articulated arm, which ended in a hand armed with a foil.

Immediately, La Billaudière-Maisonnial, turning to face us, sat down on the bench of the apparatus, and, with his body hidden from our eyes by the strange mechanism in front of him, placed his foot on the long pedal, whose function was to turn the stone.

Balbet, attired in mask, glove and fencing jacket, briskly marked a straight line in the sand with the point of his foil, then, with the sole of his left foot resting on the immutable boundary, elegantly took up his position on guard facing the articulated arm, which projected to the left so that it was clearly outlined against the white background of the altar.

The two steels crossed, and by moving his foot, La Billaudière-Maisonnial turned his mill at a considerable speed.

Suddenly, the mechanical arm, rapidly executing a sequence of skilful feints, lunged in a straight thrust at Balbet, who, in spite of his universally acknowledged talent, had not been able to parry this astonishing faultless pass.

The artificial elbow had recoiled but the mill continued to turn, and soon another series of trick exercises, completely different from the first, was followed by a second thrust which touched Balbet full in the chest.

The engagement continued in this way with numerous passes : thrusts in quarte, sixte and tierce, even in prime, quinte and octave, were interspersed with ' disengages ', ' redouble-ments ' and ' cut-overs ', to make up countless attacks, each ending in an original and complex feint, swift as lightning, which never failed to reach its target.

With his left foot riveted to the line so that he was pre-vented from giving ground, Balbet attempted only to parry the thrusts, trying to deflect the opposing foil, which was ready to slip to one side without touching him. But the mechanism, driven by the grindstone was so perfect, and the unfamiliar passes contained such bewildering ruses, that the fencer's defensive tactics were invariably frustrated at the last moment.

From time to time, La Billaudière-Maisonnial, by pushing a long, serrated rod repeatedly backwards and forwards, com-pletely changed the disposition of the various mechanisms, thus producing a new series of feints unknown even to him-self.

This process, capable of producing an infinite number of accidental results, might be compared with the light taps on the tube of a kaleidoscope, which in the visual field give rise to ever-changing polychromatic patterns of crystal mosaics.

Balbet ended by giving up the struggle and laid aside his accessories, delighted with the defeat which had furnished the opportunity of appreciating a mechanical masterpiece.

Raising the two short shafts fixed behind the bench on

which he had been sitting, La Billaudiére-Maisonnial moved slowly away, wheeling his astonishing engine with difficulty.

Following his departure, a negro lad of twelve years old, with a mischievous grin on his face, suddenly appeared, cutting fantastic capers.

This was Rhejed one of the Emperor's young sons.

Under his left arm, he held a rodent with red fur, which moved its sharp, pointed ears in every direction.

In his right hand, the child carried a light door, painted white, which looked as if it belonged to some small cupboard.

Laying the thin panel on the ground, Rhejed quite openly seized in his fist a crudely shaped dagger which was stuck in the top of his red loin-cloth.

Without hesitation, he killed the rodent outright, with one sharp stroke of the slender blade, which sank into the furry neck and remained planted there.

The boy quickly grabbed the warm corpse by the hind legs and placed it on the door.

Soon a sticky slime began to drip from the gaping mouth.

This phenomenon had evidently been foreseen by Rhejed, who, after a moment, turned the door over and held it slanting at a certain distance from the ground.

The viscous secretion, flowing on to the other side of the panel, quickly formed a circular coating which covered a considerable area.

Finally, the animal spring having suddenly dried up, Rhejed placed the rodent in the very centre of the fresh patch. Then he stood the door on one end, without worrying about the corpse, which remained firmly in the same place, held there by the strange glue.

With a sharp movement, Rhejed untied his loin cloth and glued the end of it to the first side, which had been smeared more hastily than the second.

The red material stuck without difficulty to the sticky varnish, covering it completely.

The door, laid flat again, hid a fragment of the long girdle, exposing to view the besmeared rodent.

Rhejed, turning round to unwind his loin cloth, withdrew a few paces and then stood still in an attitude of expectancy.

A strange odour, produced by the discharge of slaver, had just begun to spread, with extraordinary pungency, over Trophies Square.

Without showing any surprise at these powerful emanations, Rhejed raised his eyes as if he was watching for the appearance of some expected visitor in the sky.

Several minutes passed in silence.

Suddenly, Rhejed uttered a triumphant exclamation, pointing southwards to an enormous bird of prey, approaching rapidly at a considerable height.

To the child's great delight, the winged creature, with its brilliant black plumage, swooped down upon the door, its two thin legs, almost as long as those of a heron, landing near the rodent.

Above the hooked beak, two quivering orifices, like nostrils, seemed to possess great olfactory powers.

The tell-tale odour had undoubtedly reached the nest of the bird and, at first attracted, then guided, by an acute sense of smell, it had sought out without hesitation the prey offered to its voracity.

But its feet, held by the adhesive glue, dragged the door with them, so that this rose horizontally into the air without letting go the red cloth fastened to its underside.

In his turn Rhejed left the ground, swinging on the end of his loin cloth, a large part of which still encircled his loins.

In spite of its load, the robust fowl climbed fast, still encouraged by the cries of the child, whose laughter proved his wild jubilation.

At the precise moment he was borne away, Talu had rushed towards his son with every sign of violent alarm.

Having arrived too late, the unfortunate father followed with a look of anguish the course of the little monkey, who was flying further and further away, unaware of any danger which might befall him.

A deep amazement paralysed the onlookers, who awaited with anxiety the outcome of this terrible incident.

The preparations of Rhejed and the careful way in which he had distributed the glue from the rodent were evidence that this trip through the air had been premeditated, although the intention had not been confided to anyone.

Meanwhile the huge, flying creature, the tips of whose wings were all that could be seen over the door, continued to mount towards higher regions.

Rhejed, as he grew smaller before our eyes, was clinging frantically to the end of his loin cloth, thus increasing the chances, already so numerous, of a fatal fall, on account of the weakness of the bond uniting the red cloth and the two invisible claws to the door.

At last, worn out by its unaccustomed load, the bird showed some inclination to return to earth.

The descent soon became more rapid, and Talu, filled with hope, held out his arms to the child as if to gather him to himself.

The exhausted bird dropped at an alarming speed.

A few yards from the ground, Rhejed, tearing his loin cloth, fell gracefully, to land on his feet, while the bird, relieved of its burden, flew away to the south, still trailing the door, with a shred of red cloth clinging to it.

Too delighted to think of the scolding he deserved, Talu

rushed to his son and enfolded him in a long, rapturous embrace.

When the excitement had died down, Bex, the chemist made his entrance, pushing an enormous glass cage, which rested on a kind of mahogany platform, fitted with four low wheels of equal size.

The care taken in the construction of this conveyance, almost luxurious in its great simplicity, testified to the value of its fragile load, which it had been made to fit with precision.

It ran perfectly, without a sound, thanks to the rubber tyres protecting the silent wheels, whose thin metal spokes seemed to have been newly plated with nickel.

At the back, two upright copper shafts, elegantly curved, were joined at the upper end by a rail, with a walnut handle, which Bex grasped with both hands as he walked.

The general effect suggested a more delicate version of one of the solid trolleys which are used to move trunks and packages on railway stations.

Bex halted in the middle of the square, giving everybody time to examine the apparatus.

The glass cage enclosed a huge musical instrument, consisting of brass horns, strings, circular bows, mechanical keyboards of every sort, and a splendid paraphernalia devoted to the percussion section.

Adjoining the cage, a large space was reserved on the front of the platform for two vast cylinders, one red, the other white, each of which was connected with the atmosphere contained within the transparent walls by a metal pipe.

The fragile tube of an excessively tall thermometer rose out of the top of the cage, in which only the fine bulb, filled with a sparkling violet fluid, was inserted; the degrees marked on it

40

were divided into tenths. No frame supported the diaphanous tube which had been placed an inch or so from the side next to the two cylinders.

While all eyes were examining this curious machine, Bex, in precise terms, offered us a lucid scientific explanation.

We learned that the instrument would soon be made to work in front of us, by virtue of an electric motor concealed in its interior.

The cylinders, which were also controlled by electricity, served two opposite purposes—the red one containing a generator which produced constant heat, while the white one incessantly manufactured an intense cold, capable of liquefying any kind of gas.

Now, various components of the automatic orchestra were made of *bexium,* a new metal, chemically endowed by Bex with a prodigious thermal sensitivity. The construction of the whole machine was aimed purely at demonstrating, in a striking manner, the properties of this strange substance which the skilful inventor had discovered.

A lump of bexium, submitted to various temperatures, changed its volume, proportionately, according to a scale which could be measured from one to ten.

It was on this fact that the mechanics of the apparatus were based.

At the top of each cylinder, a handle, which turned easily, served to regulate the opening of an internal tap, which was connected by the metal duct with the glass cage; by means of this tap, Bex could change the temperature of the air inside at will; as a result of continuous alterations, the fragments of bexium, acting violently on certain springs, set in motion, and then stopped, one of the claviers, or a group of valves on a horn, and they in turn, at a given moment, were caused to vibrate in the ordinary way by grooved discs.

In spite of the fluctuations of temperature, the strings invariably retained their pitch, owing to a certain preparation devised by Bex to render them unusually rigid.

The crystal used in the walls of the cage, possessing properties of resistance which enabled it to withstand any test, was remarkably thin, and the sound, was scarcely muffled by this delicate, quivering barrier.

His exposition terminated, Bex came and stood in front of the vehicle, his eyes fixed on the column of the thermometer and his hands clenched above the two cylinders.

Turning the red handle first, he propelled a great current of heat into the cage, then quickly stopped the stream of air when he saw the violet liquid reach the desired level, after rising rapidly.

With a swift movement, as if repairing some venial omission, he let down, like the folding steps of a light carriage, a form of adaptable pedal, previously concealed between the two cylinders, which, when it opened, reached down to ground level.

To begin with, there arose a slow cantilena, tender and plaintive, with an accompaniment of calm, regular arpeggios.

A solid wheel, as in a hurdy-gurdy, passed like an endless bow across a long cord, stretched over a sound board; on this string, with its pure note, automatic hammers fell like the fingers of a virtuoso, and then were raised gently, producing all the notes of the scale without a gap.

The wheel, varying its speed, produced every shade of tone, and the effect was exactly that of a melody on a violin.

Against one of the glass walls stood a harp, each string of which was caught by a tiny wooden hook, which plucked it as it was drawn back and then, describing a curve, fell back into its original position; the hooks were attached at right angles to the top of mobile rods, whose supple and delicate play produced languid arpeggios.

As the chemist had predicted, the transparent case let through the vibrations with scarcely any dulling of their

42

sound, and the penetrating music was propagated with charm and vigour.

Without waiting for this song-without-words to end, Bex stopped the motor and left the pedal. Then, turning the red handle, he raised the temperature within, watching the thermometer as he did so. After a few seconds, he closed the hot tap and again pressed the pedal beneath his foot.

Immediately, a second bow, larger than the first, and passing across a thicker string, produced the tones of a 'cello, with great sweetness and beauty. At the same time, a mechanical keyboard instrument, whose keys moved of their own accord, began to play a rich and difficult accompaniment of perilously rapid figuration.

After this snatch from a duo sonata, Bex effected another adjustment, this time causing the violet liquid to rise just one tenth of a degree.

The pseudo-violin then joined the piano and the 'cello to blend in an *adagio* from some classical trio.

Presently, as the liquid moved one division further in the same direction, the slow solemn piece changed into a *scherzo*, almost staccato, while retaining the same combination of instruments.

Continuing to work his pedal automatically, Bex turned the white handle next and caused the violet column to fall to around zero, which was marked about half-way down the glass tube.

In obedience to his movements, a brilliant fanfare struck up, issuing from a number of horns of various sizes, clustered in a compact group. The whole family of the brass was represented in this special corner, from the huge bass to the shrill, agile cornet. Registering different degrees on the section of the thermometer below freezing, the white handle, turned several times, produced in succession a military march, a cornet solo, a waltz, a polka and a variety of noisy bugle calls.

Suddenly, opening the cold tap as far as it would go, Bex swiftly produced a terrible frost, whose effect was felt by the nearest spectators through the transparent sides. All eyes were on a gramophone with a large horn, from which emerged a rich and powerful baritone voice. A huge box, pierced with air holes and placed underneath the machine, no doubt contained a series of records, which in turn, caused the sensitive membrane to vibrate telephonically, by means of different wires, for imperceptible fluctuations in the hyperborean atmosphere, which the chemist carefully regulated, produced a number of recitatives and romances, sung by male and female voices, whose pitch and register displayed the greatest variety. The harp and the keyboard shared the secondary role, alternately accompanying the pieces of this inexhaustible repertory, which were sometimes gay, sometimes tragic.

Wishing to do full justice to the extraordinary versatility of his remarkable metal, of which not one fragment was visible, Bex spun the red handle and waited a few seconds. The icebox lost no time in changing into a furnace, and the thermometer rose to its uppermost limits. A group of flutes and fifes immediately played a stirring march rhythm, to the accompaniment of sharp, regular drum-beats. There again, different thermic variations produced unexpected results. Several fife solos, discreetly backed by a fanfare of brass, were followed by a pleasing duet which, based on the imitation of an echo, always played the same phrases twice running, performed first by a flute, and then by a flexible soprano voice from the gramophone.

The violet liquid, expanding further, rose right to the top of the tube, which looked as though it were about to burst. Several people drew back, suddenly feeling discomfort at the proximity of the burning cage, in which three hunting horns, placed not far from the harp, burst spiritedly into a noisy chorus. A slight drop in temperature then gave us a sample of the principal hunting calls, the last one of which was a mort, full of gaiety.

Having brought all the principal mechanisms of his orchestra into play, Bex volunteered to submit himself to our choice, to set in motion again one of the groups of instruments we had already heard.

Each one in turn expressed a wish, which was immediately satisfied by the chemist, who, without any other means than that of the handles, took us a second time, at random, through the various polyphonic combinations, changing the titles of the pieces out of vanity, creating imperceptible differences of temperature.

To conclude, Bex set the thermometer at a series of sub-divisions, marked in red on the tube. Thereupon, almost all the sections of the instrument played simultaneously, perform-ing a great, majestic symphony, in which was blended a choir, clearly heard, from the gramophone. The percussion, com-posed of a large set of cymbals, of the drum already used, and of several attachments with different sounds, enlivened the whole with its regular, clear rhythm. The repertory of orches-tral pieces was infinitely rich, and Bex presented all sorts of dances, medleys, overtures and variations. He finished with a wild, frenzied gallop which made heavy demands on the great bass drum, then he put up the folding pedal, before stationing himself at the back of the vehicle, which he pushed before him like a perambulator.

As he turned to leave, discussion broke out everywhere, concerning only the subject of *bexium,* and commenting on the marvellous results obtained by the use of this new metal, whose astonishing qualities the instrument had just demon-strated so clearly.

Having rapidly disappeared behind the *Bourse*, Bex soon returned, carrying upright with both hands a gigantic button-stick, a yard wide and twice as tall, made of a dull grey metal which looked like silver.

A narrow longitudinal groove was cut in the centre of the huge plate; but in this case the circular mouth through which the buttons passed, was placed half-way up the slot, and not at the bottom of it, as was usual.

Without coming closer, the chemist assured himself at a glance that he had the attention of everyone present, then he pointed out to us ten broad buttons, arranged in a vertical column, one above the other, in the lower half of the slot, naming the substance of which each was made as he did so.

Together they formed a brilliant, multi-coloured line, glinting as they reflected the light in countless different ways.

At the top, the first button, made of smooth, tawny gold, presented a shiny surface. Beneath it, the second, made of solid silver, was scarcely distinguishable from the identical background of the button-stick. The third, of brass—the fourth, of platinum—the fifth, of pewter—and the sixth, of nickel—all displayed faces of identical size and without decoration. The next four were made of numerous precious stones, skilfully joined; one was composed entirely of diamonds, another of rubies, the third of sapphires and the last of sparkling emeralds.

Bex turned the button-stick round to show us the other side. At the bottom hung a piece of blue cloth to which all the buttons were sewn.

Ten leaves of thin grey metal, attached to the fabric, were arranged one above the other some way up the slot, which was exactly the same width as they were. They occupied, on this side of the object, the place corresponding to that of the buttons on the other side, whose diameter must have equalled their length. Ten strands of metal thread had been used to anchor the precious discs firmly to the thin rectangular plates, and formed on each a criss-crossing finished with a large knot, the work of some deft craftsman.

Bex drove the base of the button-stick, which had a lightly sharpened edge, into the sand, so that it was fixed upright in front of the *Bourse* and presented the back of the buttons to the Incomparables theatre.

With a few steps he disappeared from sight, and returned carrying under each arm five long, cumbersome cylinders, made of the same grey metal as that of which the button-stick offered a huge sample.

He walked right across the esplanade, to place his heavy load in front of the red stage.

Each cylinder had a metal cap firmly fitted at one end, which made it look like a large pencil set into a common type of protector.

Bex, stacking all his equipment on the ground, arranged it in an ingenious pattern with geometrical precision.

Four enormous pencils, placed side by side, in a line on the sand, formed the base of the structure. A second line, placed on top of the first, consisted of three pencils, which lay in the narrow hollows between the rounded sides of the first layer. The next row, still shorter, contained two pencils, surmounted by the tenth and last, which was placed in a solitary position at the top of the scaffolding, whose front thus presented the shape of a triangle.

Bex had wedged the structure beforehand with two heavy stones, which he had carried in his pocket.

It was in accordance with some system and a carefully thought-out method of selection that Bex had built his pile of cylinders, taking great pains to recognise each of them by some special mark engraved at a point on their circumference.

47

The metal caps all pointed towards the distant button-stick, which served as a target for the gigantic pencils, and they were aimed in that direction like the barrels of so many cannon.

Before continuing his experiment, Bex took off his cuff-links, which were made of four golden, olive-shaped buttons. Then, removing from his clothes his watch, his wallet and his keys he handed them all to Balbet, who undertook to look after this glittering deposit.

Returning to his post and bending over in front of the stack of cylinders, Bex grasped a large ring which was fastened to the point of the top pencil cover.

By pulling gently and walking backwards, he managed to slide off the metal cap, which soon swung down like a pendulum on to the chemist's knees.

Thus exposed, the end section of the cylinder, hitherto invisible, became the cynosure of all eyes. The silver shaft, like a real pencil with a perfect point, tapered to form a cone, from which a thick amber lead projected, smooth and rounded.

Repeating the operation, Bex uncapped the ten cylinders in quick succession, and from the evenly sharpened tip of each was pointing the same yellowish, translucent lead. This task completed, the chemist crossed the esplanade again, carrying under his arms the ten short sheaths, which he put down near the button-stick.

An explanation was necessary. Bex began to speak, to disclose the purpose of his various actions.

The amber-coloured leads, enclosed in the gigantic pencils, were made of a very complex substance, prepared by Bex, and christened by him *magnetine*.

In spite of any obstacles which might find themselves in its path, the magnetine was attracted from a distance by a specific metal or a particular jewel.

Owing to certain differences in their composition, the ten

leads, which were set out in front of our eyes, corresponded to the attraction of the ten buttons, firmly held in the groove of the button-stick.

To make the handling of the newly discovered magnetine possible and practicable, the discovery of an insulating body had become indispensable. After lengthy researches, Bex had discovered *impervium*, a grey, non-shiny metal, produced by laborious processing.

A thin sheet of impervium, obstructing the field of the magnetine, totally abolished the power of attraction which the interposition of even the thickest materials could not diminish.

The pencils and the covers were all made of impervium, as were the button-stick and the ten rectangular metal strips along its slot.

The metal threads, which attached the buttons to the cloth, were braided from the same flexible metal.

By passing the shining discs, at present hidden from view, through the circular hole in the groove, Bex, his back pressed against the button-stick, would cause the sudden displacement of the cylinders, which would be precipitated with force towards the particular body which had been placed in the line of their amber-coloured leads.

This last disclosure produced a stir of panic, and the crowd of onlookers started back.

In fact we had good cause to fear numerous bruises from the pencils which, attracted by our jewellery, our watches, our money, our keys or the gold fillings in our teeth, might suddenly rush at us.

In short, the visible end of each lead projected beyond the protective end of the impervium, and fully justified our healthy apprehension.

Calmly, Bex hastened to reassure his audience. To provoke the phenomenon of irresistible magnetism, the desired object had to act rather deeply on the amber lead whose length equalled that of each cylinder. The metals and precious stones, placed in the axis of the strange battery, were alone capable of bringing them into action. And the button-stick was sufficiently wide to screen the whole danger zone; without it, the magnetic attraction would have been effective at any distance, even as far away as the ships ploughing through the Atlantic, even to the shores of America, if the curvature of the earth's surface had not rendered this impossible. Bex, being the operator, was particularly exposed, and he had, it seemed, discarded any suspect object, including the buckles on his waistcoat and trousers; the buttons on his shirt and on his clothes were made of bone, and a soft silk sash tied round his waist replaced his braces, with their inevitable metal fastenings. He had fully immunised himself at the last minute, when he had entrusted his most precious possessions to Balbet. By a happy coincidence, his teeth, in excellent condition and very white, were free of any foreign elements.

At the same time as the chemist was finishing his explanations, an unexpected phenomenon was greeted by a murmur which arose among the crowd who had slowly been moving closer.

People were showing each other with astonishment the golden coins scattered by Stella Bucharessas.

For some time, the louis, double louis and hundred-franc pieces had been stirring gently on the ground, without occasioning any surprise by their motion, which could be attributed to some capricious breeze.

In reality, the imponderable pieces of money were being subjected to the influence of the topmost cylinder, which was acting powerfully upon them; already some of the coins were flying straight towards its amber lead, and clinging firmly to it. Others followed, some round and undamaged, others bent as a result of being trampled roughly under foot.

Soon the ground was laid bare along a clearly defined strip, bordered on either side by a residue of coins which lay outside the magnetic field.

The lead was disappearing now, beneath a veritable shield of gold paper, covered with dates and effigies.

A few specks of real gold must have been used, in minute quantity, in the composition of all this wealth of tinsel.

And indeed, by its actual position, the encumbered lead corresponded unmistakably to the gold button, whose disc was the first to block the central outlet on the button-stick. Its very special property could not then have been exercised on any imitation wholly without an element of gold.

The slow reaction of the money, at first full of indecision, was due entirely to the marked insufficiency of pure gold.

Without worrying about the incident which in no way interfered with his plans, Bex took hold of the end of the strip of material and pulled it steadily towards the top of the button-stick.

The readiness and ease with which it slid along the groove made exertion unnecessary.

The cloth, as it moved up the groove, gradually covered the circular opening, which, invisible but easily detected, was soon filled by the first of the impervium plates.

Thereupon, Bex, with all the strength of both knees and his left hand, had to hold on to the button-stick which was being drawn forcibly towards the group of cylinders.

In fact, on the other side of the material, the gold button which was attached to the first metal lamina had, for the last few minutes, been framed in the round opening. Two sections of its disc, exposed without any impervium shield, thus came directly under the influence of the amber leads, which were levelled at it.

Bex's resistance caused the first cylinder to give way so that, taking flight suddenly, it flashed across the esplanade like

51

a bombshell, and reached the side of the protective plate, where it clung by its point.

Still forming a solid buttress, the chemist had taken care to slide his body to the right, in order to leave clear the estimated path of the huge pencil.

The impact rocked the button-stick, which, seized firmly by Bex, soon regained its balance.

The pencil, still now, formed a sort of gentle slope, stretching from its unsharpened end, which had just fallen to the ground, to the amber point, which was stuck fast to the gold button, in spite of the barrier of blue material.

The paper money had in no way interfered with the violent attraction of the pure metal; flattened at the moment of encounter, it still adorned the pencil lead with its factitious glitter.

Through the material, Bex felt gently for the gold button, which he wanted to hoist up into the continuation of the perpendicular slot.

But the amber lead held firm and made the process difficult.

The chemist was compelled to continue his efforts, for want of a more practical solution. All attempts to shake them apart were unsuccessful. Only the slow and gradual insertion of an impervium divider could, in the long run, overcome the extraordinary adherence of these two bodies.

A series of continuous exertions produced the desired result.

Completely blocking the opening, the gold button, still hidden from view, was once again totally eclipsed by the two side panels of the button-stick, which were joined at this point by its own steadfast and inflexible insulating plate.

Bex stood the huge crayon on its end. With the sharp edge of the pencil holders, he attempted to free the amber point from the gold paper, which still stuck to it.

The thin curved blade, scraping against the yellowish

veneer, soon got the better of the lightweight money, whose alloy contained so small a quantity of gold that it offered only a feeble resistance.

When all the coins had tumbled pell-mell to the ground, Bex fitted the pencil cover over the pencil, which he could now put on one side without risk, no matter at what point in space it was aimed.

Then, returning to the button-stick, he gently took hold of the flap of cloth, to hoist it further in the same direction.

A second experiment, identical with the first, procured the passage through the air of another pencil, whose lead hurtled violently against the unseen silver button, which was now level with the opening.

Freed by means of the same tedious procedure as had been adopted previously, the pencil fitted with a protector, was hastily set aside.

In its turn, the brass button, distinguishable behind the blue cloth, drew towards it a third cylinder which, briskly covered with its impervium cap, was placed alongside the first and second.

The two top layers were now missing from the triangular elevation, crudely formed by the stack of pencils.

Bex carried on with his unvarying operation. One by one, the buttons, raised until they were level with the opening, snapped up the amber leads, in spite of the distance which separated them, only to take cover again in the upper section of the slot.

Their function completed, the pencils, covered immediately with metal hoods, were lined up in turn on the ground.

The last four discs, extravagantly composed of precious stones, corresponded to the bottom row of cylinders, which were all that now remained in front of the theatre of the Incomparables.

Their magnetic attraction was in no way weaker than that

of the metals, and the impact of the docile amber leads was extraordinarily violent.

Having finished his experiment, Bex began to speak again and told us of the wild offers by which certain banking houses, eager to exploit his invention, had tried to seduce him.

And, indeed, his collection of cylinders could become a source of unlimited wealth, by indicating the exact whereabouts of deposits of precious stones.

Instead of relying on luck when they excavated, miners, guided infallibly by an instrument which was easy to construct, would reach the richest seams at their first attempt, and thus avoid blind groping and abortive efforts.

But it was many years since famous scientists had established, by their proverbial disinterestedness, a professional tradition that Bex wished to preserve.

And so, rejecting offers of millions and even thousands of millions, he had wisely been content with this gigantic button-stick, which together with the cylinders, amply demonstrated the virtues of his discovery, without serving any practical purpose. As he spoke, Bex had gathered up the pencils, all then secured in their covers.

He disappeared with his load, followed by Rao, carrying the button-stick, which had been quickly uprooted.

After a brief interval, the Hungarian Skariofszky appeared, in his tight-fitting, red *tzigane* jacket, and wearing on his head a forage cap of the same colour.

His right sleeve, rolled back to the elbow, revealed a thick coral bracelet, wound six times round his arm.

He was closely supervising three black porters, who, laden with various objects, halted with him in the middle of the esplanade.

54

The first negro carried in his arms a zither and a folding stand.

Skariofszky opened the stand, whose four legs rested securely on the ground. Then, on the narrow, hinged frame which opened horizontally, he set the zither, which twanged with the slight jolt.

To the left of the instrument, fixed to the frame of the stand, a metal arm rose vertically, after a slight bend, and was divided into a fork at the end; on the right, another arm, identical with the first, completed the pair.

The second negro was carrying, without difficulty, a long transparent container, which Skariofszky placed like a bridge above the zither, fitting its two ends into the two metal forks.

This new object lent itself by its form to such a mode of installation. Shaped like a trough, it was made of four sheets of mica. The largest sheets, two rectangles of equal dimensions, comprised a sloping base, their two planes obliquely joined. In addition, two triangular sections, fitted to the narrow sides of the rectangles at opposite ends, completed the diaphanous contraption, which resembled the compartment of some huge purse, made of a stiff material and wide open. A gap the breadth of a pea ran the length of the underside of this transparent trough.

The third negro had just set down on the earth a large earthenware pot, filled to the brim with clear water, whose weight Skariofszky requested one of us to feel.

La Billaudière-Maisonnial, pouring a tiny drop into the hollow of his hand, suddenly showed the liveliest surprise, exclaiming that the strange liquid appeared to be as heavy as mercury.

In the meantime, Skariofszky raised his right arm to his face, murmuring a few words of encouragement, in a voice full of gentle persuasiveness.

Then we saw the coral bracelet, which was actually a huge

55

worm, as thick as an index finger, unwind its first two coils and slowly stretch itself out to the Hungarian.

La Billaudière-Maisonnial, standing up again, was obliged to lend himself to a new experiment. At the gipsy's request, he took the worm, which slithered over his open hand; his wrist suddenly gave way under the unexpected weight of the intruder, which was apparently as heavy as solid lead.

Skariofszky removed the worm, which still clung to his arm, and placed it on the edge of the mica trough.

The reptile crawled inside the empty receptacle, drawing the rest of its body after it as it glided slowly over the bare skin of the Hungarian's arm.

Soon the reptile completely blocked the gap in the ridge at the bottom, stretching horizontally along it and suspended between two narrow inner edges of the rectangular sides.

The Hungarian raised the heavy earthenware pot, not without some difficulty, and poured its contents into the trough, which was soon filled to overflowing.

Then, resting his knee on the ground, and leaning his head to one side, he placed the empty vessel underneath the zither, on a carefully chosen spot, after running his eye up and down the back of the instrument.

Having accomplished this last move, Skariofszky, getting slowly to his feet, put his hands in his pocket as if to show that thereafter his role was that of spectator.

The worm, left to its own devices, suddenly raised a section of its body, only to let it fall back immediately after.

A drop of water, having had time to slip through the gap, landed heavily on one of the strings, which, vibrating with the shock, produced a low *C*, loud and clear.

Further along, another convulsion of the obturant body let out a second drop, which this time struck a resounding *E*.

A *G,* followed by a high *C,* attacked in the same way,

completed the common chord, which the worm then repeated in another octave.

After the third and last *C,* the seven consonant notes, played all together, provided a conclusion to this trial prelude.

After tuning up in this fashion, the worm began a slow Hungarian melody, full of tender and languid sweetness.

Each drop of water, released by a deliberate contortion of its body, correctly struck the chosen string, which cut it clean in two.

A band of felt, glued in the right place on the wood of the zither, deadened the fall of the heavy liquid, which would otherwise have produced a distracting patter.

The water, gathering in round puddles, penetrated the interior of the instrument through two circular openings cut in the soundboard. Each of the two cascades had been anticipated and fell silently on to a narrow layer of felt inside, which was specially designed to catch them.

A thin clear stream, flowing from a single outlet, soon formed beneath the zither and fell straight into the spout of the earthenware jar which Skariofszky had carefully positioned. The water, following the slope of this narrow channel, also lined with felt, ran without a sound to the bottom of the huge basin, which prevented the ground from being soaked.

The worm was still performing its musical contortions, sometimes striking two notes together, in the manner of professional zither players, who use separate sticks with their two hands.

Several tunes, both plaintive and gay, followed the first cantilena without interruption.

Then, going beyond the bounds of the usual repertory allotted to the instrument, the reptile threw itself into the polyphonic execution of a particularly lively waltz.

The accompaniment and the tune vibrated together on the

57

zither, which is generally confined to the slender output of two simultaneous sounds.

To provide some contrast in the principal part, the worm raised itself higher, thus releasing a larger quantity of water on to the string, which shook violently.

A slightly halting rhythm unobtrusively imparted to the music the unusual timbre peculiar to Hungarian gipsy bands.

After the waltz, dances of every kind gradually emptied the transparent trough.

Underneath, the earthenware pot had been filled by the continuous stream, which was now exhausted, Skariofszky took it and emptied all its contents into the light receptacle a second time, before returning it to its place on the ground.

With his supply completely replenished, the worm broke into a *czardas,* punctuated by savage and brutal variations. Sometimes great heaves of the long, reddish-coloured body produced noisy *fortissimi*; at others, imperceptible undulations allowed only tiny droplets to escape, so that the zither, suddenly hushed, was reduced to a mere murmur.

No mechanical element entered into this personal execution, full of fire and conviction. The worm gave the impression of a virtuoso performing daily, who, according to the inspiration of the moment, played differently each time a certain ambiguous passage, whose delicate interpretation was the subject of much discussion.

A prolonged operetta selection having followed the *czardas,* the liquid supply was once again exhausted. Skariofszky again went through the rapid process of decanting it, announcing the final piece.

This time, the worm, in a lively mood, began a captivating Hungarian rhapsody, every bar of which bristled with the most appalling difficulties.

Brilliant runs followed each other without respite, interspersed with trills and chromatic scales.

Soon the reptile began to accentuate with great convulsions a certain song of noble proportions, every note of which, in transcription, would doubtless have borne a heavy accent. Around this theme, established as a foundation, were woven many light ornaments which required only a shudder of the supple body.

The reptile was growing intoxicated with harmony. Far from showing the least weariness, it grew more and more excited at the contact of the musical emanations it let loose.

Its rapture communicated itself to the audience, strangely moved by the expressive tone of certain sounds like weeping, and by the incredible velocity displayed in various successions of demi-semiquavers.

A frenzied *presto* crowned the reptile's enthusiastic delirium and for several minutes it abandoned itself unreservedly to wild gymnastics.

At the end, it prolonged the perfect cadence by a sort of improvised method of amplification, repeating the last chords until the percussive liquid was completely finished.

Skariofszky held out his bare arm, around which the worm coiled itself again, after climbing up the mica slope.

The negroes came and removed the various objects, including the earthenware pot, as full now as when it had arrived.

Their procession, led by the Hungarian, soon disappeared behind the stock exchange.

# IV

IN obedience to Rao's commands, the whole of that section
of the crowd of natives who were assembled along the right
side of the square turned about and stepped back a few paces,
in order to be able to view the Incomparables theatre from
the front.

Immediately, our group drew closer to get a better view of
Talu, who had just come on to the stage, followed by Carmichael, a young man from Marseilles, whose ordinary, brown
clothes offered a striking contrast to the Emperor's elaborate
garb.

Adopting a falsetto voice, which, in its imitation of female
tones, was quite in keeping with the dress and wig he wore,
Talu performed Daricelli's *Aubade,* a song requiring the most
difficult feats of vocalisation.

Holding in his hand the music with the accompanying
French text, Carmichael prompted him a bar at a time, and
the Emperor, faithfully echoing his guide, executed numerous
flourishes, continuing his efforts for several minutes, before
ending on a reasonably pure key note, shrilling far above
his normal register.

When the ballad was finished, both singer and prompter
joined the crowd, while Juillard, the historian, the next to

appear on the stage, sat down at his lecture table on our left, equipped with an assortment of notes which he began to thumb through.

For twenty minutes, the remarkable speaker held us spellbound with his persuasive eloquence, a brief evocation, which was at the same time lucid, witty and evocative, of the history of the Electors of Brandenburg.

From time to time, he would point at one of the portraits pinned to the back-cloth, drawing our attention to a particular feature or some facial expression which he had just mentioned in one of his remarks. In conclusion, he summed up the substance of the lecture in one brilliant, final sentence, and, when he withdrew, he left us with a sense of dazzled amazement, induced by the richly coloured imagery and the animation of his delivery.


Immediately afterwards, the ichthyologist, Martignon, came to the centre of the stage, holding in both hands a perfectly transparent fish-tank, in which a strange-looking fish, whitish in colour, swam slowly around.

In a few words, the distinguished naturalist introduced the sturgeon-skate, a species hitherto unknown, which he had procured the previous day, as the result of a successful sounding in the open sea.

The fish which we saw before us was a product of cross breeding. The combination of clearly defined, dual characteristics, which the phenomenon in the tank alone possessed, could only be obtained when the eggs of a skate were fertilised by a sturgeon.

As Martignon slowly departed, never for a moment taking his eyes off the astonishing hybrid he had discovered, Tancred Bucharessas, the father of the four children whose ability had so impressed us, made a sensational entrance pushing a large instrument on castors across the front of the stage.

Laced tightly into his gipsy costume, Tancred, a limbless cripple without either legs or arms, moved very nimbly, by bobbing along on the stumps of his thighs. Without any help he climbed on to a low platform placed in the middle of the moveable contraption he had carted in, and when he turned his back on the crowd his mouth was exactly level with a broad instrument which fitted round his chin and consisted of a vertical set of pan-pipes, carefully arranged according to size, ranging from the big ones at the bottom to the small ones at the top. On his right was a large accordion, with a thick leather strap fitted to the end of the bellows, and a buckle exactly accommodated to the rudimentary biceps, less than four inches long, which stuck out from his shoulder. On the other side, a triangle hung on a thread, ready to ring when struck with an iron rod which had previously been fastened securely to the performer's left stump.

Arranging himself in the right position, Tancred, producing single-handed the noise of a whole band, vigorously struck up a sparkling overture.

Tossing his head up and down, without a pause, so that with his lips he could seek out the notes of the melody on the pipes, while his two biceps worked simultaneously—one squeezing the accordion bellows in and out, so as to play alternately the common chord and the ninth—the other bringing the iron rod down on the base of the triangle at the appropriate moment like the clapper of a bell.

On the right, seen in profile and forming one of the sides of the instrument, a big drum, with a mechanical drum-stick, had as its counterpart on the left side a pair of cymbals, fixed

62

at the end of two solid brass supports. By jumping skilfully into the air in such a way that he only moved from the shoulders down, leaving his head free, he repeatedly rocked a spring board on which he was standing; the weight of his body, landing heavily on the thin, unsteady surface, set in motion both the drum-stick and the cymbals, whose deafening sound when they clashed together merged with the resounding roll of the big drum.

The majestic overture, with its delicate and varied tones, ended with a dashing *presto,* during which the truncated legs of the human freak, jumping on the board in time to the down beat, hammered out the rhythm of a giddy tune, accompanied *fortissimo* by a loud bass part on the accordion and the constant jangling of the triangle.

After the final chord, the little man, as active as ever, left his post to vanish into the wings, while two of his sons, Hector and Tommy, came to clear the stage, without delay removing the instrument as well as the lecturer's table and chair.

When this task had been completed, an *artiste* came on to the stage, correctly dressed in a black suit and carrying a top hat in his white-gloved hands. This was Ludovic, the famous singer with four voices, whose mouth at once captured everyone's attention by its colossal size.

In a pleasant tenor voice, Ludovic softly began singing the well-known canon *Frère Jacques*, but only the left side of his mouth was moving and pronouncing the familiar words, while the rest of the enormous cavity remained closed and motionless.

Just as, after the first notes, the words: ' Dormez-vous? ' were heard in the upper third, a second buccal section began at Frère Jacques ', starting on *C.* Ludovic, as a result of long years of work, had learnt to separate his lips and his tongue into sections which functioned independently of one another, and to pronounce, at one and the same time, without difficulty, several conflicting parts, with different tunes and different words; at present the left half was moving, to show his teeth, without involving in its movements the right side, which remained motionless and tight shut.

But a third labial area soon entered into the chorus, repeating exactly the words of its forerunner; at the same time, the second voice chanted the words ' Dormez-vous?' enlivened by the first voice, which introduced a new element into the song, by matching the words ' Sonnez la matine ' to a lively, tinkling rhythm.

A fourth time the words ' Frère Jacques ' were heard, now articulated by the right end of his mouth, which had just stirred from its inactivity to complete the quartet. The first voice then ended the canon with the syllables ' Ding, ding, dong ', which provided a bass accompaniment too for ' Sonnez la matine ' and ' Dormez-vous?' sung in different tones by the intermediary voices.

Ludovic's eyes were set, and his pupils dilated, for he had need of constant mental concentration to accomplish this brilliant and unrivalled feat without faltering. The first voice had recommenced the song and the buccal regions, all going through different motions, shared the words of the canon, the four lines of which, sung simultaneously, mingled entrancingly.

Little by little, Ludovic increased the volume, to begin a rousing *crescendo* which gave the impression of a distant group of singers rapidly drawing nearer.

There were a few bars of *fortissimo* during which, progressing in a continuous cycle from one labial division to the next, the four phrases swelled loud and clear at a somewhat accelerated pace.

Then calm was restored as the imaginary band seemed to move away and lose themselves at a turn in the road; the last notes were reduced to a faint murmur, and Ludovic, exhausted by his great mental effort, walked away, wiping his brow.

After an interval lasting a minute, Philippo appeared before us, presented by Jenn, the ringmaster from whom he was never separated.

A head without a body, the head, that of a quinquagenarian, standing on a large red disc, fitted with an iron frame to prevent it from toppling over. This way was Philippo. A short, unkempt beard added to the ugliness of his face, which was rendered comic and likeable by an expression of intelligent amusement.

Holding in both hands the flat disc, which was a kind of round table without legs, Jenn showed the crowd this trunkless head, which began to chatter gaily, with a flow of the most original sayings.

The lower jaw was very prominent, and the mouth, spluttering at every word, sent out a shower of saliva, which landed some distance in front of him.

Here, there was no possibility of any of the subterfuges usually adopted for the well-known 'talking-head' trick; there was no system of mirrors under the table, which Jenn moved carelessly, without taking any suspicious precautions. Besides, the showman walked to the edge of the stage and held out the round platform to any spectator who wanted to examine it.

Skariofszky took a few steps forward and was handed Philippo, who thereafter, passing from hand to hand, held a short, and surprisingly witty, conversation with each person; some held the table at arm's length in order to avoid, as far as possible, the shower of spray from the mouth of the freak, whose astonishing rejoinders caused us to burst out laughing continuously.

After going the complete round, Philippo returned to his starting point and was restored to Jenn, who still stood on the stage.

Immediately, the showman pressed a hidden spring which caused the red table to open like an extraordinary flat box, for it in fact consisted of two sections joined by a narrow hinge.

The lower disc, seen from the side, dropped open at right angles, while Jenn held the circle which, until a moment ago, had formed the lid and which, remaining horizontal, still supported the bearded face.

Underneath it, clad in the classic flesh-coloured tights, hung a tiny human body, which, on account of its total atrophy, had until then fitted into the narrow hiding place in the hollow table, which was barely an inch thick.

This sudden vision completed the person of Philippo, a talkative dwarf, who, showing a normally developed head, lived in perfect health, in spite of the diminutive size of his remarkable anatomy.

While he continued to talk and spit, the extraordinary chatterbox moved his puppet-like limbs in all directions, as if to give free play to his gaiety and all his tireless exuberance.

Soon, grasping Philippo by the neck, after removing the iron frame which worked on hinges fitted with catch-fasteners, the impresario lowered the upper disc, whose opening was easily large enough to enable the weightless, pink-clad body to slip through. The agile midget, whose head, bigger than Jenn's, was as long as the rest of the body, suddenly took advantage of his new-found freedom of movement to scratch his beard furiously without interrupting the shower of speech.

As Jenn carried him off into the wings, he quickly grasped

one foot in each hand and disappeared, jigging up and down, while a final jest scattered thousands of drops of his abundant saliva.

At once the Breton, Lelgoualch, dressed in the traditional costume of his province, came forward flourishing his round hat in greeting, while the boards of the stage resounded to the thud of his wooden leg.

In his hand he held a hollow bone with distinct holes pierced in it like a flute.

Speaking with a strong Breton accent, the newcomer recited a ready-made patter, giving us the following details concerning himself.

At eighteen, Lelgoualch, following the craft of a fisherman, coasted along the shores near his native town of Paimpol, in his little boat.

The owner of a set of Breton bagpipes, the boy was considered the best player in the region. Each Sunday, people gathered in the public square to hear him play, with a truly individual charm, an inexhaustible host of Breton airs stored up in his memory.

One day when there was a festival in Paimpol, climbing to the top of a greasy pole, Lelgoualch fell from the top to the ground and broke his leg. Ashamed of his clumsiness, which the entire village had witnessed, he got to his feet and began the ascent again, succeeding by the sheer strength of his arms. Then he returned home as best he could, still making it a matter of pride to hide his pain.

When, after waiting too long, he at last sent for the doctor, the damage had been excessively aggravated, and gangrene had set in. It was deemed necessary to amputate.

Lelgoualch, when he was told, put a brave face on it and,

only thinking how he might make the most of the situation, simply asked the operating surgeon to keep his tibia for him since he intended to put it to some mysterious use.

His request was granted, and one day the poor cripple, sporting a brand new wooden leg, called on a violin maker and, with precise instructions, left in his hands a carefully wrapped parcel.

A month later, Lelgoualch received a black case lined with velvet, which contained the bone of his leg, fashioned into a flute, whose tone was strangely clear.

The young Breton quickly learned the new fingering and then embarked on a lucrative career, playing tunes of his country in music-halls and circuses. The weird instrument, whose origin was explained each time, drew curious crowds, and everywhere the takings increased.

It was already twenty years since the operation, and meanwhile the tone of the flute had all the while improved, like that of a violin which mellows with age.


As he finished the story, Lelgoualch raised his tibia to his lips and began to play a Breton melody, full of languid melancholy. The pure, velvet tones were like nothing we had ever heard; the quality of the instrument, which was both warm and crystal-clear, with an indescribable purity, were wonderfully suited to the particular charm of the gentle, singing melody, whose expressive phrasing bore the listener away to the heart of Armorica.

Several ballads, joyful or patriotic, romantic or lively, followed the first song, preserving throughout a perfect unity from which the local colour vividly emerged.

After a last soft lament, Lelgoualch withdrew with brisk strides, his wooden leg tapping across the boards.

Urbain, the circus rider, then made his appearance, wearing a blue coat, leather breeches and boots with turnovers and leading a magnificent black horse, a powerful thoroughbred. Only an elegant halter adorned the head of the animal, whose mouth was free of any bit or trammel.

Urbain took a few steps across the stage, and turned the splendid charger round to face us, introducing it by the name of Romulus, called in circus jargon 'the horse with the gift of the gab'.

At the spoken request of the horseman, who asked a number of the audience to mention any word which came into his head, Juillard called out 'Equator'.

Immediately, repeating slowly, one at a time, the syllables which Urbain spoke aloud, the horse quite distinctly pronounced the word 'E-qua-tor'.

The animal's tongue, instead of being square like that of its kind, was pointed, like those which gabble in the human gob.

This peculiarity, which he had noticed by chance, persuaded Urbain to attempt the education of Romulus, who, after two years' work, had got into the habit of repeating distinctly any sound he heard, like a parrot.

The horseman repeated the test, now asking the onlookers for whole sentences, which Romulus repeated with him. Soon, managing without his prompter, the horse fluently recited his whole repertory, including numerous proverbs, fragments of fables, oaths and commonplaces, gabbled at random, without any sign of intelligence or comprehension.

At the end of this amazing display, Urbain led Romulus away, the horse still murmuring vaguely to itself.

The man and the horse were replaced by Whirligig, looking light and slender in his clown's costume and with flour on his face, who carried by the brim, one in each hand and one in his teeth, three separate baskets which he set down on the stage.

Cleverly aping an English accent, he introduced himself by saying that he was a lucky fellow who had just made a big profit from two different games.

At the same time he showed us the baskets, containing, respectively, money, dominoes and dark-blue playing cards.

Taking first the basket of cash, which he moved towards the right, Whirligig, scooping out handfuls of copper coins, built a curious construction on the edge of the stage, against the wall.

Large and small coins were quickly piled on top of each other by the clown's expert fingers which seemed accustomed to the task undertaken. Soon the base of a feudal dungeon became recognisable, with a large door cut in it, the top of which was still missing.

Without a moment's rest the nimble craftsman continued his task, to the accompaniment of noisy, cheerful clinking metal. In places, narrow slits were left in the round wall, which grew higher as we watched.

When he drew level with the top of the door, Whirligig took from his sleeve a long, flat, narrow bar, whose brown colour matched the muddy hue of the coins. This sturdy beam, placed across the two door-posts like a bridge, enabled the clown to continue his work on a firm and solid foundation.

The money still piled up abundantly, and when the basket was empty, Whirligig proudly pointed to a high tower, artistically crenellated, which looked like part of the exterior of some old building of which one corner formed part of a stage set.

With a stack of dominoes which he took in armfuls from the second basket, the clown set out to build a kind of unsupported wall at the right-hand side of the stage.

The uniform rectangles, arranged one deep, were placed on top of each other in perfect symmetry, many with their black sides showing, the rest turned outwards, their white faces showing various numbers of spots.

Soon a large panel, which rose up in a perfectly vertical plane, showed, on a white background, the black outline of a priest in a long cassock, wearing the traditional hat; some on their sides, some standing on one end, according to the needs of the pattern, their black and white faces skilfully alternated, the only materials used in the execution of the design were the dominoes, which appeared to have been glued together along their narrow edges. Such was the precision with which the work was accomplished.

Continuing in this way, without trowel or mortar, Whirligig in a few minutes completed a wall nine feet long, which, extending towards the back of the stage at a slightly oblique angle, formed a strictly homogenous block. The first motif was repeated the length of the mosaic, and there now appeared a whole procession of clerics, who looked as though they were walking in little groups towards a single unknown objective.

Going over to the third basket, the clown took out and unfolded a large piece of black cloth, which had rings fixed to two corners so that it could be hung up without difficulty on two hooks which had been fixed to the back-cloth and the left wall of the stage before the performance.

The black drape, falling right to the floor, thus formed a wide, broken surface, on which the wall of dominoes converged, stretching in a straight line from the tower of money.

The side of the cloth which was turned outwards, newly

exposed to the air, was covered with a moist coat of some kind of fresh, shiny paste.

The clown planted himself gracefully in front of this huge target and, with extraordinary dexterity, began to throw at it the playing cards, which he drew in fistfuls from his supply.

Each light projectile, spinning through the air, infallibly landed with its blue back to the black curtain and remained imprisoned there by the sticky liquid coating it.

The thrower seemed to be playing a kind of patience, as the cards landed in symmetric patterns, so that black and red, strong and weak, lay haphazardly side by side, without regard to value or suit.

Before long, diamonds, clubs, spades and hearts, following one upon the other in straight rows, sketched out the shape of a roof on the black background; then came the front of a house, complete with several windows and a large door, on whose threshold Whirligig, using a whole pack, carefully drew the outline of an ecclesiastic in a hat, who seemed to be stepping out of his house to welcome the group of colleagues who were coming towards him.

When the game of patience was over, the clown turned round to give this explanation of his three masterpieces: " A group of reverend gentlemen leaving the tower of an old cloister to visit the parish priest in his rectory."

Then, as light and agile as ever, he folded up the cloth with all the cards it contained and demolished the decorative wall and brown tower in a few seconds.

Everything was quickly returned to the stout baskets, and Whirligig vanished with them like a sprite.

A moment later, the Belgian tenor, Cuijper, appeared on the stage, buttoned into a tight frock-coat.

72

He held between his fingers a fragile metal instrument, which he held out for the audience to see as best they could, turning it slowly round to display each side in turn.

It was a *squeaker,* a larger version of those toys with a nasal sound which are used to imitate Punch's voice.

Cuijper briefly recounted the story of this bauble, his own invention, which by amplifying his voice a hundredfold, had been able to shake the Monnaie theatre in Brussels to its foundations.

We all remembered the sensation in the press caused by *Cuijper's Squeaker,* which no manufacturer of musical instruments had been able to imitate.

The tenor jealously guarded the secret concerning the composition of the metal and the shape of its many circumvallations, which gave the precious trifle its fabulous qualities of resonance.

Fearful of increasing the chances of theft and indiscretion, Cuijper had restricted himself to the manufacture of a single specimen, the object of his constant vigilance; thus we were now looking at the same squeaker which, throughout one season, had aided him in singing principal roles on the stage of the Monnaie.

As he finished these preliminary explanations, Cuijper announced the great aria from *Gorloès* and put the squeaker to his mouth.

Suddenly a superhuman voice, which, it seemed, must have been audible for miles around, issued from his throat, causing the listeners to tremble.

This tremendous volume in no way marred the charm of his tones, and the mysterious squeaker, the cause of this unbelievable burst of sound, instead of distorting it, brought out more clearly his elegant pronunciation of the words.

Avoiding all effort, Cuijper, as if for his own amusement, shattered the stillness of the atmosphere, without any shrill

73

tone spoiling the purity of his notes, which recalled both the flexibility of the harp and the power of the organ.

Alone, he filled the air better than a huge choir; his *forte* would have drowned the roar of thunder, and his *piano* retained tremendous breadth, while giving the impression of a faint murmur.

The final note, opening softly, then swelling with true art, and cut off at the height of its glory, produced a sense of amazement among the crowd, which lasted until Cuijper departed, his fingers once more toying with the strange squeaker.

A thrill of curiosity roused the audience again as the great tragic actress, Adinolfa, entered, clad in a simple black dress which accentuated the fatal sadness of her countenance, whose very aspect was darkened by her fine, velvety eyes and her thick brown hair.

After a short announcement, Adinolfa began to declaim in Italian the noble, ringing verses of Tasso; her features were expressive of intense sorrow, and there was a tremor in her voice which verged on a sob; she wrung her hands in anguish, and her whole being trembled with grief, intoxicated with exaltation and despair.

Soon, real tears sprang from her eyes testifying to the disturbing sincerity of her terrible emotion.

Sometimes she would kneel, her head bent beneath the weight of her affliction, then she would get up, her fingers joined and stretched out to Heaven, whither she seemed fervently to address her rending cries.

Tears streamed from her lashes, while the poems of Tasso, illustrated by her affecting mime, echoed harshly, spoken in savage, stirring tones, designed to evoke the most dreadful mental torment.

With a last emphatic line, each syllable of which was hurled forth separately in a voice hoarse with effort, the inspired tragedienne walked slowly away, holding her head in her hands, her clear, abundant tears falling to the last.

Immediately two curtains of red damask, drawn by an unseen hand, moved simultaneously from the furthermost ends of the empty stage, screening it completely as they met at a point in the middle.

# V

TWO minutes passed, during which Carmichael entered and took up his position on the left-hand side, in front of the theatre, which bustled with unseen, noisy activity.

Suddenly the curtains opened again on a *tableau vivant* with an air of picturesque gaiety.

In a loud voice, Carmichael, pointing to the motionless apparition, made this brief pronouncement:

' The Feast of the Gods on Olympus.'

In the centre of the stage, which was hung with black draperies, Jupiter, Juno, Mars, Diana, Apollo, Venus, Neptune, Vesta, Minerva, Ceres and Vulcan, seated in full dress at a sumptuously laden table, smilingly raised their brimming cups. On the point of drinking a toast, Mercury, represented by the comedian Soreau, seemed to be held aloft by the wings on his sandals, and floated above the banquet without any perceptible means of support from the beams of the roof.

The curtains closed again, hiding the immortal assembly from our sight, then they reopened after a great deal of bustle which lasted a few moments, to reveal in a different setting a rather elaborate spectacle.

The left half of the stage suggested a peaceful scene with a stretch of water, hidden by a hedge of reeds.

A coloured woman, who, from her costume and her adornments, appeared to belong to a savage North-American tribe, stood motionless in a light boat. Alone with her in the frail craft, a little girl of white origin held in her hands a fishing rod by which, with a quick jerk, she lifted from the water a pike, which had been caught in a trap; underneath, the head of the fish could be seen poking through the mesh, about to plunge back into its native element.

The other half of the stage represented a grassy bank. In the foreground, a man, apparently running as fast as his legs would carry him, bore on his shoulders a pasteboard snout, which hid his face completely and made him look like a boar with a human body. A piece of wire, forming a wide arch, was attached by both ends to the wrists of the runner which he held at different heights in front of him. A glove, an egg and a wisp of straw, arranged to look as if they were flying through the air, were threaded to the metal wire at three points in its graceful curve. The fugitive's hands were held open to the sky, as if he were juggling with the three objects, fixed in their upward course. The arc, sloping away from him gave the impression that the juggler was being swept swiftly and irresistibly onwards. Seen only in rear profile, and apparently drawn by an invincible force, the juggler was moving towards the back of the stage.

In the centre of the stage a live goose was rooted to the spot by some kind of glue which held her feet wide apart in a great stride so that she looked as if she were running at a dizzy speed. Her two white wings were stretched open, as if to aid her in her wild flight. Behind the bird, Soreau, clad in floating robes, represented the raging west wind; from his mouth there issued a long cardboard funnel, grey-blue in colour, marked with longitudinal stripes and copied from those great puffs of wind that artists drew coming out of the mouths of zephyrs, which skilfully represented the gust of a storm; the open end of the light cone pointed at the goose, which was driven forward by the current of air. Boreas was also carrying in his right hand a rose on a long, thorny stalk and was preparing to strike the fugitive, to hasten her flight. The goose, which was almost facing the audience, was on the point of crossing the juggler's path, each of them apparently following, in opposite directions, the sharp curve of the same parabola.

In the background stood a gold grating, behind which the she-ass Milenkaya, was straining to reach an untouched trough of bran with her jaw closed by a suture, passed through it from top to bottom. Certain peculiarities made it possible to tell what trick had been employed to simulate the painful impediment which was forcing her to starve. Only the two rowels which showed were really there, fastened to the nose of the she-ass and both crossed by a small piece of stick. At a superficial glance, the artifice produced an effective impression of completely locking the jaw, thus condemning the animal perpetually to the torment of Tantalus.

Carmichael, pointing to the little girl standing up in the boat, who was none other than Stella Bucharessas, proferred this explanation in a clear voice.

' Ursula, accompanied by the Huron Maffa, goes to the aid of the bewitched people on Lake Ontario.'

The characters all remained as motionless as statues. Soreau, holding the point of the long, sky-blue horn between his teeth, blew out his smooth, puffed cheeks, without letting the rose, which he held at arm's length, tremble as he did so.

The curtains were closed again, and immediately, from behind their impenetrable barrier, could be heard a continuous uproar produced by feverish and hurried activity.

Suddenly the stage was revealed, completely transformed.

The centre was entirely taken up by a staircase which wound upwards and was lost among the rafters.

Half-way up, an old blind man, in mid-eighteenth-century costume, appeared facing us, at a turn in the staircase, in the process of descending. In his left hand he held a dark bunch of greenery, consisting of a number of sprigs of holly. By examining the bottom of the spray closely, it was possible after a while, to distinguish all the colours of the rainbow, in the form of seven silk bows, tied individually to each of the stems in the bunch.

With a goose quill which he held in his free hand, the blind man was writing on the balustrade to his right, which, by reason of its flat rail and pale colour, offered a convenient smooth surface.

Several minor characters, crowded on the steps around, were solemnly following the old man's movements. The nearest among them, who was holding an inkwell, seemed to be watching the pen to see when it needed recharging.

Pointing at the stage with his finger, Carmichael addressed these words to the audience :

' Handel composing the theme of his oratorio, *Vesper*, by a mechanical process.'

Soreau, in the part of Handel, had made himself up in the conventional manner to suggest blindness, by colouring his eyelids, which he kept almost completely lowered.

The scene disappeared behind the veil of draperies, and an interval of some length was indicated only by whispering among the audience.

' The Czar Alexis discovers the assassin Plehtcheiev.'

This sentence, uttered by Carmichael just as the curtains were being drawn along their rod, applied to a Russian scene of the seventeenth century.

On the right, Soreau, playing the Czar, held up to his eyes a circle of red glass which had the appearance of the setting sun. His gaze, passing through this round pane, rested on a group of commoners to his left, clustered round a dying man, with face and hands quite livid, who had fallen into their arms in a fit.

The scene was of short duration and was followed by an

interlude which ended with this announcement by Carmichael: ' Constantine Canaris evoking the scent of flowers, borne to him on the echo in the woods of Argyros.'

Soreau, in the part of the famous sailor, stood sideways on the front of the stage, his hands cupped to his mouth like a trumpet.

Near him, several of his companions stood in attitudes of surprise and astonishment.

Without moving, Soreau pronounced clearly the word, 'rose ', which was quickly repeated by a voice off-stage.

At the very moment that the echo was heard, a strong, pervasive scent of roses spread over Trophies Square, reaching the nostrils of everyone there, only to fade almost immediately.

The word ' carnation,' which Soreau pronounced next, produced the same phonetic and odoriferous effect.

One by one, lilac, jasmine, lily-of-the-valley, thyme, gardenia and violet were called aloud, and each time the echo diffused exhalations of strong perfume, which corresponded exactly to the word it had obediently repeated.

The curtains were drawn on the poetic scene, and the air was immediately cleared of all trace of the intoxicating scents.

After a tedious wait, a scene was abruptly uncovered, and Carmichael pointed to it, accompanying the gesture with these words :

' Prince Savellini, the multi-millionaire, robbing tramps in the slums of Rome.'

For the first time Soreau appeared in modern dress, enveloped in an elegant fur overcoat, and bedecked with precious stones which glittered on his tie and on his fingers. Nearby, a circle of sinister-looking thugs stood around, out of curiosity watching two men fighting, armed with knives. Taking advantage of the concentration of the onlookers, who were too absorbed in the duel to notice his presence, the man in the fur coat, standing just behind them, was furtively going through their filthy pockets and removing the sordid contents. His probing hands were at that moment clutching a dented watch, a grubby purse and a huge check handkerchief, still almost buried in the depths of a patched jacket.

When the usual smooth mechanism which closed the curtains hid this antithetical oddity from view, Carmichael left his post, thus marking the end of the series of scenes without action.

The stage was soon exposed to view once again, for the entrance of the old ballerina, Olga Chervonenkova, a fat Latvian with a moustache, dressed as a dancer and garlanded with leaves, who made her appearance riding on Sladky, the elk, crushing him under her tremendous weight; the graceful creature paced twice up and down the stage, then returned to the wings, relieved of the stout amazon, who took her place for the ' Dance of the Nymph '.

With a smile on her lips, the erstwhile star began a series of rapid turns, which still showed some trace of her former talent; beneath the stiff folds of her tulle skirt, her monstrous legs, moulded in close-fitting pink tights, performed their skilful movements with sufficient agility and some of her past gracefulness, which occasioned considerable surprise.

Suddenly, as she was crossing the stage with tiny steps, her feet raised on the tips of her toes, Olga fell heavily, with cries of pain.

Doctor Lefleuve left our group and rushed on to the stage where he ascertained the pitiful state of the invalid who had been forced to stop by a torn ligament.

At the moment of the accident, Talu, as if to avoid any interruption in the performance, gave some discreet instructions to Rao.

Suddenly, drowning the distant cries of poor Olga, a huge chorus, composed of deep, ringing, male voices, burst into song.

On hearing the sound, everyone turned towards the west side of the esplanade, in front of which the black warriors, kneeling by their weapons which they had laid on the ground, were singing the whole of the *Jeruka,* a boastful epic, composed by the Emperor, who had taken as his subject the recital of his own exploits.

The tune, which had a strange rhythm and tonality, consisted of a single, short motif, repeated indefinitely with a constant change of words.

The singers beat time to each couplet, clapping their hands in perfect unison, and a rather splendid impression was produced by the glorious lament which was performed not without nobility and distinction.

Nevertheless, the constant repetition of the single phrase gradually induced acute boredom, accentuated by the inevitable likelihood of its continuance, since the *Jeruka* was a faithful account of the Emperor's whole life, in which great deeds had been numerous.

The Ponukelian words, completely incomprehensible to European ears, were unfolded in meaningless verses, doubtless full of momentous events, and night began to fall without any sign that this wearisome chant was drawing to its close.

Suddenly, when we despaired of ever reaching the last verse, the choir, ceasing of its own accord, was replaced by a female voice—a wonderful, sharp voice, which rang out with great purity in the now deep dusk.

All eyes, searching for the spot from which this new voice came, made out Carmichael, standing at the end on the left, in front of the chorus, who was finishing the *Jeruka* alone, singing an additional chapter devoted to *The Battle of the Tez,* without any change in the time of the music.

His astounding head-voice, imitating the vibrations of the female throat to the life, rose to perfection in the great sonority of the open air, without seeming in the least troubled by the difficult pronunciation of the unintelligible syllables of which the verses were composed.

After a few moments, Carmichael, at first so sure of himself, was forced to stop, betrayed by his memory, which denied him a word in the string of unintelligible syllables he had conscientiously learned by heart.

Talu prompted from a distance in a loud voice with the fragment which the young man from Marseilles had forgotten, and, picking up the thread of his story, he reached the end of the last couplet without further hesitation.

Immediately the Emperor said a few words to Sirdah, who, translating into excellent French the sentence dictated by her father, was compelled to inflict on Carmichael three hours' detention as a punishment for his momentary lapse.

# VI

THE black warriors, all getting to their feet together, had just picked up their weapons.

Reassembling under the direction of Rao, the first party, together with our group and most of the Incomparables, set out, walking fast in a southerly direction.

We crossed the south district of Ejur at a lively pace, and the plain soon appeared, bounded by the great trees of the Behuliphruen, a magnificent garden, stocked with strange and wonderful plants.

Suddenly Rao halted the huge column of men who had now reached a vast stretch of open country, the size of which made it suitable for certain experiments with long-distance acoustics.

Stephen Alcott, a sturdy old man with a protruding chest, stepped from among the ranks with his six sons, whose extraordinary thinness was strikingly apparent under the plain, close-fitting red jerseys they wore.

Their father, dressed in the same way, took up his stand on a spot chosen at random, with his back to the setting sun, then, carefully turning a half-point of the compass, he suddenly stopped dead, assuming the immobility of a statue.

Starting from the very spot on which Stephen was standing, the oldest of the six brothers walked obliquely towards the Beluliphruen, following the exact path of his father's line of vision and counting out loud the long, slow strides which he was at pains to make strictly equal. He stopped on reaching the number one hundred and seventeen, and, turning to face west, followed the paternal example by striking a studied pose. The next brother, who had accompanied him, took a similar walk in a south-westerly direction and after sixty-two paces of mechanical uniformity became as stiff as a dummy, his breast turned towards the east. In their turn, the four youngest brothers performed a similar action, each one taking as his starting point the predetermined goal reached by the previous marker and exercising, in the performance of his remarkably controlled, brief progress, a mathematical precision usually reserved to the craft of the surveyor.

When the youngest brother was in his place, the seven confederates, situated at unequal distances from each other, were spaced out in a strange, crooked line, whose five unequal angles were strictly marked by the position of each brother's heels.

The apparently meaningless figure they formed was the deliberate result of a calculated number of even strides, each one's individual total ranging from a minimum of sixty-two to a maximum of a hundred and forty-nine.

Once at their posts each of the six brothers violently drew in his chest and stomach, with a painful muscular effort, to make a great hollow, each holding his arms around this to form a circle which extended the sides of the cavity and made it even deeper. Their jerseys still clung to their skin all over, held in place by some sticky substance.

Cupping his hands to his mouth to make his voice carry, the father, addressing the eldest son, called out his own name in a deep, resonant voice.

85

Immediately, at regular intervals, the four syllables—
*Ste-phen Al-cott*—were repeated in turn at the six points of
the enormous zig-zag, without the participants making the
slightest movement with their lips.

It was the voice of the head of the family himself which
had just reverberated against the thoracic cavities of the six
young men; for, on account of their extreme emaciation,
carefully maintained by a rigorous diet, they exposed to the
sound a surface of bone, hard enough to reflect all its vibrations.

This first attempt did not satisfy the executants, who
changed places slightly and altered their positions.

The adjustment took several minutes, during which time
Stephen often called out his name, testing the result, which
his sons each time improved, sometimes by shifting their feet,
a little and moving a centimetre in one direction or another,
sometimes by leaning over more, the better to assist the swift
passage of the sound.

It was apparently a question of some imaginary instrument,
difficult to tune properly, which above all required for its
regulation minute care and patience.

Finally, after a satisfactory test, Stephen, with one short
word which inevitably reverberated six times, ordered the
emaciated sentinels to stand quite still.

Then the real display began.

Stephen, at the top of his voice, called out all sorts of
names, interjections and common words with an infinite
variety of pitch and intonation. And each time the sound,
rebounding from chest to chest, was reproduced with crystal
clarity, at first loud and strong, then more and more faintly,
down to the last murmur which was barely a whisper.

No echo, in forest, grotto or cathedral, could have competed
with this artificial combination, accomplishing a true miracle
in acoustics.

The Alcott family had worked out the geometric pattern of the crooked line after months of study and groping, and the irregularities, arrived at scientifically, depended on the particular shape of the individual chest in so far as the anatomical structure of each possessed resonant powers of a greater or smaller range.

Several members of the procession stood close to each vibrating sentinel and were able to ascertain that there was no trickery involved. The mouths of the six young men remained tight shut and the initial call alone was responsible for the multiple sound.

Stephen, wishing to give the experiment the broadest possible application, quickly pronounced some short sentences which were slavishly repeated by the six voices of the echo; some lines of verse, pentameters recited one at a time, were distinctly heard without any overlapping or confusion; different types of laughter, a deep ' Ah ', a shrill ' Oh ', and a piercing ' Ee ' produced a wonderful impression of empty, heartless derision. Cries of pain or alarm, sobbing, exclamations of pity, loud coughing and comical sneezes were all recorded in turn with the same perfection.

Proceeding from the spoken word to song, Stephen produced a few loud baritone notes which reverberated perfectly at the different angles in the line and were followed by fragments of recitative, trills and snatches of tunes, and a gay popular ballad, relayed in sections.

To end with, the soloist, taking a deep breath, sang the arpeggios of the common chord repeatedly up and down the scale, making full use of his voice and producing the effect of a choir, faultlessly in harmony, by means of the rich, sustained polyphony produced by the combined echoes.

Suddenly Stephen stopped short for want of breath and became silent, and the artificial voices, robbed of their musical source, died away one by one; the six brothers, resuming their normal positions with visible relief, were able to relax comfortably, heaving great sighs.

The procession quickly reformed and moved off again in a southerly direction.

After a short and easy march through the encroaching darkness, the advance-guard reached the shore of the Tez, a broad, placid river, whose right bank was soon crowded with people as the columns spread themselves out along it.

A canoe, manned by native oarsmen, took Talu and Sirdah off the bank and carried them to the other shore.

There, emerging silently from a bamboo hut, the black witch-doctor Bashku came up to the young blind girl, an ivory cup in his hand, and, taking her by the shoulder, led her towards the water.

Then they waded out into the river-bed together, gradually sinking lower as they moved further from the shore.

After he had taken several paces, Bashku stopped, up to his breast in water, holding high, in his left hand, the cup, half full of a whitish fluid, while near him Sirdah had almost completely disappeared beneath the dark, rushing waters.

Dipping two fingers in the milky balm, the witch-doctor gently rubbed the young girl's eyes, then waited patiently for the remedy to take effect. After some delay, he struck the ball of each of her eyes sharply with his thumb to complete the cure, quickly detaching the scales, which dropped into the current and soon disappeared, carried downstream towards the sea.

Sirdah gave a cry of joy, proving that the operation had been wholly successful and had in fact just restored her sight.

Her father responded with an excited cry, followed by a noisy outburst of enthusiastic shouts from the whole procession.

Returning quickly to dry land, the delighted child threw herself into the arms of the Emperor, who clasped her in a long embrace with touching emotion.

Then they both resumed their places in the canoe, which crossed the river to set them down on the right bank, while Bashku returned to his hut.

Sirdah treasured the moisture that still clung about her, coming as it did from the sacred waters of the river which had been the scene of her recovery.

Under the leadership of Rao, the column remounted the slope along a hundred yards of its length, and halted in front of a huge machine, suspended between four posts, which reached out across the stream like the arch of a bridge.

Night had fallen slowly, and on the bank an acetylene beacon, fixed to the top of a post, illuminated the astonishing object which met our eyes, by means of a powerful reflector carefully directed on to it.

The whole apparatus, made of metal, looked at first glance distinctly like a loom.

In the middle of it, parallel to the current, was stretched a horizontal warp, consisting of an indefinite number of blue threads, placed side by side in a single row, which took up no more than six feet by reason of their extraordinary fineness.

Several *healds,* made of perpendicular strings, each fitted with an eyelet, formed a line of vertical divisions right across the warp, from one edge to the other. In front of them hung a *batten,* a sort of huge metal comb, with countless imperceptible teeth, which smoothed out the warp as if it were hair.

On the right, along the edge of the warp, a large panel about a yard square was made up of a number of compartments, separated by thin partitions; each of these sockets contained a narrow shuttle around whose *spool*, a thin bobbin fixed at back and front, was wound a supply of thread of one colour.

Every imaginable shade, every subtle variation of the seven colours of the prism, was represented by the contents of the inside of the shuttles, which must have numbered almost a thousand. The threads, more or less unwound according to their spacing, converged at the first corner on the right-hand side of the warp and composed a curious, multi-coloured network.

Underneath, almost touching the water, a number of paddles, arranged in a square like a squadron, formed the entire base of the machine, supported on one side by the bank and on the other by two piles driven into the bed of the river. Each paddle, suspended between two narrow rods, was apparently geared to turn a driving-belt on the left, which passed round a small boss, from which its two parallel bands rose vertically.

Between the paddles and the warp, there lay a kind of oblong case which presumably contained the mysterious mechanism required to drive the whole machine. The four posts were surmounted by a rectangular ceiling from which hung the healds and the batten.

The paddles, the case, the ceiling, the shuttle-box, the posts and all the connecting parts, without exception, were made from fine steel, light grey in colour.

Having placed Sirdah in the front row so that he might initiate her in the automatic method of manufacturing a cloak which he wished to present to her, Bedu the inventor, the hero of the moment, pressed a spring in the box to set in motion the precious machine, born of his industry and perseverance.

Immediately, various paddles dipped half-way into the water, submitting their blades to the power of the current.

Operated out of sight by the driving belts, whose upper section disappeared into the depths of the case, the shuttle box slid forward horizontally, following the direction of the current of the river. In spite of the change of position, the innumerable threads, attached to the corner of the warp, were held perfectly rigid, by means of a system of reverse winding with which all the shuttles were equipped; left to itself, each *quill* or *spindle,* fitted with a bobbin, was turned the opposite way from the direction in which it unwound by means of a spring which offered a very slight resistance to the unreeling of the silk. Some threads were thus mechanically shortened while others were lengthened and in this way the network retained its original firmness with no sagging or entanglement.

The shuttle-box was held in place by a thick vertical rod, bent at right angles to fit horizontally into the inside of the box; there, presumably, a long groove which we could not see from the bank permitted the slow run sideways which had begun a moment ago.

Soon the shuttle-box stopped and began to move upwards. The vertical part of its stem was gradually extended, uncovering a set of sliding sections like those of a telescope; controlled by a combination of internal wires and pulleys, it required only the release of some powerful coil-spring to start this gradual ascent, which ended a moment later.

The movement of the shuttle-box had coincided with a

91

slight adjustment in the healds, some of whose threads were lowered while the others were raised. The operation took place out of sight, within the thickness of the ceiling which only had narrow slots for the great fringe of strings to pass through, so that they might hang almost down to the case, pulled tight by a legion of small weights fixed to the ends. Each silk thread in the warp, passing singly through an eyelet in one of these strings, was at present being raised or lowered several centimetres.

Suddenly, swift as lightning, a shuttle, ejected from the box by a spring, passed between the rows of silk threads which were held at two different levels and, crossing their whole width, ended up in a single compartment, fixed in the correct place for that purpose. Unwound from the fragile device, a pick or transverse thread now ran through the middle of the warp to form the beginning of a weft.

Pulled from below by a mobile rod in a groove in the case, the batten came down on the weft with its numerous teeth, only to resume its vertical position immediately afterwards.

The strings of the healds, changing places again, wrought a complete change in the disposition of the silks, which performed a swift general post, shifting up or down.

Expelled by a spring from the compartment on the left side, the shuttle, with increased speed, crossed the warp in the opposite direction, to regain its socket; a second weft thread, unrolled from the spool, received a hard knock from the batten.

While the healds moved backwards and forwards in a curious fashion, the shuttle-box, faithful to a single plane, simultaneously employed its two modes of changing position to move diagonally; when it was set in the correct position, a second socket took advantage of the pause to eject a shuttle which shot like a rocket along the race between the silks, disappearing into the compartment still fixed firmly on the opposite side.

The descent of the batten on the new weft-thread was followed by a considerable rearrangement among the healds, to prepare the way for the return of the shuttle, thereupon promptly restored to its own tray.

The work continued according to an invariable process. By means of its remarkable mobility, the shuttle-box brought particular shuttles, one by one, into position opposite the stationary compartment, and their two-way passage corresponded perfectly with the functioning of the batten and the healds.

Little by little, the warp moved further in our direction, carried along by the slow rotation of the *loom-roller,* a wide transverse cylinder to which all the threads were attached. The weaving proceeded rapidly, and soon a rich cloth appeared before our eyes in a narrow, even band, its colours delicately blended.

The paddles underneath drove the whole machine without any assistance, by means of their own complex and precise action—some of them remaining immersed almost continuously, while others were only dipped in the current for a few seconds at a time; several of the smallest only brushed the water with their blades for a moment and quickly rose again, dropping back in the same fleeting manner after a brief pause. Their number, their graduated sizes, the way they plunged into the water, separately or together, briefly or for a longer period, all these factors provided an endless variety of combinations, favouring the execution of the boldest designs. One might have mistaken it for some silent musical instrument, striking chords or playing arpeggios, some simple, others extremely intricate, whose rhythm and harmony were constantly recurring. The driving-belts, by reason of their elasticity, lent themselves to this continual lengthening and shortening.

93

The whole apparatus, remarkable both in its assembly and in its lubrication, ran with a silent perfection which gave the impression of a true mechanical marvel.

Bedu drew our attention to the healds, worked only by the paddles, which transmitted power from the case to the ceiling by means of an electro-magnet. The lead wires were hidden inside one of the two posts at the back, and this method did away with the perforated cards used in a Jacquard machine. There was no limit to the number of variations which could be obtained by the raising of certain groups of threads, coinciding with the lowering of others. Together with the host of multi-coloured shuttles, this multiplicity of successive patterns depending on the way the warp was divided, made practicable the production of fairy-like fabrics, resembling the pictures of the old masters.

Manufactured on the spot according to some anomalous condition of the extraordinary machine, which had been specially constructed to operate before an attentive audience, the strip of cloth grew fast, showing every detail in the powerful beams of the beacon. The design of the material represented a great stretch of water, in which men, women and children, wide-eyed with terror, were clutching at a few pieces of wood from a wreck, which floated here and there amid every kind of debris; and so great was the ingenuity of the wonderful mechanism of the loom that the result could bear comparison with the finest water-colours; the faces were full of savage expression, and the colour of flesh had been admirably captured, ranging from the weather-beaten bronze of an old man to the milky whiteness of a young woman and the youthful rosiness of a child; the waves, running through the whole gamut of blues, were covered with shimmering reflections, and the degree of transparency varied from place to place.

Moved by a driving-belt, which passed through an opening

in the huge case to which it was attached by two supports, the roller drew in the cloth which was already being wound round it. The other end of the warp put up quite a strong resistance, because of a steel bar which served as an end-piece and was held between two parallel runners fixed to the box by a number of vertical rods. It was on the left of the runner that the stationary compartment, in which each shuttle came to a brief halt, had been screwed.

The picture on the cloth was slowly completed, and we saw a mountain appear, towards which the groups of human beings and every sort of animal were swimming; at the same time every part of the sky was striped with hundreds of transparent, diagonal lines which provided a key to the subject, borrowed from the account of the Flood in the *Bible*. Calm and majestic on top of the waves, Noah's ark soon reared its regular and solid shape, peopled with tiny figures, moving around in the midst of a large menagerie.

All eyes were drawn to the shuttle box, on account of the remarkable precision of its smooth, agile gymnastics. The most varied shades were used in turn, to be woven into the warp in the form of weft threads, and the general effect of the silks suggested a palette infinitely rich in colours. Sometimes the box shifted its position considerably, in order to use, one after the other, shuttles which were a long way apart; at other moments several shuttles belonging to the same area required only the slightest adjustment. The point of the selected shuttle always found a path through the other threads, issuing from the neighbouring sockets and all extending in a single direction, which presented an open-weave incapable of causing any obstruction.

On the cloth, a mountain, half-submerged by the waves, was now visible up to the summit. Everywhere on its sides, wretched victims of the flood, kneeling on this last refuge, soon to be denied them, seemed to be crying out to Heaven with wild gestures of distress. Torrential rain poured down in cataracts in every part of the picture, which was scattered with wrecks and islets, where the scenes of despair and supplication were multiplied.

The sky broadened out in the zenith, and great clouds suddenly took shape, from a combination of grey silks, ranging from the clearest tones to the murkiest shades. The thick bank of swirling vapour rolled majestically across the sky, harbouring in its flanks an inexhaustible reservoir of water, ready to feed the terrible deluge indefinitely.

At this moment Bedu stopped the machine by pressing another spring in the box. Immediately the paddles became still, and ceased to transmit energy to the various parts which thereupon stood stiff and idle.

Turning the roller in reverse, Bedu, using a well-sharpened blade, cut all the loose threads around the edges of the material which was thus quickly freed from its frame; then, with a needle and silk, threaded in readiness, he lost no time in making gathers in the top, where there was a border of streaming rain clouds.

The cloth, wider than it was long, when made up in this way, was shaped like a simple, flowing cloak.

Bedu went up to Sirdah and placed about her shoulders the folds of the wonderful garment which gracefully enveloped the happy, grateful girl down to her feet.

The sculptor Fuxier had just approached the searchlight to show us some blue pastilles which lay in the palm of his hand, and which, to our knowledge, contained within them all sorts of images *in posse,* the work of his own hand. He took one and threw it into the river, a little downstream from the loom, which now stood inactive.

96

Presently, in the beam of the acetylene lamp, the water became unmistakably disturbed and the ripples on its surface took on the appearance of a quite distinct raised outline which many of us recognised as that of Perseus, bearing Medusa's head.

It was the capsule alone which, as it dissolved, had suddenly created this deliberate, artistic stir in the river.

The apparition lasted a few moments, then the water gradually became calm again, and its mirror-like smoothness was restored.

Skilfully aimed by Fuxier, a second pastille landed in the current. The concentric rings which spread out as it fell had scarcely dispersed when a new picture appeared, composed of numerous fine ripples. This time, dancers with mantillas, on a table laid for a meal, were executing a lively dance among the food and the dishes, keeping time with their castanets, to the applause of the guests. The liquid drawing was so detailed that in places the shadows of the crumbs on the cloth could be distinguished.

When this gay scene had been effaced, Fuxier repeated the experiment by dissolving a third pastille, the effect of which was not long in appearing. The water, becoming suddenly ruffled, conjured up a larger picture of a dreamer sitting by a spring, who was jotting down in a notebook the fruits of his inspiration; behind him, leaning against the rocks of some newly-formed waterfall, an old man with a long beard, looking like the personification of a river, was leaning towards the individual and reading over his shoulder.

' The poet Giapalu allows himself to be robbed of the great poetry of his genius by old Var,' explained Fuxier, who soon after cast yet another pastille into the stream, now calm again.

This time, as the water began to froth, it took on the appearance of one half of a clock-face, with unusual signs on it. The word ' NOON ', written in raised letters on the water, occupied the place usually reserved for the third hour; then, reading downwards, came all the divisions from one o'clock to eleven o'clock contained within one quarter of the circle; at the bottom end instead of the figure ' VI ' was the word ' MIDNIGHT ', written in full along the axis of the diameter; then, continuing towards the left, eleven more sections ended in a repetition of the word ' NOON ', which took the place of the ninth hour. Playing the part of a solitary hand, a long piece of rag, resembling the point of a pennant, was attached to the precise spot where the centre of the complete clock-face would have been; supposedly blown by the wind, the flimsy streamer was swept to the right, registering five o'clock in the evening with its narrow, outstretched point. The clock, supported on top of a firmly planted pole, stood in a stretch of open countryside, with a few people walking past, and the accuracy and realism of the whole liquid portrayal were amazing.

' The wind-clock in the land of Cockaigne,' resumed Fuxier, who amplified his announcement with the following commentary :

In the happy country in question the wind, which was perfectly regular, benevolently undertook to tell the inhabitants the time. Precisely at noon, it blew strongly from the west and dropped gradually until it reached midnight, a poetic hour when a perfect calm reigned. Thereafter a light breeze sprang up from the east and rose continuously until noon next day, when it was at its height. At this hour, the wind suddenly swung round and at once blew up from the west again, to recommence its course of the previous day.

Remarkably adapted to suit these unvarying conditions, the clock which had been submitted in effigy to our appreciation fulfilled its function better than an ordinary sundial, whose work, confined to daylight hours, is constantly impeded by passing clouds.

The land of Cockaigne had vanished from the stretch of water, and the stream, growing smooth again, swallowed up the last of the pastilles which Fuxier dropped in it.

The surface, rippling in artistic folds, bore the outline of a man, half-naked and holding a bird on his finger.

'The Prince of Conti and his jay,' said Fuxier, showing us his empty hand.

After the undulations in the river had been smoothed away, the procession set off again along the road to Ejur, plunging into the black darkness, which the light from the beacon no longer dispersed, since Rao had promptly extinguished it.


We had been walking for several minutes when, on our right, a firework display lit up the darkness.

A shower of rockets rose into the sky, and soon, reaching the height of their ascent, their glowing cases burst with a sharp bang, scattering through space a thousand luminous portraits of the young Baron Ballasteros, which it was intended should be substituted for the normal, commonplace succession of golden rain and stars. Each image, as it burst from its case, unfolded of its own accord, to float at large with a gentle, swaying motion.

These drawings, brilliantly executed in lines of flame, represented the elegant man-about-town in a great variety of poses, each of them distinguished by a special colour.

Here, the wealthy Argentinian, sapphire blue from head to foot, appeared in evening dress, his gloves in his hand and a flower in his button-hole; there, a ruby-coloured sketch showed him dressed for the fencing school, ready for the attack; elsewhere a portrait of his head and shoulders alone, of colossal proportions, seen full-face and drawn in gold, showed beside a brilliant violet print in which the young man, in top hat and buttoned overcoat, was portrayed in profile, down to his knees. Further away, a diamond sketch showed the brilliant sportsman in tennis clothes, gracefully brandishing a racquet and about to hit the ball. Other radiant likenesses were displayed on every side, but the chief attraction was without doubt a particularly large portrait in emerald green, in which an impeccable rider, mounted on a horse, proceeded at a trot; the hero of this phantasmagoria respectfully greeted some unseen amazon as he passed by. The procession had halted to gaze in leisure at this alluring spectacle.

The portraits, falling slowly through the air and casting their powerful, multi-coloured light over a wide area, lasted some time without losing any of their brilliance. Then, one by one, they burned out without a sound, and darkness gradually covered the plain.

Just as the last streak of fire faded into the night, the manufacturer Luxo came to join us, proud of the splendid effect produced by his pyrotechnical masterpiece.


Suddenly, a distant, prolonged rumbling was heard; the detonation of the rockets had evidently precipitated a storm which had been brewing for some time in the overheated atmosphere; immediately the same thought struck us all : ' Jizme is about to die !'

At a sign from Talu, the procession set off again and, briskly crossing the southern district of Ejur, poured back into Trophies Square.

The storm was already nearer; flashes of lightning followed each other in rapid succession, preceding the thunder claps, each louder than the last.

Rao, who had gone on ahead, soon appeared leading his men, heavily laden with a curious couch which they set down in the middle of the esplanade. By the brightness of the lightning, it was possible to examine the strange construction of this piece of furniture, which appeared both comfortable and terrifying.

The body-work, raised on four wooden legs, was spread with a soft, white mat, covered all over with fine, separate drawings, which resembled by their size and shape the tail-pieces placed at the ends of chapters in certain books; the most varied subjects were brought together in this collection of unconnected, self-contained *vignettes*; landscapes, portraits, dreaming couples, groups of dancers, ships in distress and sunsets, had all been treated with a conscientious and naïve art, which was not without its charm or interest. A cushion had been slipped under one end of the mat, which was thus raised to support the sleeper's head; behind the place where the back of the neck was eventually to rest, stood a lightning-conductor, with a long rod which dominated the length of the reclining seat. An iron skull-cap, attached by a lead wire to the base of the tall spike, appeared to have been made ready to encompass the brow of some person condemned to a spec-tacular death, after being summoned to lie down on the fatal bed; in front of it, two metal shoes, placed side by side, were connected to the earth by another wire, the end of which Rao himself had inserted in the ground.

Reaching its height with the meteoric rapidity common in equatorial regions, the storm now broke with extreme violence; a terrible wind was driving great black clouds across the sky incessantly ablaze with lightning.

Rao had opened the prison to release Jizme, a young native woman of marked grace and beauty who had remained alone behind the grim bars since the triple execution earlier on.

Jizme, without offering any resistance, lay down on the

white mat of her own accord, placing her head in the iron cap and her feet in the rigid shoes.

Prudently, Rao and his assistants stood back from the dangerous instrument, which remained completely isolated.

Then Jizme took in both hands a slip of parchment, which hung on a fine cord about her neck, and gazed at it for a long time, occasionally taking advantage of the flashes of lightning to show it to everyone with a look of joy and pride; a name in hieroglyphics was written in the middle of the pliant rectangle, and underneath, on the right side, with a gap between, was a minute, threefold diagram, representing three different phases of the moon.

Presently, Jizme dropped the card, so diverting her gaze, which had rested on the red stage, that it was now fixed obliquely on Naïr; the young man, still fastened to his pedestal, had abandoned his delicate task on the appearance of the condemned woman, devouring her with his eyes.

At that moment, the thunder was roaring without interruption, and the lightning was becoming frequent enough to give the illusion of artificial daylight.

Suddenly, accompanied by a terrible crash, a blinding zigzag of fire rent the whole sky, striking the tip of the lightning conductor.

Jizme, who had just stretched out her arms to Naïr, was unable to accomplish the gesture, the lightning had passed through her body, and the white mat now bore only her corpse with wide-open eyes and inert limbs.

During the short lull in the storm which followed the deafening thunder clap, dreadful sobs drew our attention to Naïr, who was shedding bitter tears as he gazed at the dead girl.

The porters picked up the apparatus without disturbing Jizme's body, then in sorrowful amazement we awaited the gradual appeasement of the elements.

The wind was still blowing the clouds southward, and the thunder became rapidly more distant, every minute losing something of its force and duration. Little by little, the sky cleared all around, and bright moonlight shone down on Ejur.

# VII

IN the pale light, ten slaves appeared, carrying a heavy burden which they set down on the very spot where Jizme had just expired.

This new object consisted principally of a white wall, set down facing us, held upright by means of two long, iron struts which rested on the ground on one side.

From the top of the wall a broad canopy jutted out, its two foremost corners corresponding with the outer ends of the struts, and suspended six feet above them.

The porters departed, while the hypnotist Darriand came forward slowly, leading by the hand the negro Seil Kor, a poor madman aged about twenty who, as he walked, uttered soft, incoherent words in a French completely devoid of expression.

Darriand abandoned his patient for a moment to take a look at the white wall, and in particular at the canopy, to which he seemed to give his full attention.

Meanwhile, Seil Kor, left to his own devices, gesticulated good-naturedly, revealing in the bright moonlight the eccentricities of his carnival costume, which consisted of a cap, a black velvet mask and a ruff, all three cut out of paper.

The ruff was cut entirely out of the blue covers of the magazine *Nature*, whose title showed in several places; the mask displayed all over its surface a compact and numerous group of different signatures, printed in facsimile; on the top of his cap, the word 'Tremble' was spaced out in large letters, visible with certain movements of the head of the young man, who, in this garb, resembled a nobleman in some charade, who was supposed to frequent the court of the last of the Valois.

The three articles, too small for Seil Kor, seemed better suited to the measurements of a twelve-year-old child.

Darriand, calling for the public's attention with a few words, had just tilted the white wall backwards in order to show to all the onlookers the interior of the overhanging ceiling, which was entirely covered with reddish plants, giving it the appearance of an upturned flower stall.

Setting the structure straight again, the hypnotist provided us with a few facts about a certain experiment he wished to try.

The plants we had just seen, rare and valuable plants whose seeds he had discovered during a distant voyage to Oceania, possessed magnetic qualities of extraordinary power.

A subject placed beneath the scented roof would feel disturbing emanations penetrate his being, immediately plunging him into a true hypnotic trance; thereafter, his face turned to the wall, the patient would see passing across the white background, by means of a system of electric projections, all sorts of coloured pictures which the momentary over-stimulation of his senses made him mistake for realities; the view of a hyperborean landscape would immediately lower the temperature of his body, causing his limbs to tremble and his teeth to chatter; on the other hand, a picture simulating a glowing hearth would cause him to perspire heavily and in the end spread serious burns over all the surface of his skin. By presenting Seil Kor in this manner with a striking episode from his personal biography, Darriand counted on arousing the memory and the sane reason which the young negro had recently lost, following a head wound.

When he had finished his announcement, Darriand took Seil Kor by the hand again and led him under the canopy, his face turned to look at the reflection on the white wall. The poor lunatic was immediately seized with violent agitation; his breathing quickened and with the tips of his fingers he touched his ruff, his cap and his mask, seeming to rediscover, at the unfamiliar contact of these three objects, some sad, personal memory.

Suddenly, lit up by an unseen battery, an electric lamp, inserted at the very centre, deep inside the broad canopy, brilliantly projected on the wall a large square of light due to the combined effects of a lens and a reflector. The actual source of the glare remained hidden, but the dazzling shaft of light could be seen sloping downwards and growing progressively larger until it met the barrier partly obscured by Seil Kor's head.

Darriand, who had produced this lighting himself, was now slowly turning a silent crank-handle, fitted level with his hand on the far left of the wall. At once, some coloured film, placed in front of the lamp, cast a picture on the white screen, setting in front of Seil Kor a charming little girl with fair hair, aged about twelve and extremely pretty and graceful; above the portrait were these words: *The Young Candiot.*

At the sight of her, Seil Kor, overcome with excitement, knelt down as if before a deity, crying: 'Nina . . . Nina . . .' in a voice trembling with joy and passion. Everything in his attitude showed that the sharpening of his senses, increased tenfold by the pungent odours of the Oceanian plants, made him admit the real, living presence of the adorable child and rapturously call her name.

After a moment's pause, Darriand turned the handle again, thus, by means of a system of spools and diaphanous strips, whose unseen workings were detectable, controlling a series of pictures ready to pass in front of the luminous lens.

The portrait slipped to the left and disappeared from the screen. On the bright surface we could now read the name: *Corrèze*, set in the middle of a map of one of the *départements* of France, on which the prefecture, a large black spot, was labelled only with a question mark, instead of the name *Tulle*. Faced with this abrupt question, Seil Kor seemed to fidget nervously, as if searching for some answer which eluded him.

But under the title: *Fishing for Cramp-Fish*, a sad picture soon replaced the geographical map. Here, wearing a navy-blue dress and weighed down by a long, pliant fishing line, the little girl whom Seil Kor had called Nina was fainting as she took in her fingers a white fish that wriggled on the end of the hook.

Darriand continued to wind, and scenes with titles succeeded each other without a break, making a profound impression on Seil Kor, who was still kneeling down and showed his growing exaltation by sighs and exclamations.

After *Fishing for Cramp-Fish* came *Martingale*, which showed a young Negro, no more than a child, standing on the steps of a large building, rattling silver coins in his hand, and approaching a doorway, surmounted by these words: *The Casino in Tripoli.*

*The Fable* consisted of a page from a book, propped up against a huge sponge-cake.

*The Ball* presented a gay party of children, dancing in couples around a great hall. In the foreground, Nina and the young negro with the silver coins were approaching each other, holding out their arms, while a woman with a benevolent smile seemed to encourage their tender embrace.

Soon *The Oo Valley*, a deep, green landscape, was followed by *Bolero in the Coach House*, in which Nina and her friend were seen dancing in a primitive setting cluttered with carts and harnesses.

*Leaving a Trail* represented an impenetrable forest through which Nina was courageously advancing. Nearby, apparently marking out his line of retreat like Tom Thumb, the young black boy was dropping on the ground with a shake of his knife a white crumb which, he had no doubt, just that minute cut from a heavy Swiss cheese in his left hand.

Lying asleep on a bed of moss in *The First Night of Advent*, in *Taking Bearings* Nina reappeared standing up, pointing with her finger at the stars.

Finally, *The Coughing Fit* pictured the young girl, racked by a terrible cough and sitting with a pen in her hand in front of a sheet of paper which was almost covered. In a corner of the picture a large page, placed there to be read, was apparently an enlarged reproduction of the writing under the little girl's hand; beneath a group of scarcely legible lines was this heading : *Resolution*, followed by an unfinished sentence which suggested the conclusion of an analysis of the catechism.

Throughout this series of pictures Seil Kor, in a state of extreme agitation, never ceased to throw himself about, holding out his arms to Nina, whom he upbraided tenderly.

Letting go of the handle, Darriand quickly turned off the lamp and, raising Seil Kor to his feet, dragged him outside, for the young negro's frenzy had reached a stage of paroxysm, and there was reason to fear the disastrous effects of spending too long beneath the bewitching vegetation.

Seil Kor soon recovered his calm. Stripped of his paper trappings by Darriand, he suddenly looked around him like a sleeper just awakening, then murmured softly :

' Oh ! I remember, I remember now . . . Nina . . . Tripoli . . . The Valley of the Oo . . .'

Darriand watched him anxiously, joyfully detecting the first signs of a cure. Soon, the hypnotist's triumph became amazingly evident, for Seil Kor, recognising all our faces, began to answer rationally a shower of questions. The experiment, a brilliant success, had restored his reason to the wretched madman who was full of gratitude towards his deliverer.

Thousands of congratulations were bestowed on Darriand, while the porters carried away the marvellous projector, whose power had just been demonstrated in so happy a fashion.

A moment later, we saw a Roman chariot approaching from the left, drawn without difficulty by a slave, its two wheels, as they turned, producing a continuous, high $C$, pure and accurate, which vibrated clearly through the night.

On the narrow platform of the vehicle was a cane chair containing the thin, sickly body of the little Kalj, one of the Emperor's sons; beside the axle walked Meisdehl, a charming, pretty girl who chattered gaily to her listless companion.

Each of the two children, aged between seven and eight, wore a reddish head-dress, contrasting with their ebony skin; that of Kalj, a simple, brimless hat cut out of a page from an illustrated paper, displayed on its crown, illuminated by the face of the moon, a charge of cuirassiers in bright colours with the name: 'Reichshoffen' underneath, an incomplete scrap of the explanatory caption; as for Meisdehl, hers was a tight cap made of similar material, in shades of red, the colour of the flames of a fire which figured prominently and were accounted for by the word 'Commune', legible on its rim.

The chariot crossed the square, still emitting its loud $C$, then stopped near the Incomparables theatre.

Kalj got out and disappeared towards the right, dragging Meisdehl with him, while the crowd gathered again in front of the little stage to watch the final scene from *Romeo and Juliet,* staged with numerous additions from the original manuscript of Shakespeare.

The curtains opened to show the profile of Meisdehl who, lying on a raised couch, enacted Juliet plunged in her death-like trance.

Behind the bier, greenish flames, coloured with sea-salt, rose from a burning brazier, hidden in the base of a dark metal receptacle, of which only the top was visible.

After a few moments Romeo, played by Kalj, appeared silently to contemplate with sorrow the corpse of his idolised partner.

Instead of the traditional costumes, two reddish caps in the style of the legend were enough to conjure up the Shake-spearian lovers.

Exalted by the last kiss which he impressed on the forehead of the dead girl, Romeo raised to his lips a small flask, which he threw far away after draining its poisonous contents.

Suddenly, Juliet opened her eyes, sat up slowly and came down from her bed before the eyes of the distracted Romeo.

The two lovers, held in each other's arms, exchanged a thousand caresses, abandoning themselves to a frenzy of joy.

Then Romeo, running to the brazier, drew from the flames an asbestos thread, the end of which was hanging over the side of the metal receptacle. This fire-proof cord had several burning coals suspended along its length, which, cut like precious stones and glowing red from the heat, looked like sparkling rubies.

Returning to the front of the stage, Romeo fastened the strange necklace around Juliet's throat and her skin endured the terrible jewels without a tremor.

But the dreadful spasms of death seized the lover at the height of his happiness, just as he was radiant with hope and confidence. With a gesture of despair, he showed the potion to Juliet who, contrary to the accepted version, discovered a little of the liquid left in the bottom of the phial which she swiftly drained with joy.

Half reclining on the steps of the bier, Romeo, under the influence of the deadly potion, was about to become the plaything of inescapable hallucinations.

Everyone awaited this moment to see the effect of certain red pastilles which owed their existence to the art of Fuxier and which, when thrown into the brazier one at a time by Adinolfa, who was hiding behind the funeral couch, were supposed to throw out billows of smoke in lifelike shapes.

The first apparition suddenly rose from the flames in the form of a thick vapour, fashioned in great detail, which represented the temptation of Eve.

In the middle, the serpent, coiled round the trunk of a tree, was extending his flat head towards the beautiful, unconcerned Eve, whose hand was manifestly raised to ward off the evil spirit.

The outlines, clear at first, grew more blurred as the cloud floated up into the air; soon all the details were lost in a swirling confused mass which quickly disappeared into the sky.

A second efflux of smoke reproduced the same picture; but this time Eve, without further struggle, held out her fingers towards the apple which she was about to pick.

Romeo turned his wild eyes towards the blaze, whose green flames cast a tragic glow on the boards of the stage.

A thick smoke, minutely sculptured, again burst from the fire, creating a gay bacchanalian rout before the dying man; women were executing a frenzied dance for a group of rakes with sated smiles; in the background a man who appeared to be playing the part of Amphitryon was pointing out, for the admiration of his guests, the lewd, supple dancers.

Romeo, as if he recognised the vision, murmured these disjointing words :

' Thisias . . . the orgy in Sion ! . . . '

Already the scene was rising into the air, breaking up in patches as it did so. After it had evaporated, more smoke, issuing from the same source, presented the same characters rearranged in a different pose; pleasure having given way to terror, the dancers and the libertines, on their knees in dismay, bowed their heads before the apparition of God the Father, whose angry face, motionless and threatening in mid-air, dominated the various groups.

Abruptly a new fantasy of moulded smoke replaced the interrupted ballet and was greeted by Romeo with these words :

' St. Ignatius ! '

This time the smoke formed into two subjects, one above the other, which could be considered separately. In the bottom one nothing remained of St. Ignatius, who had been delivered to the beasts in the arena, but a tragic corpse, inert and mutilated; above, a little further back, a second image of the saint, more transparent than the first, to show that his soul had departed from his body, was borne towards a Paradise peopled with haloed brows and represented as an isle, encircled by a calm sea.

' Pheior of Alexandria ! '

This exclamation from Romeo greeted a phantom, chiselled out of a patch of cloud, who had emerged from the burning coals after St. Ignatius; he was standing in the centre of an attentive crowd and looked like one of the *Illuminati,* sowing the good word; his coarse robe hung loosely on his ascetic's body, which looked as if it had grown thin through fasting, and his emaciated face made his prominent temples seem larger by contrast.

This presentation constituted the opening of a story which was promptly continued by a second volley of smoke with a clear outline. This time, in the middle of a public place, two groups occupying two exact squares distinctly marked out on the ground, were composed respectively of old people and of young men; Pheior, after some violent reprimand, had been exposed to the anger of the young men, who had knocked him to the ground without pity for the weakness of his wasted limbs.

A third aerial episode showed Pheior on his knees in an attitude of ecstasy, caused by the appearance of a courtesan, passing by with a retinue of slaves.

Little by little, the smoke which formed these human groups spread an intangible, drifting veil over the scene.

' Jeremiah . . . the silex ! '

After uttering these words, inspired by a sombre, fleeting eruption which raised, above the flames, the figure of Jeremiah being stoned by a large crowd, Romeo, his strength exhausted, fell dead before the eyes of the distracted Juliet, and she, still wearing the necklace whose redness had now faded, in her turn fell prey to the hallucinatory potion.

A light shone suddenly to the left, behind the back-cloth, illuminating a figure visible through a narrow painted grating, which until then had seemed as opaque and homogeneous as the fragile wall of which it was part.

Juliet turned towards the patch of light, crying :

' Father . . . ! '

Capulet, played by Soreau, was standing there in a long, flowing, golden silk gown; his arm was stretched out to Juliet in a gesture of hatred and reproach, clearly referring to the guilty marriage she had secretly celebrated.

Then darkness reigned once more, and the vision disappeared behind the wall, which had resumed its normal appearance.

Juliet, kneeling in an attitude of supplication, got up, shaken by sobs, and remained a few moments covering her face with both hands.

A new beam of light caused her to raise her head and drew her over to the right, before a vision of Christ, mounted on the legendary ass, slightly veiled by a second painted grating in the partition, the fellow of the other.

It was Soreau who, having changed quickly, played the part of Christ, whose very presence seemed to accuse Juliet of having betrayed him in seeking death by her own hand.

Motionless, the divine apparition, suddenly darkening vanished behind the high wall, and Juliet, as if she had gone out of her mind, began to smile gently at the thought of some new dream which was about to delight her imagination.

At that moment, the bust of a woman, borne on a wheeled pedestal, which some unseen hand must have directed laterally from the wings to the left by means of a straight rod hidden at floor level.

The pink and white bust, resembling a hairdresser's dummy, had large blue eyes with long lashes and a magnificent head of fair hair divided into slender tresses, which hung down naturally on all sides. Some of these tresses, visible by chance as they fell on her bosom or shoulders, revealed numerous pieces of gold, attached externally here and there.

Juliet, fascinated, went towards the visitor, pronouncing this name:

' Urgela ! . . . '

Suddenly the pedestal, shaken to right and left by means

of the rod, communicated this jolting to the bust and the golden hair swung violently. Countless pieces of gold, carelessly attached, fell in an abundant shower, proving that the unseen tresses at the back were no less richly adorned than the others.

For some moments, the fairy scattered her dazzling riches unstintingly, until, drawn by the same conjectural hand, she vanished silently.

Juliet, as if grieved by this desertion, allowed her gaze to wander, and it fastened naturally on the fire which was still alight.

Once again, a cloud of smoke rose from the flames.

Juliet drew back, crying out in a tone of lively terror :
' Pergovedula . . . the two heifers . . . !'

The transient and intangible form resembled a woman with dishevelled hair who, sitting down to a monstrous meal, consisting of two heifers cut up in large portions, eagerly brandished a huge fork.

The smoke dispersed to reveal, behind the fire, a tragic apparition, which Juliet referred to by the same name ' Pergovedula,' uttered with mounting horror.

It was the tragedienne Adinolfa who had suddenly arisen, made up by a curious art; her whole face, coated with a yellow ochre cream, was in violent contrast to her green lips, which had taken on the colour of mildew, opening in a terrifying wide grimace; her unkempt hair marked a resemblance to the last vision created by the fire, and her eyes pierced Juliet insistently, filling her with dread.

A thick smoke, this time lacking any determinate form, once more arose from the coals, obscuring Adinolfa's face, no longer visible after the ephemeral veil had evaporated.

Not so brilliantly adorned by the necklace whose fires were gradually dying, Juliet, by this time on the point of death, sank down on the steps of the couch, her arms hanging loosely and her head falling back. Her eyes, henceforth empty of expression, finally rested gazing up at a second Romeo who slowly descended towards her.

The new character, played by one of Kalj's brothers, impersonated the airy, living spirit of the inert corpse, which lay stretched out near Juliet. A reddish head-dress like that of the original, adorned the brow of this perfect double, who, stretching out his arms with a smile, came to fetch the dead girl and conduct her to the immortal abode.

But Juliet, who appeared to have lost her reason, turned her head away with indifference, while the spectre, contrite and repudiated, fled silent into the darkness.

After a few last, feeble, unconscious movements, Juliet fell dead beside Romeo, just as the two curtains of the stage were closing rapidly.

Kalj and Meisdehl had astonished us all by their wonderfully tragic mime and by their few lines of French, pronounced without fault and with no accent.

Returning to the esplanade, the two children immediately took their leave.

Drawn by the slave, and with the escort of the faithful Meisdehl, the chariot, once more emitting its high, continuous note, carried off to the left the sickly Romeo, visibly exhausted by the exertion of his versatile performance on the stage.

The *C* was still vibrating in the distance when Fuxier came towards us, clasping to his breast, with his right hand spread round it, an earthenware pot from which sprouted a vine.

In his left hand he held a transparent, cylindrical jar, fitted with a cork with a metal tube running through it, and displaying in the bottom a heap of chemical salts, blossoming into beautiful crystals.

Placing his two burdens on the ground, Fuxier took from his pocket a small dark-lantern which he set down quite flat on the surface of the soil, so that it was just touching the inside edge of the stone pot. An electric current, turned on in the heart of the portable lamp, suddenly projected a dazzling beam of white light, directed towards the zenith by a powerful lens.

Then, picking up the jar, which he held horizontally, Fuxier turned a key placed at the end of the metal tube, from which an outlet, carefully directed at a particular part of the vine, sprayed out a heavily compressed gas. A brief explanation by the operator informed us that this fluid, on coming into contact with the atmosphere, at once produced an intense heat which, combined with certain very peculiar chemical properties, would ripen a bunch of grapes before our eyes.

He had scarcely finished his commentary when already the sight he had announced began to appear visibly in the form of a minute cluster of grapes. Fuxier, possessing the power which legend attributes to certain fakirs of India, was accomplishing for our benefit the miracle of sudden blossoming.

Under the influence of the chemical current, the embryo fruit developed rapidly, and soon a single bunch of white grapes, heavy and ripe, hung on the side of the vine.

Fuxier replaced the jar on the ground, after closing the tube with another turn of the key. Then, drawing our attention to the bunch of fruit, he pointed out tiny figures imprisoned in the centre of the translucent spheres.

By executing in advance on the incipient fruit modelling and colouring processes more intricate even than those involved in the preparation of his blue and red pastilles, Fuxier had deposited in each seed the embryo of a pleasing picture whose development had just followed the phases of the ripening so quickly achieved.

Through the skin of the grapes, which was particularly fine and transparent, it was possible, by standing near them, to study without difficulty, the different groups which were lit from above by the electric beam.

The modifications carried out in the germinal phase had resulted in the suppression of pips so that nothing disturbed the clarity of the translucent, coloured, Lilliputian statues, whose material was provided by the pulp itself.

' A glimpse of ancient Gaul,' said Fuxier, pointing with his finger at the first grape, in which a number of Celtic warriors were preparing for battle.

Each of us admired the delicacy of the lines, so effectively thrown into relief by the luminous effulgence.

' Odo being sawn up by a demon in the dream of Count Valtguire ' continued Fuxier, indicating the second grape.

This time one could distinguish, within the delicate skin, a sleeper in armour lying at the foot of a tree; a wisp of smoke which seemed to issue from his forehead, to represent a dream, contained in its fine coils a devil armed with a long saw, whose pointed teeth were cutting into the body of one of the damned, contorted with pain.

Another grape, summarily explained, showed the circus in Rome, packed with a large crowd, watching with excitement a fight between gladiators.

'Napoleon in Spain.' These words of Fuxier's referred to a fourth grape, in which the Emperor, dressed in his green costume, rode as a conqueror on horseback among the inhabitants, who seemed to revile him by their sullen, menacing attitude.

'From the Gospel of St. Luke,' Fuxier went on, lightly touching three grapes which hung side by side from the same parent stalk, divided into three branches, and in which the three scenes which follow were composed of the same characters.

In the first instance, Jesus was seen stretching out his hand to a little girl with her lips half-open and a fixed stare in her eyes, who seemed to be singing some light, long-drawn-out trill. Beside her on a straw pallet a little boy, lying motionless in the sleep of death, clutched between his fingers a long wand of osier; near the death-bed the father and mother, overcome by grief, wept silently. In the corner a sickly, hunch-backed girl remained humbly in the background.

In the middle grape, Jesus, turning towards the bed of straw, was looking at the dead child who, miraculously restored to life, was plaiting the light, flexible wand of osier like a skilled basket-weaver. The family, filled with wonder, showed their joyful amazement with ecstatic gestures.

The last scene, in the same setting, and with the same characters, glorified Jesus, as he touched the crippled girl, who suddenly became beautiful and erect.

Leaving this short trilogy to one side, Fuxier lifted up the bottom of the bunch and showed us a splendid grape, commenting on it with these words:

' Hans the woodcutter and his six sons.'

Inside, a remarkably robust old man was carrying on his shoulder a tremendous load of wood, consisting of whole trunks, mixed with bundles of fire wood, tied together with creepers. Behind him, six young men were all bent, severally under a burden of the same type, but infinitely lighter. The old man, half turning his head, seemed to be mocking the laggards, who were less enduring and less vigorous than himself.

In the penultimate grape, a youth, clad in the costume of the reign of Louis XV, while out for a stroll, gazed with emotion at a young woman in a flame-red gown who was sitting in her doorway as he passed.

' The first pangs of love, experienced by Jean-Jacques Rousseau's *Émile*,' explained Fuxier, who, turning the grape in his fingers, caused the electric beams to play among the bright red reflections of the gaudy dress.

The tenth and last grape contained a superhuman duel which Fuxier presented to us as the reproduction of a painting by Raphael. An angel, hovering a few feet from the ground, was driving the point of his sword into the breast of Satan, who staggered back, dropping his weapon.

Having thus surveyed the whole cluster, Fuxier extinguished the dark-lantern, which he replaced in his pocket, then went away, once more, as at his entrance, carrying the earthenware pot and the cylindrical container.

# VIII

We were still following the bunch of evocative grapes with our eyes when Rao appeared leading his slaves, weighed down under a large object, somewhat elongated in shape.

Beside the party, Fogar, the Emperor's eldest son, walked in silence, holding in his right hand a magnificent violet flower, whose stalk bristled with thorns.

This new burden was set down on the usual spot, and Fogar remained alone on guard, while the others quickly departed.

The object, which was clearly revealed in the light of the moon, was nothing more than a primitive bed, a comfortless sort of cot, bearing a number of strange emblems.

On the right, fastened behind the raised section intended for the sleeper's head, was an earthenware pot, enclosing the root of a huge, pale plant which bent over in the air of its own accord to form a tester.

Above this graceful canopy a lamp, at present unlit, was supported on a metal stem with an inflected tip.

On the end of the bed which was furthest from us stood several ornaments, arranged with care.

Almost at the right-hand corner a long triangular piece of of material, like a pennant, was stretched sideways, unfolding from the top of a thin wooden peg, painted blue. The general effect was of a flag representing some unknown nation, on account of the colours of the bunting—namely, a cream background scattered with rather asymmetrical red lines, and two black dots fairly close together, arranged one above the other near the vertical base of the triangle.

A little further to the left was a tiny portico, about eight inches wide. Hanging from the upper beam, the fringe of a dress or a costume at the slightest touch swung its numerous even, whitish threads, all of which ended in a red point.

Continuing one's scrutiny in the same direction, the next article one saw was a shallow container from which emerged a cake of white soap, covered with thick lather.

Then came a metal recess containing a fine large sponge.

Beside the recess, a fragile shelf supported an amphora of a strange shape, against which was lying a cylindrical object, fitted with a propeller.

Finally, completing this incongruous collection of ornaments, at the left end stood a round zinc plate, balanced horizontally on a narrow column.

The side of the cot facing the plant and the lamp was no less burdened.

At the corner next to the zinc plate could be seen first, a kind of gelatinous block of a dullish yellow colour.

Nearer, in the same line, was spread a thin coat of dry cement, stuck to a piece of carpet, in which a hundred thin, sharp jet bugle-beads were set upright in ten equal rows.

The block and the carpet lay side by side on a short plank, only just large enough to hold them.

Three gold bars, so skilfully disposed that they seemed to prolong the median line of the bed, rose from iron holders which gripped them firmly in their claws. No one could distinguish between them, so uniform and alike was the shape of these cylinders with rounded ends.

Bordering the narrow space occupied by these three precious ingots, a second plank, closer to us, matched the first.

On it were, first, a basket containing three cats, lent by

Marius Bucharessas, which were none other than three of the *greens* from the game of prisoners' base, still wearing their ribbons.

Next to them, a fragile object, resembling the door of a cage, consisting of two thin pieces of wood placed horizontally an inch or so apart, supported two slender vertical posts between their four inner extremities. Filling in the rectangle thus formed, black horse-hairs, stretched tight, were spaced at short distances, threaded through imperceptible holes drilled in the two wooden slats, and knotted on the outside at top and bottom. On the same spot lay one half of a very straight twig, cut lengthwise to show an internal section which was slightly resinous.

Finally, standing upright on the board against the third corner of the cot, was a large candle, and next to it two dark pebbles.

Near the middle of the cot, on the left of the future sleeper, was a metal rod, which at first rose vertically, then bent sharply to the right and ended in a handle curved like a crutch.

Fogar had just finished a close examination of the various parts of the bed. On his ebony face gleamed a precocious intelligence whose spark was astonishing in this young boy who had scarcely reached adolescence.

Availing himself of the whole of that side which remained unencumbered, he climbed on to the cot and slowly stretched himself out, in such a way that his left armpit rested on the curved handle, which fitted under it exactly.

With his arms and legs completely straight, he lay still in a corpse-like position, placing the violet flower within reach of his right hand.

124

His eyelids had ceased to flutter over his staring eyes, which were empty of expression, and his respiratory movements gradually grew weaker under the influence of a powerful death-like slumber which little by little came over him.

After a while, his prostration was complete. The youth's breast remained as still as if he were dead, and his half-open mouth seemed to have been robbed of breath.

Bex, taking several steps forward, drew from his pocket an oval mirror which he held above the young negro's lips; no mist clouded the shining surface which retained all its brightness.

Then, placing his hand over the patient's heart, Bex made a negative sign to indicate the absence of any beat.

A few seconds passed in silence. Bex quietly withdrew, leaving the ground clear around the cot.

Suddenly, as if in the depths of his torpor he found some remnant of consciousness, Fogar moved his body imperceptibly so that his armpit pressed on the handle.

Immediately the lamp lit up, directing straight down, towards the earth, an electric beam of dazzling whiteness whose brilliance was increased tenfold by means of a newly polished reflector.

The white plant, which curved to form a tester over the bed received the full blast of this intense light which seemed to have been directed at it. Because of its transparency we could see in the overhanging part a delicate picture, clear and vigorous, which was an integral part of the vegetable substance whose whole thickness was coloured.

The general effect was of a stained glass window, remarkably smooth and unbroken because of the absence of any divisions or broken reflections.

The diaphanous picture represented a scene in the Orient. Under a clear sky lay a splendid garden, full of exotic flowers.

In the centre of a marble basin a fountain of water spouting from a jade tube gracefully traced its slender curve.

Beside it rose the walls of a sumptuous palace, and framed in an open window stood a couple embracing each other. The man, a stout person with a beard, dressed like a merchant from the *Arabian Nights,* wore on his smiling face an expression of effusive and changeless joy. The woman, a pure Morisco by her dress and her looks, remained listless and melancholy in spite of her companion's good humour.

Beneath the window, not far from the marble basin, stood a young man with curly hair, whose attire, in time and place, seemed to correspond with that of the merchant. Raising towards the couple the face of an inspired poet, he sang some elegy of his own composition, with the help of a speaking-tube of dull silvery metal.

The Morisco followed the poet eagerly with her eyes and he in turn stood in ecstasy before her sensational beauty.

Suddenly a molecular alteration took place in the fibres of the luminous plant. The picture lost its clarity of colour and outline. The atoms all vibrated at once, as if endeavouring to rearrange themselves according to some other inevitable grouping.

Presently, a second scene rose up, as splendid as the other and similarly embodied in the delicate and transparent vegetable structure.

This time, a high dune of golden tone retained on its arid slope the marks of several footsteps. The poet of the first picture, kneeling on the crumbling soil, gently put his lips to the deep imprint of a tiny, graceful foot.

After a few moments of immobility, the atoms once more began to swim dizzily, recommencing their agitated motion which resulted in a third view, full of life and colour.

This time the poet was no longer alone; beside him was a Chinaman in a violet robe, pointing at a great bird of prey, whose majestic flight no doubt had some prophetic significance.

A new disturbance within the sensitive plant presented the same Chinaman in his curious laboratory, receiving from the poet some pieces of gold in exchange for a manuscript offered and received.

Each strange phase of the plant lasted the same length of time; one after another, the series of pictures faded on the overhead screen.

The laboratory was followed by a richly decorated banqueting hall. Seated at a table ready laid, the fat, bearded merchant was sniffing a dish which he held in his hands. His eyes closed drowsily under the influence of the appetising smell with which there mingled some perfidious substance. Facing him, the poet and the Morisco watched happily the approach of this heavy slumber.

After this there appeared a paradisal scene on which the burning rays of the mid-day sun shone steadily down. In the background flowed the waters of a beautiful waterfall tinged with green reflections. The poet and the Morisco were sleeping side by side in the shade of a fantastic flower which looked like some giant anemone. On the left, a negro approached in haste, as if to warn the lovers of some imminent danger which threatened them.

The same setting, reappearing a second time, now showed the two lovers mounted on a prancing zebra, poised ready to break into a wild gallop. Seated sideways behind the poet, who was firmly astride in the saddle, the Morisco laughingly waved a purse containing a few gold coins. The negro watched the departure with a respectful gesture of farewell.

The delightful spot vanished completely, to give way to a sunny road, on the side of which stood a stall, laden with food. Lying in the middle of the road, supported by the anxious poet, the Moorish maiden, pale and exhausted, received nourishment at the hands of an eager, attentive shopkeeper.

On her next appearance, the Morisco, restored to health, was wandering with the poet. Near her, a man of strange appearance seemed to be uttering gloomy forebodings to which she listened with uneasiness and distress.

One last picture, which, according to the evidence, contained the tragic ending of the idyll, showed a terrible abyss, the side of which was covered with jagged rocks. The Morisco, battered by these innumerable spikes, was reaching the end of a terrible fall, submitting to the vertiginous lure of hundreds of eyes, without faces or bodies, which had in them a cruel expression full of menace. From above, the poet in despair, hurled himself into the gulf after his loved one.

This dramatic scene was unexpectedly replaced by the portrait of a wolf with blazing eyes. The animal's body alone took up as much space as any of the preceding sketches; underneath in large capitals was this description in Latin: ' LUPUS '. There was no similarity in proportion or colours to connect this gigantic silhouette with the Oriental sequence, whose unity remained patently obvious.

The wolf soon faded, and we saw the opening picture reappear, with the garden and the marble basin, the singing poet and the couple standing at the window. All the pictures were run through a second time in the identical order, separated by intervals of the same duration. The wolf concluded the series, which was followed by a third cycle, exactly like the two previous ones. The plant repeated indefinitely these curious molecular revolutions, which seemed to be bound up with its own existence.

When the original garden with the basin returned for the

fourth time, all eyes, wearing of the monotony of the spectacle, turned away to look down at the still inanimate figure of Fogar.

The young negro's body and the objects placed on the edges of the bed were covered with multi-coloured reflections from the strange canopy.

Just as flagstones in the floor of a church reflect the finest details of a stained-glass window in the sunlight, the whole area occupied by the bed slavishly reproduced the shapes and colours cast on the screen. It was possible to recognise the characters, the fountain, and the walls of the palace, magnified by projection, as they tinged the various obstacles and irregularities on which their rich colours chanced to fall, reproducing their infinitely varied forms.

The polychromatic light spilled freely over the earth, casting fantastic shadows here and there.

Without even looking up at the plant, it was impossible not to notice each punctual change, bringing with it by reflection another familiar, predictable picture.

Then Fogar's slumber was broken. His chest rose slightly, marking a resumption of the respiratory functions. Bex placed a hand over his heart, which had stopped for so long, then returned to his place, telling us of faint pulsations, as yet barely noticeable.

Suddenly the eyelids fluttered, assuring us of his complete return to life. His eyes lost their abnormally fixed stare, and Fogar, with a quick movement seized the violet flower which lay where he had dropped it, near his right hand.

With a thorn from its stem he made a lengthwise gash along the inside of his left wrist, thereby opening a prominent, swollen vein; and from it he removed a clot of greenish blood, wholly congealed, and placed it on the bed.

Then, sharply tearing a petal from the flower and squeezing it between his fingers, he produced a few drops of some efficacious liquid which, as they fell on the vein, immediately joined the two gaping edges together.

Thenceforward, his circulation, free from any obstruction, was able to resume its course freely.

Two further operations of an identical nature, performed by Fogar himself on his chest and near the bend at the back of his right knee, produced two more blood clots, similar to the first. Afterwards, two more petals, required for sealing the blood vessels, were missing from the violet flower.

The three clots, which Fogar held side by side in his left hand, looked transparent and tacky, like sticks of angelica.

The young Negro had obtained the desired result by his voluntary catalepsy, whose only purpose had in fact been to influence a partial condensation of the blood, calculated to provide the three solidified fragments, which gleamed with delicate variations of colour.

Turning to the right and looking at the point of the flag with the red stripes, Fogar picked up one of the clots, which he slowly raised up against the blue staff.

Suddenly a quiver of life ran through the whitish bunting, which was covered with light reflected from above. The triangular pennant which had hung motionless until this moment began to climb down, clinging to its pole as it did so; instead of a simple piece of material, we saw before us some strange animal, endowed with instinct and the power of movement. The stripes, in shades of red, turned out to be salient blood vessels and the two symmetrical spots were a pair of restless, staring eyes.

The vertical base of the triangle was attached to the staff by numerous suction pads which a series of contortions had for some time now been moving steadily in one direction.

Fogar, still raising his green clot, soon encountered the animal which was accomplishing its descent at a regular pace.

Only the upper suction pads now remained fastened, while the lower ones, detaching themselves from the staff, greedily snatched the blood clot, which the young man relinquished.

By means of a kind of sucking action, the gluttonous mouths, assisting each other in the process, hastened to absorb this diet of blood of which they seemed remarkably fond.

Having finished their meal, they fastened themselves once more on to the flagstaff, and, again becoming motionless, the creature resumed its earlier appearance of a stiff flag with unfamiliar colours.

Fogar placed his second clot near the frail portico, which stood on the left of the flag-post on the edge of the bed.

Immediately the fringe, hanging on the underneath of the horizontal span, shook itself feverishly, as if lured by some attractive bait.

Its upper edge consisted of a system of suction pads like those of the triangular animal.

By some acrobatic movement, it managed to reach one of the door posts and to travel down it towards the delicacy it was offered.

Its flowing tentacles, endowed with life and strength, delicately gripped the clot, and passed it to some of the suckers which, unfastening themselves from the post, feasted upon it without delay.

After the prey had been completely assimilated, the fringe hoisted itself up to the high span by the same route, and returned to its former position.

The last clot was placed by Fogar at the bottom of the receptacle containing the white soap.

Suddenly the thick lather, spread over the top of the smooth, shiny cake, was seen to move.

A third animal had just revealed its presence, which until then had been concealed by complete immobility, as well as by its misleading appearance.

A sort of snowy carapace covered the body of this strange beast, which, as it crawled slowly forward, let out at regular intervals a sharp, plaintive hiccup.

The reflections from overhead assumed a quite particular brilliance on the immaculate tegument and the colours were remarkably clear.

Reaching the edge of the soap, the animal crept down a perpendicular side in order to reach the flat bottom of the container; there, full of impatient gluttony, it swallowed the clot of blood, then silently settled into immobility in order to embark ponderously on a calm, voluptuous period of ingestion.

Fogar got to his knees on the bed in order to reach more easily the objects which were further away.

With the tips of the fingers he moved a thin lever fixed externally to the metal recess next to the cake of soap.

At that very moment, a brilliant light set the sponge ablaze, exposing it to all eyes. Several glass tubes, through which passed an electric light current, were arranged horizontally one above the other on the inner wall of the recess, which was suddenly flooded with light.

Thus visible in its transparency, the sponge revealed through its almost diaphanous tissue a real human heart in miniature, to which was connected a most complicated system of blood circulation. The aorta, clearly marked, carried a host of red corpuscles which, through infinite ramifications of every kind of vessel, distributed life to the farthest parts of the organism.

Fogar picked up the amphora next to the recess and slowly poured over the sponge several pints of pure, limpid water.

But this unexpected aspersion seemed to displease the astonishing specimen which, of its own accord contracted violently to expel the unwelcome liquid.

A central opening, running downwards from the lower shelf of the recess, provided a way out for the rejected water which flowed on to the ground in a thin trickle.

The youth recommenced the same experiment several times.

In the heart of the electric radiation the little drops, changing into diamonds, sometimes flashed like other precious stones, due to the perpetual renewal of the multi-coloured projections.


Fogar put the amphora back in its place and took the cylinder with the propeller down from beside it.

This new object, made completely of metal and rather small in size, contained a powerful battery which the young man turned on by pressing a button.

As if in obedience to an order, the propeller, fixed to the end of the cylinder as to the stern of a ship, began to turn rapidly, making a faint noise as it did so.

Presently, the instrument, held by Fogar, hung over the horizontal zinc plate, still balanced on top of the post.

The propeller, fixed underneath, continuously fanned the greyish surface, whose appearance was gradually changing.

The breeze, caressing all the points of the perimeter in

turn, produced a distortion of the strange disc, which bulged in the middle like a dome; it might have been taken for a gigantic oyster, contracting on contact with an acid.

Without prolonging the experiment, Fogar turned off the electric fan which he put back beside the vase.

No longer fanned by the breeze, the edges of the dome slowly opened out again and in a few seconds the disc resumed its former rigidity and to judge from its misleading appearance, might be thought to have lost the animal life which had just been manifested in it.

Turning to the left, towards the other side of the bed Fogar picked up the gelatinous block and placed it carefully on top of the jet bugles, planted upright in their cement bed; when the youth released it, the inert mass of flesh slowly subsided because of its own weight.

Suddenly, at the sensation of pain caused by the pricking of the hundred black points, a feeler, attached to the front of the block, shot up in a signal of distress and, at the end of it, three divurgent branches opened out, each one ending in a thin suction pad with its base showing.

Fogar took the three cats out of their basket, half asleep. As he did so, the shadow cast by his body ceased to cover the block, on which part of the wolf was projected, returning, for the tenth time at least, to the thick screen of vegetation.

One by one, the cats were attached by their backs to the three suckers which, looking as if they belonged to the arms of an octopus, held on to their prey with an irresistible force.

Meanwhile, the hundred jet spikes penetrated still further into the flesh of the shapeless beast, whose increasing pain was shown by a sudden spiral motion of the three arms, which turned like the spokes of a wheel.

134

The spinning, at first slow, accelerated feverishly, to the great danger of the cats, who struggled hopelessly, unsheathing their claws.

Everything soon became confused in a frantic whirl, punctuated by a furious, mewling chorus.

This phenomenon never once caused any torsion of the feeler, which remained stable throughout, acting as a support. By means of some delicate and mysterious mechanism, the whole effect exceeded in force and interest the illusory appearance of the wheels of the rotifer.

The speed of revolution was increased still further under the influence of the hundred punctures, ever deeper and more agonising; the violent displacement of air produced a continuous humming whose pitch rose constantly; the cats, thrown into confusion, merged into an unbroken circle with green stripes, from which there escaped savage wails.

Fogar lifted the block off again and returned it to its original position.

The suppression of the pain brought with it a sudden slowing down, and then the astonishing gyration stopped completely.

With three violent shakes, Forgar released the cats, which he placed, stunned and whimpering, in the basket, while the tentacle with its three arms fell lifeless, among the constantly changing reflections.

Bending over to the right, the youth picked up the amphora again and poured over the white soap a certain quantity of water which soon dripped down in a shower from underneath, through small holes in the bottom of the receptacle.

The amphora, quite empty by this time, was replaced beside the cylinder with the propeller, and the young man grasped firmly in his hand the slightly elongated cube of soap which was wet on all its six flat sides.

After this, drawing back as near to the head of the bed

as possible, Fogar, closing his left eye, took careful aim at the three gold bars which he could see, one behind the other, in a straight line, between the basket of cats and the carpet with the hundred black spikes.

Suddenly, with a lithe movement, he stretched out his arm.

The soap appeared to execute a series of perilous bounds, then, describing a graceful curve, landed on the first ingot; from there it rebounded, still spinning like a wheel, on to the second bar of gold, which it only brushed for an instant; a third trajectory, this time accomplished only with two slow somersaults, brought it to the third heavy cylinder, on which it balanced, upright and immobile.

The deliberate slipperiness of the object thrown, combined with the rounded top of the three ingots made the success of this feat of skill most noteworthy.

Having returned the soap to its container, Fogar continued his voyage of discovery and carefully took in his left hand the contraption constructed like the door of a cage.

Then, wiping three fingers of his right hand on his loin-cloth, he took hold of the split stick which had been divided in half lengthwise.

By using this last object as a bow, he was able to scrape it across one of the black horse-hairs stretched between the two sides of the small rectangular harp, as if it were a violin string.

It was the inside edge of the twig which was applied and a resistant glaze, produced by some natural secretion, successfully fulfilled the function of resin.

The horse-hair vibrated with force, thanks to a certain very curious nodosity producing simultaneously two perfectly distinct sounds, separated by an interval of a fifth; one could see, above and below, two quite separate and obviously different areas of vibration.

Fogar, changing his position, passed his bow over another horse-hair, which alone played a major third of perfect accuracy.

Each resonant string in turn, individually tested by the bowing of the twig, gave out two simultaneous sounds of equal volume. Whether they were in tune, or dissonant, all the intervals were different, giving the experiment an amusing variety.

The young man, putting the harp and bow away, picked up the two dark-coloured pebbles which he struck sharply together above the thick candle standing on the corner of the bed; a shower of sparks fell from them at the first impact and landed partly on the highly combustible wick, which immediately burst into flame.

The startling strangeness of the substance of which the candle was made was revealed in the surrounding light from the still, straight flame, and it was seen to resemble in texture the delicious, porous flesh of certain fruits with delicate membranes.

Suddenly, the atmosphere was disturbed by a loud crackling, coming from the candle which, as it burned, imitated the noise of thunder.

A short silence separated the first rumbling from a second peal, more violent still, itself followed by several dull rumbles which marked a period of calm.

The candle burned rather quickly, and soon the evocation of a storm reached almost perfect, lifelike proportions. Thunder-claps of a terrible violence alternated with the distant voice of prolonged, dying echoes.

The dazzling moonlight contrasted strangely with the raging din which characterises a storm, and all that was lacking was the howling of the gale and the flash of lightning.

When the candle, growing shorter and shorter, had almost entirely disappeared, Fogar blew on the wick to extinguish it, and the peaceful silence was instantly restored.

Immediately, the black porters, who had returned a few moments previously, lifted the narrow bed on which the youth was lying unconcernedly.

The party moved off without a sound, with the ever-changing lights from the polychromatic projections continuing to play on them.

The solemn moment had now arrived when we must proceed to the distribution of the awards.

Juillard drew from his pocket, in the form of a pendant cut out of a thin sheet of tin-plate, an equilateral triangle representing the Greek capital *delta*, which had a tiny ring at one of its corners so twisted as to stand perpendicular to the rest.

This bauble, which looked as if it were nickel-plated, attached to a broad blue ribbon by its suspension ring, constituted the *Grand Decoration of the Order of the Delta*, whose holder must have enriched the well-advised shareholders who had placed their trust in him.

Choosing as his only criterion the attitude of the negro audience during each performance, Juillard, without any hesitation, named Marius Bucharessas, whose kittens, playing at prisoners' base, had aroused endless enthusiasm among the Ponukelians.

Speedily decorated with the supreme insignia, the child returned, proud and happy, admiring upon his breast the effect of the blue ribbon, which lay diagonally across his pale pink jersey, while at his left side the shining pendant flashing in the moonbeams, showed up clearly against the black background of his velvet shorts.

Among the group of speculators, cries of delight broke out, uttered by Marius's shareholders, among whom a premium of ten thousand francs was soon to be distributed.

After the presentation of the Grand Decoration, Juillard had suddenly displayed six *deltas*, smaller than the first, but identical in shape and made out of the same metal. This time, the ring by which each one hung was level with the whole, and through it passed a ribbon, no more than an inch or two long, with two slightly curved pins fastened vertically to the double thickness at the top.

Still guided impartially by the amount of native approval bestowed on the different candidates, Juillard asked Skariofszky, Tancred Bucharessas, Urbain, Lelgoualch, Ludovic and La Billaudière-Maisonnial to come forward, and pinned on the bosom of each in turn, without any sort of formality or address, one of the six new decorations symbolising the rank of *Knight of the Delta*.

It was time to retire to bed.

At an order from Talu, who, departing with long strides, gave the signal to withdraw, the natives dispersed through Ejur.

Our party, keeping together, reached the special district which was reserved for us in the heart of this strange capital, and soon we were all asleep in the shelter of our primitive huts.

# IX

THE following day, Norbert Montalescot woke us before it was light.

Dressing hurriedly, we set out in an orderly band along the road leading to Trophies Square, enjoying with a sensuous pleasure the comparative coolness of the early morning.

The Emperor and Sirdah, who had also been roused by Norbert, came out on to the esplanade at the same time as we did. Abandoning the apparel he had worn the previous day, Talu was clad in the clothes he usually wore as befitting an African chief.

Norbert beckoned us towards the hut where Louise had spent the whole night engaged in her work. Having got up with the first glimmerings of dawn, he had come to receive his orders from his sister who, raising her voice but not appearing, had enjoined him to rouse us from our sleep immediately.

Suddenly, making a sharp tearing noise, a gleaming blade seemed to slash through one of the black walls of the hut without the aid of any hand.

The sharp edge cut firmly through the thick cloth, finally completing a large rectangle; the knife was being wielded from inside by Louise herself and soon, pulling away the piece of cloth which she had cut out, she rushed into the open carrying an enormous travelling bag, crammed full.

'Everything is ready for the experiment,' she cried with a smile of triumphant delight.

She was tall and beautiful, her warrior's garb completed by a pair of full breeches, gathered into fine riding boots.

Through the gaping hole so recently made could be seen scattered over a table all sorts of flasks, retorts and flat dishes, which made the hut look like a laboratory.

The magpie had just escaped to flutter freely from one sycamore to another, intoxicated by its independence and the fresh air.

Norbert took the heavy bag from his sister and set out at her side towards the southern end of Ejur.

The whole escort, with Talu and Sirdah at their head, followed the brother and sister, who walked quickly along as the day grew brighter.

After leaving the town, Louise continued walking for a moment longer, then, attracted by certain combinations of colour, she stopped on the very spot where, the previous evening, we had watched the firework display.

The dawn, shining from behind the magnificent trees of the Behuliphruen, produced curious, unexpected lighting effects.

Talu himself chose a favourable spot for the fascinating test which had been promised, and Louise, opening the bag her brother carried, unpacked a folded object which, once it was opened into its normal position, formed a strictly vertical easel.

A new canvas, stretched tightly over its inner frame, was placed half-way up the easel and held firmly in place by a screw clamp, which Louise lowered to the required level. Next, the young woman, with great care, took from a box, made to protect it from any contact, a palette, prepared in advance, which fitted exactly into a special metal holder fixed to the right side of the easel. The colours, placed well apart in little heaps, were arranged in a semi-circle with geometrical precision, on the upper part of the thin wooden board, which like the empty canvas, was set up facing the Behuliphruen.

In addition, the bag contained a hinged stand, similar to a camera tripod. Louise picked it up, then lengthened the three extending legs, which she set down on the ground not far from the easel, anxiously adjusting the height and stability of the apparatus.

At that moment, Norbert, obeying the instructions of his sister, took from the case, to place it behind the easel, a heavy chest whose glass lid revealed several batteries arranged next to each other inside.

In the meantime, Louise was slowly unpacking, with infinite caution, a utensil, doubtless very fragile, which looked to us like some thick, solid plate, protected by a metal lid which corresponded exactly with its rectangular shape.

Distinctly recalling the skeleton of a weighing-machine, the top part of the three-legged support consisted of a sort of fork, with two widely diverging prongs, which ended abruptly in two vertical arms, on which Louise was able to fix one of the long sides of the plate, cautiously assembling it by using two small, deep holes, correctly placed at the point where two grooves at the back, carved out to facilitate the sliding movement of the sides encompassing the lid, projected.

In order to appraise the disposition of the various articles, the young woman, screwing up her eyes, stepped back towards the Behuliphruen, in order to judge their relative distances more accurately. From this position she could see on her right the stand, on her left the easel with the chest behind it, and, in the centre, the palette with the paints.


The lid of the rectangular plate, with a ring in the centre by which it could be grasped, was directly exposed to the light of the dawn; from its back, completely unconcealed, sprang a myriad of exceedingly fine metal wires, giving it the appearance of a head of hair growing too evenly, which seemed to connect every imperceptible area of the surface with a kind of machine charged with a supply of electric energy. The wires were twisted together to form a thick coil, wrapped in insulating material, which ended in a long bar, and this, Louise, returning to her post, bent down to plug into a socket in the side of the box of batteries.

The bag also furnished a strong vertical tube, somewhat in the form of a photographic head-rest, standing firmly on a circular base and fitted at the top with a screw, which turned easily, and could fix an iron rod inside at a convenient height.

Placing the device in front of the easel, Louise pulled the movable rod up out of the tube and tightened the screw, carefully verifying the level reached by its highest point, which was exactly opposite the still untouched canvas.

On this single, steady point, as if it were a game of cup and ball, the young woman planted a large metal sphere, fitted horizontally with a short hinged arm on a pivot extending in the direction of the palette, in whose tip were inserted some ten paint brushes, radiating like the spokes of a wheel lying on its side.

Soon the operator had contrived to establish communication between the sphere and the electric box by means of a double wire.

Before beginning the experiment, Louise, uncorking a little oil can, poured a drop of oil on the hairs of each paint brush. Norbert moved away the bulky suitcase, almost empty now that he had extracted the metal sphere.

Throughout these preparations, the day had been slowly breaking, and dazzling rays of light flashed among the trees in the Behuliphruen, turning it into a many-coloured fairyland

143

Louise could not stifle a cry of admiration as she turned to look at the splendid garden which seemed to have been illuminated by magic. Judging the moment incomparable and miraculously propitious for the realisation of her plans, the young woman went up to the stand with its threefold ramification and seized by the ring the lid which fitted over the metal plate.

All the onlookers crowded round the easel so as not to offer any impediment to the luminous rays.

Louise was clearly moved when the moment came to undergo the great test. Her musical respiration quickened, increasing the frequency and the power of the monotonous chords continually emitted by the tags of her shoulder-knot. With a quick movement she snatched off the lid, then, retreating behind the tripod and the easel, joined us to watch the movements of the mechanism.

Deprived of its shutter, which the young woman still held between her fingers, the plate now stood exposed, revealing a smooth, brown, shiny surface. All eyes were fixed eagerly on this mysterious substance, endowed by Louise with strange, photo-mechanical properties. Suddenly, opposite the easel, a slight shudder ran through the automatic arm, which consisted of an ordinary, bright, horizontal blade, bent in the middle; the adjustable angle of the elbow tended to open as wide as possible, owing to a powerful spring, whose effect was counteracted by a flexible metal wire, which, emerging from the sphere, was fastened round the furthest tip of the arm and thus regulated the gap; at present the wire was being stretched to allow the angle to become progressively greater.

This first sign of activity caused a slight stir among the restless, uneasy audience.

The arm slowly extended towards the palette, while the horizontal, rimless wheel, created on the end of it by the star of brushes, was gradually raised to the top of a vertical axle, wound upwards by a cogged ring which was directly connected to the sphere by a highly elastic driving belt.

The two actions combined brought the tip of one of the brushes on to a thick supply of blue paint, in a pile near the top of the palette. The hairs quickly became stained, then, after a short descent, spread the particles they had picked up over a clean section of the surface. A few specks of white, gathered in the same way, were deposited on the place which had recently been stained blue, and the two shades mixed perfectly by a prolonged stirring, gave a very subdued pale blue.

Slightly shortened by the tautening of the metal wire, the arm swivelled a little and stopped higher up, in front of the left corner of the canvas fixed on the easel. Immediately the brush, impregnated with the delicate shade, automatically drew a narrow, vertical strip of sky down the side of the future picture.

A murmur of admiration greeted this first broad brush stroke and Louise, thereafter assured of her success, let out a long sigh of satisfaction, accompanied by a noisy fanfare from her aglets.

The wheel of brushes, coming back to face the palette, suddenly began to turn, driven by a second belt made of the same expandable material, which disappeared inside the sphere. There was a sharp snap as a stop-catch fixed another brush with new, unblemished hairs firmly in the place of honour. Soon several primary colours, mixed on another part of the palette, made up a golden yellow pigment full of fire, which was carried to the picture and continued the vertical band already begun.

Turning to look at the Behuliphruen again, it was possible to verify the absolute exactness of this sharp juxtaposition of the two shades which composed a line clearly marked in the sky.

The work proceeded with precision and speed. Now each time the palette was visited, several brushes in turn concocted their various mixtures of colour; returning to the picture, they followed each other in the same order, all laying on the canvas, sometimes in minute quantities, their particular new tint. This process made it possible to achieve the most subtle gradations of tone, and, bit by bit, one corner of a landscape, vividly true to life, spread itself before our very eyes.

Without taking her eyes off the mechanism, Louise gave us some useful explanations.

The brown plate alone set the whole process in motion, by means of a system based on the principle of electro-magnetisation. In spite of the absence of any lens, the polished surface, owing to its extreme sensitivity, received enormously powerful light-impressions, which it transmitted by means of the countless wires inserted in the back to activate a whole mechanism contained within the sphere, whose circumference must have measured more than a yard.

As we were able to ascertain with our own eyes, the two vertical arms which terminated the fork at the top of the tripod were made of the same brown substance as that of which the metal plate itself was composed; because they were so perfectly adapted to each other, they formed together a homogeneous block and were now contributing, in their special field, to the continued progress of photo-mechanical communications.

According to the disclosures of Louise, the sphere contained a second rectangular plate, fitted with another network of wires, conveying the polychromatic sensations of the first, and, through this a thin metal wheel moved from section to section, while the current it set up drove a complete series of crank arms, pistons and rollers by electricity.

The work advanced progressively from left to right, still in vertical strokes, sketched in rapid succession, from top to bottom. Each time the rimless wheel revolved in front of the palette or in front of the canvas, a sharp click could be heard as the catch fell shut to hold one brush after another steady throughout the duration of its task. This monotonous noise was like a very slow imitation of the whirligigs at a fair.

The whole surface of the palette was now touched-in or broadly smeared; the most incongruous mixtures of colours were placed side by side, constantly being altered by the fresh addition of one of the primary colours. There was no confusion, in spite of the disconcerting bright medley, and each brush was assigned to a particular category of shades, so that it was confined to a certain, more or less limited speciality.

Soon the whole of the left side of the painting was finished. Louise followed with delight the movements of the apparatus which had functioned so far without any mishap or error.

This success was never once threatened during the completion of the landscape, the second half of which was painted with amazing assurance.

A few seconds before the end of the experiment, Louise had once again passed behind the easel and then behind the tripod in order to take her place near the sensitive plate. By this time there only remained in the top right-hand corner of the canvas a narrow white line which was quickly filled in.

After the last stroke of the brush, Louise promptly replaced the obturating cover on the brown plate, stopping the hinged arm by this simple action. Then, free from any anxiety concerning the mechanical process, the young woman was able to examine at leisure the picture which had been executed in such a curious fashion.

The tall trees of the Behuliphruen were faithfully reproduced with their magnificent branches, whose leaves, of a strange colour and shape, were covered with bright reflections. On the ground, large flowers, blue, yellow or scarlet, sparkled among the moss. In the distance, through the trunks and the branches, shone the sky; at the bottom, a first horizontal belt of blood-red faded into a strip of orange just above it, which in turn became lighter, giving birth to a bright golden-yellow; next came a pale blue, almost white, in the heart of which, on the right, shone one last, late star. The finished work, seen as a whole, gave an impression of uncommonly intense colouring and remained strictly true to the original, as each person was able to confirm by a quick glance at the actual garden.

With the help of her brother, Louise, unwinding the clamp of the easel, replaced the painting with a block of the same size, consisting of a thick pile of sheets of white paper, placed one on top of the other and joined at the edges; then removing the last paint brush to have been used, she inserted a carefully sharpened pencil into the empty space.

In a few words we were informed of the aim of this ambitious young woman, who now wished to submit for our examination a simple drawing, whose lines would naturally be more precise and more detailed than those of the painting and which required her only to press a certain spring in the top of the sphere to make a slight adjustment to the internal mechanism.

In order to provide a complex and animated subject, fifteen or twenty of the spectators went, at the request of Louise, to arrange themselves in a group a short distance away. Seeking to produce an effect of life and movement, they posed as passers-by in a busy street; several of them, suggesting by their position that they were walking with rapid strides, bent their heads with a look of deep concentration; others, more relaxed, gossiped together like couples taking a stroll, while two friends exchanged familiar greetings as they passed each other at a distance.

Instructing them, like a photographer, to maintain the utmost immobility, Louise standing near the plate, sharply removed the cover and then made her usual detour, to come and watch the action of the pencil from near at hand.

The mechanism, reset at the same time as it had been adjusted by the action of pressing the spring on the sphere, slowly swung the jointed arm to the left. The pencil began to run up and down the white paper, following the same vertical sections, previously marked out by the paint brushes.

This time, there were no journeys to the palette, no changes of instrument, or mixing of paint to delay the work, which made swift progress. The same landscape appeared in the background, of secondary importance this time, and was blotted out by the figures in the foreground. The gestures, taken from life—the mannerisms, very marked—the silhouettes, strangely amusing—and the faces, blatant likenesses—all had the desired expression, sometimes gloomy, sometimes gay. One person's body, leaning slightly towards the ground, seemed to be bent by the impetus of walking briskly forward; another's beaming face denoted pleasant surprise at an unexpected meeting.

The pencil glided lightly over the page, leaving it often, and in a few minutes it was covered. Louise, returning to her post at the appropriate moment, replaced the shutter over the plate, then beckoned to the models, who came running to admire the new picture, delighted to move around after their prolonged immobility.

In spite of the contrast of the setting, the drawing gave the exact impression of a street of busy traffic. Each one recognised himself without difficulty among the compact group, and the warmest congratulations were lavished on Louise, who was excited and happy.

Norbert set about dismantling all the accessories, to pack them back in the suitcase.

In the meantime, Sirdah conveyed to Louise the complete satisfaction of the Emperor, who had been amazed at the perfect manner in which the young woman had fulfilled all the conditions he had strictly imposed.


Ten minutes later we were all back in Ejur.

Talu dragged us as far as Trophies Square, where we perceived Rao, accompanied by a native warrior.

In front of us all, the Emperor pointed to Carmichael, explaining his gesture in a few terse words.

Immediately, Rao went up to the young man from Marseilles, whom he led towards the sycamores next to the red theatre.

The warrior was placed on guard to watch the poor culprit, who stood with his face turned to the trunk of the tree, beginning the three hours' detention, during which he had to revise without a pause *The Battle of Tez*, which he had recited imperfectly the previous day.

Fetching Juillard's chair from the deserted wings, I came and sat down underneath the branches of the sycamore, offering my aid to facilitate Carmichael's task. He immediately handed me a large, loose sheet of paper, on which the barbaric pronunciation of the Ponukelian text had been carefully transcribed into French. Spurred on by the fear of further failure, he began reciting the strange lesson attentively, humming the tune under his breath, while I followed each line syllable by syllable, ready to correct the slightest mistake or to prompt him with any fragment he might have forgotten.

The crowd, forsaking Trophies Square, had slowly dispersed through Ejur, and, in the great silence of the early morning, only slightly absorbed by my purely mechanical task, I could not help musing over the many adventures which had filled my life during the past three months.

# X

ON the 15th of March preceding, intending to pursue a
long journey through the curious regions of South America, I
had embarked at Marseilles on the *Lynceus,* a huge and
speedy liner on its way to Buenos Aires.

The first days of the crossing were calm and the weather
superb. Thanks to the familiarity resulting from our meals in
common, I quickly established relations with some of the
other passengers, a list of whom is here summarily drawn
up :

1. The historian Juillard, who, being possessed of a desirable
fortune, travelled almost continuously for pleasure, here and
there giving lectures renowned for their luminous wit and
charm.

2. The aged Olga Chervonenkova, a Latvian, formerly
a *prima ballerina* in St. Petersburg,—now grown fat and
bearing a moustache. For the past fifteen years, Olga, leaving
the stage in good time and surrounding herself with numerous
animals whom she cared for tenderly, had lived in quiet seclu-
sion on a small farm she had bought in Latvia, not far from
her native village. Her two great pets were Sladky, an elk, and
Milenkaya, a she-ass, who both came running at her least
call and often followed her indoors. Recently, a cousin of the
former *ballerina,* settled in the Republic of Argentina from
his early youth, had died leaving a small fortune made as a
coffee planter. Sole heiress, Olga, informed of her windfall

by the deceased man's lawyer, resolved to betake herself to the spot and supervise matters herself. She set off at once, leaving her menagerie in the care of a woman friend and neighbour who was devoted to the animals. At the last moment, unable to face so grievous a separation, she bought two open crates for the elk and the donkey and had them carefully deposited in the guard's van. At every stop, the solicitous traveller visited her two prisoners, caring for them even more tenderly on the boat.

3. Carmichael, a young man of twenty from Marseilles, already well-known for his remarkable head-voice, easily mistaken for that of a female soprano. Over the past two years, Carmichael had enjoyed cabaret triumphs throughout France, dressed as a woman and singing, each in its requisite *tessitura,* with impeccable flexibility and virtuosity, all the most difficult items in the soprano repertoire. He had booked his passage on the *Lynceus* in pursuance of a highly advantageous engagement in the New World.

4. Balbet, pistol and fencing champion of France, the favourite in an international competition for arms of every sort organised in Buenos Aires.

5. La Billaudière-Maisonnial, maker of precision tools, anxious to show at the same competition a mechanical foil capable of executing the most varied and transcendental thrusts and parries.

6. Luxo, firework manufacturer, in whose vast works at Courbevoie all Paris's great pyrotechnic displays were planned. Three months before embarking, Luxo had been visited by the young Baron Ballesteros, a rich Argentinian who, for some years past, had led a wildly extravagant and ostentatious life in France. On the point of returning to his own country and being married, Ballesteros wanted, on the occasion of his marriage, to give a truly royal firework display in the huge park of his country house near Buenos Aires; apart from the agreed

cost of this, Luxo was to be paid a considerable fee to come in person and supervise the proceedings. The manufacturer accepted the offer and undertook to see everything through to the end. Before taking his leave, the young Baron, somewhat intoxicated by the deserved renown of his good looks, formulated a thought which, though it betrayed the flashiness of his mentality, yet lacked neither unexpectedness nor originality. He wanted, for the final set-piece, rockets which, as they burst, should spangle the air with pictures of himself in various guises, instead of the multi-coloured stars and caterpillars whose banality seemed to him tedious. Luxo declared the project practicable and next day received a voluminous collection of photographs intended to serve him as models and showing his client in a diversity of costumes. A month before the marriage was due to be celebrated, Luxo had set out with his full cargo, not forgetting the famous crowning-piece packed separately and with special care.

7. The great architect Chènevillot, invited by the same Baron Ballesteros, who, wishing to have important structural alterations made to his house while he was away on his honeymoon, had concluded that only a French contractor would do. Chènevillot took with him a number of his best workmen, who would keep a sharp scrutiny on all that would have to be done by indigenous labour.

8. The hypnotist Darriand, desirous of making known in the New World certain mysterious plants whose hallucinatory properties he had discovered and whose odour could so raise the acuteness of a subject's perceptions that he would take for reality mere luminous projections from finely coloured films.

9. The chemist Bex, who during the past year had travelled widely abroad with the disinterested purpose of popularising two marvellous scientific discoveries, the fruit of his ingenious and patient exertions.

10. The inventor Bedu, taking to America a new type of loom, which, thanks to a curious system of paddle-blades, would, if set up in the flow of a river, automatically weave the richest materials. Setting up on the Rio de la Plata this apparatus constructed to his design, the inventor counted on receiving lucrative orders for similar looms from all the manufacturers in the area. Bedu himself designed and selected colours for the different silks, damasks or chintzes he wanted; the functioning of its countless blades once governed by the relevant combination, his machine reproduced any pattern indefinitely without aid or supervision.

11. The sculptor Fuxier, who, by means of a miraculously subtle internal modelling, inserted into red lozenges or pastilles of his own making the germ of numerous seductive images, ready to unfold in the form of smoke when brought into contact with any source of intense heat. Other lozenges, of a uniform bright blue, dissolved at once in water to produce veritable *bas-reliefs* on its surface due to the same interior preparation. With the aim of making his discovery widely known, Fuxier was taking to Buenos Aires a new and abundant supply of the two substances compounded by him, so that he might execute on the spot whatever might be requested in the way of a light group enclosed in a red pastille or liquid *bas-relief* contained potentially in a blue one. This method of sculpture by sudden opening-forth, is a third application served to create delicate subjects in grapes capable of ripening in a few minutes. Fuxier had provided himself for his experiments, with a number of vine-stocks growing in large earthenware pots whose watering and aeration he carefully supervised.

12. The two banking partners Hounsfield and Cerjat, called to the Argentine by affairs of high importance and accompanied by three of their clerks.

13. A theatrical company, which, proceeding to Buenos

Aires to play a large number of operettas, counted among its members the play-actor Soreau and the star singer Jeanne Souze.

14. The ichthyologist Martignon, engaged to form part of a scientific mission which, embarking at Montevideo on a small steam yacht, was to take soundings in the South Seas.

15. Dr. Leflaive, the ship's doctor.

16. Adinolfa, the great Italian tragic actress, about to appear for the first time before an Argentinian public.

17. The Hungarian Skariofszky, a zither-player of great talent, who, dressed in gipsy costume, performed on his instrument with a virtuosity for which concert organisers on both sides of the Atlantic paid enormous fees.

18. The Belgian Cuijper, no less highly paid, and justly so, for his fine tenor voice, to which a contrivance in rare metal added a formidable magic quality.

19. A strange assortment of freaks, animal trainers and acrobats engaged at great cost for three months at a circus in Buenos Aires. These incongruous persons included the clown Whirligig,—the horseman Urbain, owner of the horse Romulus, Tancred Bucharessas, an individual without arms or legs, accompanied by his five children, Hector, Tommy, Marius, Bob and Stella,—Ludovic, a singer,—Lelgoualch, a Breton,— Stephen Alcott and his six sons,—Jenn the ringmaster and Philippo the dwarf.


For a week our passage was calm and uneventful. But, in the middle of the eighth night, a terrible hurricane smote us in mid-Atlantic. The screw and the wheel were shattered by the violence of the waves, and, after two days of wild drifting, the *Lynceus,* borne along like so much dead wreckage, ran aground on the coast of Africa.

Nobody failed to answer when the roll was called, but with the ship itself stove in and its boats useless, all hope of putting to sea again had to be abandoned.

Hardly had we gone ashore when we saw bounding and gambolling towards us some hundreds of negroes, who gaily flocked around us manifesting their joy by a noisy clamour. They were led by a young chief of open, intelligent countenance, who, introducing himself by the name of Seil Kor, plunged us into astonishment by replying to our first questions in fluent and correct French.

A few brief exchanges informed us of Seil Kor's mission. He had been charged with conducting us to Ejur, capital of the Emperor Talu VII, his lord, who, expecting for some hours past that our ship would presently run aground as a native fisherman had stated that it inevitably must, proposed to keep us in his power until he received adequate ransom.

We had to bow to the force of numbers.

While the negroes were occupied in unloading the ship, Seil Kor, yielding to our entreaties, was kind enough to offer us some description of our future residence.

Seated upon a narrow piece of rock, in the shadow of a high cliff, the youthful orator began by recounting his own story to the attentive group we formed, spread out here and there on the soft sand.

At the age of ten, wandering in this same region to which chance had just brought us, Seil Kor had met a French explorer called Laubé, who, attracted doubtless by the child's lively appearance, had resolved to attach to his person and take back to his own family this living souvenir of his travels.

Landing on the west coast of Africa, Laubé had sworn never to return upon his tracks; accompanied by a valiant escort, he pushed forward to the east, then, bearing northward, crossed the desert by camel and finally reached Tripoli, the point of arrival he had determined on beforehand.

During the two years this took, Seil Kor had learnt French by listening to his companions; struck by such aptitude, the explorer was at pains further to give the child many fruitful lessons in reading, history and geography.

In Tripoli, Laubé expected to rejoin his wife and daughter, who, according to the calculations they had made beforehand, should already have been installed for two months at the Hôtel de l'Angleterre to await his return.

The explorer felt the tenderest emotion on learning from the hotel porter of the presence of the two dear ones he had left so long deprived of his loving care.

Seil Kor, discreetly, went out to look round the town, not wishing to intrude upon the first expansive moments of a reunion so impatiently anticipated by his protector.

Returning, after an hour, into the large entry hall, he perceived Laubé, who led him to his own room, situated on the ground floor and brilliantly lighted by a broad, open window looking out on the hotel gardens.

Having already spoken to Seil Kor as a very learned person, the explorer wished to put the child through a sharp course of test and revision before presenting him to the two new companions of his existence.

A few questions on the major facts of history received satisfactory replies.

Taking next the geography of France, Laubé asked for the main towns of a number of *départements* picked at random.

Seated facing the window, Seil Kor had not yet made any mistake in his almost mechanical recital, when suddenly, on the point of naming the prefecture of Corrèze, he felt as though he were about to faint; a mist swam before his eyes, and his legs started trembling, while the heart in his breast beat loud and hurriedly.

This perturbation was caused by the sight of a ravishing child about twelve years of age, who, just now passing through the garden, had briefly met Seil Kor's dazzled gaze with a glance from the depth of her blue eyes.

Meanwhile Laubé, having observed nothing, went on repeating with some impatience :

' Corrèze, principal town . . . ?'

The vision had faded, and Seil Kor was able to regain command of himself sufficiently to reply in a murmur :

' Tulle.'

The name of this town would eternally remain linked in Seil Kor's mind with the overwhelming apparition.

His examination over, Laubé conducted Seil Kor to his wife and his daughter Nina, in whom the young negro, in an ecstasy and with a joy that was almost divine, recognised the fair-haired child of the garden.

The life of Seil Kor was thenceforward illuminated by the continual presence of Nina, for the two children, being of the same age, were together unbrokenly at play and at study.

Laubé, at the moment of Nina's birth, had been living with his wife in Crete, because of a voluminous work he was preparing on *Candia and its Inhabitants*. It was thus in a foreign land that the little girl's first years had been spent, tenderly brought up by a Candiot nurse, a trace of whose soft and charming accent she retained.

This accent enchanted Seil Kor, whose love and devotion increased hourly.

He dreamed of holding Nina for a moment in his arms; in the depths of his imagination he saw her a prey to countless dangers, from which he rescued her before the anguished and grateful eyes of her parents.

These fancies were soon to be exchanged for sharp reality.

One day, standing on a terrace of the hotel washed by the

sea, Seil Kor was fishing with his friend, who looked ravishing in a navy-blue frock he cherished particularly.

Suddenly Nina uttered a cry of joy on seeing at the end of her line, which she had just lifted out of the water, a big, wriggling fish. Drawing it towards her, she seized her prey in order to take it off the hook. But immediately on contact she received a shock and fell unconscious to the ground. The fish, inoffensive in appearance and rather like a ray or skate, was in fact a *torpedo* or cramp-fish, whose electrical discharge had caused this unexpected result.

Seil Kor raised Nina in his arms and carried her to the hotel, where, as her mother and father appeared promptly, she recovered her senses after moments of a torpidity which was not serious.

Once his first misgivings had been removed, Seil Kor blessed the misadventure which, bodying forth his dream, had allowed him to embrace his beloved companion briefly.

Nina's birthday occurred several days after this incident. For the occasion, Laubé proposed to give a small children's ball to which the few European families living in the town were to be invited.

Resolved to celebrate the great day by making up a story for his friend, Seil Kor devoted part of his nights to cultivating his memory and his intonation in secret.

Thinking also to offer the little girl a present, he promised himself to risk at the gaming tables the few pieces of silver he owed to the generosity of Laubé.

One casino in Tripoli, easily accessible, featured a game with little horses in which the stakes were suitable to the most modest purses.

Favoured by the luck which, they say, goes with beginners, Seil Kor promptly won with a martingale and was able to order, at the best pastry-shop in the place, an enormous Savoy cake destined to appear in the midst of the celebrations.

The ball, started in the course of the day, filled the great hall of the hotel with joyful animation. At about five o'clock, the children trooped into the next room and sat down at a huge table loaded with fruit and other delicacies. At that moment the famous cake was brought in, on Seil Kor's behalf, and greeted with noisy acclamation. All eyes were fixed on the donator, who rising without embarrassment, delivered his fable in a clear and resonant voice. At the last verse applause broke out on all sides, and Nina, rising in her turn, proposed a toast to Seil Kor, thus for an instant lord of the banquet.

When the guests had eaten, the ball continued. Seil Kor and Nina waltzed together, then, exhausted by a series of rapid turns, stopped suddenly beside Mme. Laubé, who stood there calmly, delightedly contemplating the beautiful childish joy with which she felt herself surrounded.

Seeing her daughter approach with her companion, the worthy woman, grateful for all Seil Kor's attentiveness, turned smiling to the young negro, and said in a gentle voice, pointing to Nina : ' Kiss her !'

Seil Kor, almost dizzy, put his arms about his friend and placed on her blooming cheeks two chaste kisses which left him swaying as though intoxicated.

After this family solemnity, Laubé, recovered from his fatigue after a stay in Tripoli, resolved to go back to France. The explorer owned, in the Pyrenees, near a village called Port d'Oo, a modest country house whose peace and isolation he valued highly. There he would be well situated for drawing up, with the help of his notes, a detailed account of his travels.

Seil Kor was delighted with his new abode; the house was situated in the beautiful Oo valley, and every day the young African set off with Nina on long expeditions in the forest, profiting by the last rays of a mild and clement autumn.

One evening, their walk having taken them into the village, the two children suddenly perceived a troupe of wandering players who, crowded together on a wagon or on foot in streets full of curious observers, gave out countless handbills, attracting the crowd with patter and by beating on the big drum.

Two handbills were given to Seil Kor, who read them with Nina. The first, drawn up as an advertisement, began with a long phrase announcing in large letters the sensational arrival of the Ferréol troupe, composed of acrobats, dancers, tight-rope walkers; the second part of the sheet contained a bombastic discourse adjuring the French to remain vigilant, in view of the presence upon their soil of the chief of the band, the famous wrestler Ferréol, capable with his own hands of destroying armies and tearing down ramparts; the exhortation began thus: 'Tremble, people of France . . .!' and the word 'Tremble', designed to catch the eye, was displayed in bold type, set out as a heading on its own.

The other handbill, of more modest dimensions, bore this simple attestation: 'We were beaten by Ferréol', followed by an innumerable list of signatures reproduced in facsimile and emanating from the most formidable professionals put to the floor by the illustrious champion.

Next day, Seil Kor and Nina betook themselves to the village square to watch the promised display. A wide platform stood in the open air, and the two children were greatly diverted by the jugglers, clowns, spinners of cartwheels and performing animals, who for two hours passed before their eyes.

At one point, three men came out and set up, at the right-hand end of the platform, a fragment of Renaissance architecture, with a balcony and a large window on the first floor.

Presently, a corresponding set appeared to the left on the far side of the trestles, and one of the stage-hands carefully fixed a steel wire between the two balconies, facing each other.

No sooner were these preparations complete than the right-hand window opened discreetly and allowed passage to a young woman dressed like a princess in the reign of Charles IX. This unknown person made a sign with her hand, and at once the other window yielded to the pressure of a lord, richly attired, who in his turn appeared on the balcony. The new-comer, in embroidered doublet, short knickerbockers and velvet cap, wore also a stiffened ruff and a black mask appropriate to the clandestine adventure upon which he seemed about to embark.

After an exchange of signs indicative of advice and promises, the lover, climbing over the balustrade, placed his foot on the steel wire, then, arms extended like those of an equilibrist, set himself to the task of crossing, by the aerial route presented to his audacity, the distance separating him from his fair neighbour.

But of a sudden, lending ear towards the interior of the house as though listening for the footfall of some jealous one, the young woman returned precipitately the way she had come, warning her intrepid lover with a gesture, whereupon he, with long strides, regained his point of departure and disappeared behind curtains.

A few moments later the two windows opened again, and the perilous voyage started all over with new hope. This time the crossing was accomplished without false alarm, and the two lovers fell into each other's arms, amid a prolonged ovation.

The steel wire and the two sets were removed without delay, and a young Spanish couple, abruptly on stage, were dancing a vigorous *bolero,* accompanied with cries and foot-stamping. The woman, in a mantilla, the man, in short jacket and *sombrero,* both held in their right hand a tambourine, upon which they applied vigorous wrist strokes. After ten minutes of unbroken turns and jerks of the hip, the two dancers ended in a graceful and smiling immobility, while the electrified crowd enthusiastically applauded.

The performance ended with the famous Ferréol flooring a number of victims, and night was already falling when Seil Kor and Nina, delighted with the afternoon's proceedings, went off, arm in arm, along the road to the great house in which they lived.

Next day, kept indoors by a fine, steady drizzle, the two children had to abandon their daily walk. Fortunately, a coach house among the outbuildings offered a wide space propitious to the wildest games; the mischievous darlings went there to play.

Haunted by the previous evening's display, Nina had brought her work-basket, with the idea of concocting for Seil Kor accoutrements like those of the tightrope dancer. At the far end of the coach house, two carts facing each other, their shafts touching, provided a convenient and safe field for experiment to an equilibrist yet unpractised.

Armed with a pair of scissors, a threaded needle and the two handbills which Seil Kor had kept, Nina set to work; from the first sheet she cut out a cap, and from the second a domino with two threads designed to pass behind the ears.

The ruff required a larger quantity of paper; in a corner of the coach house, put out there for throwing away, lay a bundle of old copies of *Nature,* a magazine to which Laubé both subscribed and contributed. Tearing off the blue covers of a large number of issues, Nina succeeded in putting together an elegant collarette of uniform colour, and soon, adorned with the three articles carefully executed by the adroit little needlewoman, Seil Kor embarked upon his funambulistic career, crossing from end to end the narrow and somewhat precarious way provided by the shafts of the two carts.

Encouraged by this first success, the children then proposed to copy the *bolero* of the Spanish couple. Seil Kor removed his paper disguise, and the dance began, at once turning wild and febrile; Nina particularly put a curious fervour into her miming, clapping her hands together to imitate the tambourine's rhythmical chatter, and prolonging her joyful gambols without thought of becoming tired or breathless. Suddenly stopped in the midst of all this effervescence by the dinner-bell, the two dancers left their outbuilding for the house.

The weather had turned cold with the onset of twilight, and a kind of sleet fell from the dull sky.

In a sweat from the delirious and prolonged dance, Nina was seized with a dreadful shivering, which stopped when she reached the dining-room, where burned the first fire of the season.

Next day, the sparkling sun had reappeared, lighting one of those last translucid and pure days which every year precede the coming of winter. Wishing to take advantage of this serene afternoon which perhaps marked the last farewell of the fine weather, Seil Kor joyfully proposed to Nina a long walk in the forest

The little girl, who in fact had a fever but believed herself merely to be out of sorts for the moment, accepted her friend's invitation and set out at his side. Seil Kor carried a full luncheon-basket swinging upon his arm.

After an hour's course in the depth of the woods, the two children were confronted by an inextricable tangle of trees, which marked the beginning of a large thickset area known to the countryfolk as the *maquis*. This designation was justified by an extraordinary interlacing of branches and creepers; nobody entered the *maquis* without risk of losing himself for ever.

Until then, on their mad expeditions, Seil Kor and the

little girl had wisely skirted this area. But, from the attraction of the unknown, they had promised themselves that one day they would boldly venture into the heart of this mysterious region. The occasion seemed to them ripe for the realisation of this project.

Presently, Seil Kor resolved to mark out the way back like Tom Thumb. He opened his basket of provisions, but, remembering the discomfiture of the well-known hero, instead of crumbling bread he picked a Swiss cheese of dazzling whiteness, fragments of which, no temptation to birds' stomachs, would stand out clearly against the dark ground of moss and heath.

The exploration began; every five paces, Seil Kor picked at the cheese with the point of a knife and threw the light fragment to the ground.

For half an hour, the imprudent pair penetrated thus into the *maquis* without discovering any end to it; the light was beginning to fail, and Seil Kor, suddenly worried, sounded a retreat.

For a while, the boy easily traced his path, uninterruptedly marked. But soon the markers gave out; some hungry animal, fox or wolf, sniffing out the odorous track, had licked up the bits of cheese, thus snapping the thread meant to lead back the two who were now lost.

Slowly the sky darkened, and it was night.

Almost out of his mind, Seil Kor persisted for a long time, but in vain, in the attempt to find a way out of the *maquis*.

The exhausted Nina, shivering with fever, was barely able to follow and feared at every moment to feel her strength leave her. In the end, the poor child, giving way against her will and uttering a cry of distress, lay down on a bed of moss beneath her steps, while Seil Kor stood beside her anxious and disheartened.

Nina fell into an unwholesome sleep; it was now quite dark, and there was a sharp chill in the air; it was just at the beginning of Advent, and a feeling of winter penetrated the damp, glacial atmosphere.

Deeply moved, Seil Kor took off his coat to cover the little girl, fearful of depriving her of a rest of which she seemed to have so much need.

After a long doze shot through with ceaseless dreams, Nina awoke of herself and stood up, ready to travel on again.

In a clear sky, the stars now gave out their most brilliant fires. Nina knew how to find her bearings; she pointed out the pole star with her finger, and the two children, thenceforward taking an undeflected course, at the end of an hour reached the outskirts of the *maquis;* a further lap brought them to the house, where the little girl fell into the arms of her parents, pale with anxiety and fear.

Next day, still wishing to battle against a rapidly progressing illness, Nina arose as usual and went into the schoolroom, where Seil Kor was going over a French exercise prescribed by Laubé.

Since her return from Africa, the little girl had been learning her catechism at the village church; that morning, she had to finish a piece of apologetics to be given in the following day.

Half an hour's concentration sufficed for her to finish her task and reach the set analytical conclusion.

Having written the first words : ' I resolve that I shall . . .' she turned to Seil Kor to ask his advice on how she ought to go on, when a terrible fit of coughing seized her, racking her from head to foot with gasps and wheezing.

The frightened Seil Kor approached the sick girl, who between spasms avowed all : the shivering she had felt on leaving the coach house—and the fever, which not having abated since last evening, had certainly been aggravated by that dangerous slumber upon the bed of moss.

Nina's parents were at once called, and the little girl was thereupon put to bed.

Alas! neither the resources of science nor the constant attention of a frantic household were able to triumph over the terrible sickness, which, in less than a week, carried the poor child off from her family's near-idolatrous concern.

After this sudden death, Seil Kor, out of his mind with despair, could no longer bear the scenes till then divinely illuminated by his friend's presence. The sight of all those places so often contemplated with Nina made odious the horrible contrast between his present grief and happiness past.

The onset of cold weather, moreover, troubled the young negro, who, in his heart, still preserved a nostalgia for the African sun. One day, leaving upon the table, addressed to his dear protector, a letter full of affection, gratitude and regret, he fled from that large country house bearing with him as though they had been holy relics the cap, ruff and domino made by Nina.

By means of casual labour at the farms he passed through on his way, he managed to put together a large enough sum of money to get to Marseilles. There he enlisted as stoker aboard a vessel chartered to sail down the West African coast.

When the vessel put in at Porto Novo, he deserted and went back to his native territory, where his intelligence and culture before long secured him a position of importance near the Emperor's person.

We had listened in silence to Seil Kor's recital. He, stopped for a moment by the emotion inherent in so many poignant recollections, then spoke again and informed us about the master he served.

Talu VII, whose origins were illustrious, boasted of having European blood in his veins. At a period already remote, his ancestor Suan had gained the throne by an act of daring, then undertaken to found a dynasty. This is the traditional account of what ensued.

A few weeks after the accession of Suan, a large ship, tempest-driven, had foundered within sight of the shores of Ejur. Sole survivors of the disaster, two young girls of fifteen, clinging to an isolated piece of wreckage, succeeded in reaching land after passing through countless hazards.

The shipwrecked girls, ravishing twin sisters of Spanish nationality, were so alike in appearance that one could not be told apart from the other.

Suan was much taken with these charming adolescents, and, in his impatient desire to procreate abundantly, married them both on the same day, happy to confirm the superiority of his birth by the adjunction of such European blood as, in times present and to come, must capture the fetichistic imagination of his subjects.

It was also on a single day, and at the same hour, that the two sisters, in their proper time, were brought to bed each of a son.

Talu and Yaour—thus were the children named—thereafter caused their father some anxiety, since, baffled by the unexpected event of two simultaneous births, he did not know how to decide upon the heir to his throne.

The exact similarity in appearance between his two brides made it impossible for Suan to be certain about anteriority of conception, which alone could have given one of the brothers superior rights.

In a vain attempt to elucidate this point, the two mothers were interrogated; with the help of a few native words painfully acquired, each testified boldly in favour of her son.

Suan decided to have recourse to the judgement of the Great Spirit.

Under the name of 'Trophies Square', he had just laid out in Ejur a vast quadrangular esplanade, where he proposed to hang, on the trunks of sycamores planted all round, numerous spoils of war taken from redoubtable foes who had bitterly striven to bar his way to power. Posting himself at the northern extremity of the new site, he caused to be sown at the same instant, in a plot of ground conveniently prepared, the two seeds of a rubber tree and a palm, each previously assigned before witnesses to one of his sons; a token of the divine will, the tree first to spring from the earth would indicate the future sovereign.

The two fertilised spots of earth were tended and watered with impartial care.

It was the palm tree, planted to the right, which first showed above the surface of the soil, thus proclaiming Talu's rights to the detriment of Yaour, whose rubber tree appeared a whole day later.

Four years after their arrival in Ejur, the twin sisters, catching a fever, perished almost at the same time, laid low by the terrible ordeal of a particularly broiling summer. At the time of the shipwreck, they had contrived to salvage a miniature portrait representing them side by side wearing the national mantilla; Suan preserved this image, a precious document when it came to establishing the superior essence of his race.

Talu and Yaour grew up, and so did the two trees planted at their birth. The presence in their veins of Spanish blood manifested itself in the two young brothers only by a slightly paler coloration of their black skins and somewhat less accentuatedly thick lips.

Watching over the stages of their growth, Suan sometimes felt uneasy at the thought of the bloody quarrels which might one day break out over the succession. Fortunately a new conquest partly dispelled his anxiety, providing him with the occasion to carve out a kingdom for Yaour.

The empire of Ponukele, founded by Suan, was bordered to the south by a river called the Tez, the mouth of which lay not far from Ejur.

Beyond the Tez lay Drelshkaf, a rich land which Suan, after a campaign which had gone in his favour, contrived to establish under his dominion.

Thenceforward, Yaour was destined by his father one day to ascend the throne of Drelshkaf. Compared with the neighbouring empire, the appanage seemed modest certainly; Suan hoped nevertheless by this compensation to soothe the jealousy of his disinherited son.

The two brothers were twenty years old when their father died. Things followed their natural course, and Talu became emperor of Ponukele, Yaour king of Drelshkaf.

Talu I and Yaour I—thus were they designated—took to themselves numerous wives and founded two rival houses always ready to enter into conflict. The Yaours laid claim to the empire to which they contested the Talus' rights, while these, for their part, strong in their knowledge of the divine intervention which had chosen them for supreme rank, demanded the crown of Drelshkaf, of which they had been deprived by a mere caprice on the part of Suan.

One night, Yaour V, king of Drelshkaf, direct and legitimate descendant of Yaour I, crossed the Tez with his army and penetrated by surprise into Ejur.

The Emperor Talu IV, great-grandson of Talu I, was forced

to flee to escape death, and Yaour V, realising the dream of his ancestors, united Ponukele and Drelshkaf under one sceptre.

At this epoch the rubber tree and palm in Trophies Square had finally come to their full growth.

The first task of Yaour V on taking the title of emperor was to burn down the palm sacred to the abhorred race of the Talus and to grub out every root of the accursed tree whose first appearance above the earth had dispossessed his kin.

Yaour V reigned for thirty years and died at the height of his power.

His successor, Yaour VI, a coward and incapable, made himself unpopular by his continual blundering and his cruelty. Talu IV, leaving the place of exile in which he had so long languished, was thus able to gather about him a great many partisans who fomented a revolt among the discontented people.

Yaour VI fled in terror without awaiting battle and took refuge in his kingdom of Drelshkaf, whose crown he succeeded in retaining.

Renamed Emperor of Ponukele, Talu IV planted a new palm-shoot on the spot laid bare by Yaour V; soon a tree sprang up, like to the first, whose emblematic significance it evoked, proclaiming the restoration of the legitimate branch.

Since that time everything had taken place normally, without violent usurpation or difficulties concerning the succession. At present Talu VII reigned over Ponukele and Yaour IX over Drelshkaf, both keeping alive the traditions of hatred and jealousy which, at all times, had divided their forebears. The mark of European blood, long effaced by a succession of purely indigenous unions, had left no trace upon the persons of the two sovereigns, who resembled their subjects both in feature and in skin colour.

In Trophies Square, the palm planted by Talu IV now dwarfed by its magnificent appearance the rubber tree half dead with old age which stood there as its mere appendage.

# XI

A T this point in his narration, Seil Kor paused for breath, then touched on more intimate details affecting the Emperor's private life.

At the beginning of his reign Talu VII had married a young and ideally beautiful Ponukelian woman, called Rul.

Much in love, the Emperor refused to select other female companions, despite the usages of the country, where polygamy was an honoured custom.

One stormy day, Talu and Rul, then three months gone with child, walked lovingly upon the beach of Ejur to admire the sublime spectacle offered by the raging sea, when they saw far out a ship in distress which, having struck a reef, sank like a stone before their eyes.

Speechless with horrror, the pair remained unmoving for a long time, gazing at the fatal spot, where floated some few pieces of wreckage.

Presently the corpse of a woman of white race, evidently proceeding from the vanished ship, floated towards the shingle, tossed this way and that by the waves. The floating figure, laid flat, face to the sky, was dressed in a Swiss costume of dark skirt, embroidered apron in many colours and red velvet corset which, reaching only to her waist, enclosed an open-necked white blouse with broad puffed sleeves. At the back of her head might be seen, shining through the transparency of the waters, long gold pins set in the form of a star about a firmly braided coil of hair.

Rul, much inclined to finery, was immediately fascinated by the red corset and the golden pins with which she dreamed of tricking herself out.

At her request the Emperor summoned a slave, who, putting out in a canoe, set himself to the task of bringing the shipwrecked woman to shore.

But the heavy weather made his task arduous and Rul, whose morbid desire was sharpened by the difficulties to be overcome, followed anxiously, with alternating hope and discouragement, the perilous manoeuvres of the slave, who saw his prey constantly evade him.

After an hour of unceasing struggle with the elements, the slave finally reached the corpse, which he contrived to hoist into his canoe; the body of a child of two was then discovered, on the back of the dead woman, whose neck remained convulsively encircled by the two small arms, still clenched. The poor child was no doubt the nursling of the shipwrecked woman, who, at the last moment, had attempted to swim to safety bearing the precious burden with her.

Nurse and child were transported to Ejur; presently Rul entered into possession of the gold pins, which she pricked out in a circle in her hair, then of the red corset, which she fastened trimly over the cloth which girded her loins. Thenceforward she never left off these ornaments which were her great joy; as her pregnancy advanced, she let out the lace, which slid smoothly through eyelets finely ringed with metal.

For some time after the wreck, the sea continued to throw up on the coast, amid flotsam and jetsam of all kinds, decorated boxes, which were carefully brought in. Among the debris was discovered a sailor's cap bearing the word: *Sylvander,* the unlucky ship's name.

Six months after the storm, Rul gave birth to a daughter who was called Sirdah.

The anxious hour spent by the young mother before the body of the Swiss woman reached land had left its mark. The child, otherwise healthy and well-formed, bore on her forehead a red birthmark of unusual shape, set about, like the points of a star, with yellow lines reminiscent of the celebrated gold pins.

The first time Sirdah opened her eyes, she was seen to squint dreadfully; the mother, very proud of her own beauty, felt humiliated at having produced anything so ill-favoured and took an aversion to this child who wounded her vanity. On the other hand, the Emperor, who had ardently wished for a daughter, conceived a deep love for the poor innocent, whom he surrounded with tenderness and care.

At this period Talu had as his counsellor an individual by the name of Mossem, a tall negro, at once magician, doctor and man of letters, who acted as prime minister.

Mossem had become infatuated with the charming Rul, who for her part was attracted by the seductive counsellor, whose majestic bearing and wide knowledge she admired.

Their intrigue followed its inevitable course, and Rul, a year after the birth of Sirdah, brought into the world a son bearing a marked facial likeness to Mossem.

Talu, fortunately, did not notice the fatal resemblance. His son, nevertheless, failed to gain in his heart any place like that held by Sirdah.

In accordance with a law instituted by Suan, every sovereign, at his death, was succeeded by his first born, whether girl or boy. Twice already, in each of the rival clans, daughters should therefore have reigned; but in every case their premature death had caused the reversion of supreme rank to a brother.

Mossem and Rul conceived the dreadful project of bringing about the disappearance of Sirdah in order that their son might one day be emperor.

In the midst of all this, Talu, possessed by bellicose instincts, set out on a protracted campaign, leaving his power in the hands of Mossem, who, during the absence of his monarch was to exercise absolute authority.

The two accomplices did not let slip an occasion so favourable to the execution of their plan.

To the north-east of Ejur stretched the Vorrh, an immense virgin forest where none dared venture, because of a legend which peopled its darkness and maleficent spirits. It was enough to abandon Sirdah there; her body, shielded by superstition, would never be found, since none would look for her.

One night, Mossem set out, carrying Sirdah in his arms; next evening, after a long day's march, he reached the skirts of the Vorrh and, too intelligent to believe in tales of the supernatural, fearlessly penetrated beneath the haunted branches offered to his view. Coming to a vast open space, he placed the little sleeping Sirdah down on the moss, then regained open country by the very path he had himself just cleared through the dense mass of branches and creepers.

Twenty-four hours later he returned to Ejur by night; both departure and return had gone unwitnessed.

During his absence, Rul had stationed herself upon the threshold of the imperial hut, in order to bar entry to it. Sirdah was seriously ill, she said, and Mossem was staying by the child's bedside to give her every care. After her accomplice's return, she announced the death of Sirdah, and next day a solemn funeral was celebrated.

Tradition demanded, upon the demise of any member of the royal family, a death certificate setting forth in detail the last hours of the deceased. Possessed of all the secrets of Ponukelian script, Mossem undertook this task and drew up on parchment an imaginary account of how Sirdah had met her end.

The Emperor's grief was extreme when, on his return, he learned of the death of his daughter.

But there was nothing to make him suspect the plot concocted against Sirdah; the two accomplices, drunk with joy, thus saw realised to their hearts' content the odious scheme which made their son sole heir to the throne.

Two years passed during which Rul did not again conceive. Disappointed by this sterility, Talu, without on that account repudiating her whom he still believed faithful, finally resolved to take other wives, in the hope of having a second daughter, whose features might recall the image of his beloved Sirdah.

He was disappointed in his purpose; he begot only sons, who did not succeed in making him forget the vanished dear one.

Only war distracted him from his grief; endlessly, he undertook new campaigns pushing back the bounds of his vast domain and nailing countless spoils to the sycamores in Trophies Square.

Endowed with a poet's sensibility, he had begun an enormous epic, each of whose cantos celebrated one of his major feats of arms. This work he called the *Jeruka*, a Ponukelian word denoting triumphant heroism. Full of pride and ambition, the Emperor was determined in his own person to eclipse all the princes of his race and to transmit to future generations a poetic account of his reign, which he meant to make predominating and full of glory.

Each time he completed a fragment of the *Jeruka,* he taught

178

it to his warriors, who chanted it in unison to a slow and monotonous kind of recitative.

The years went by without any shadow falling between Mossem and Rul, who continued to love each other in secret.

But one day the Emperor was informed of their relations by one of his new wives.

Unable to believe what he took for audacious slander, Talu gaily recounted the thing to Rul, begging her to take care of the jealous hatred her overwhelming beauty provoked among her rivals.

Though reassured by the Emperor's jovial tone, Rul smelled danger and vowed to redouble her precautions.

She suggested to Mossem that he should take a mistress upon whom he would ostentatiously bestow honours and riches in order to divert the monarch's suspicions.

Mossem approved of this plan, whose prompt realisation seemed to him, as to Rul, urgently necessary. His choice fell upon a young beauty called Jizme, whose ebony countenance revealed, when she intoxicatingly smiled, teeth of a dazzling whiteness.

Jizme quickly grew accustomed to the privileges of her lofty station; Mossem, bent on playing his part well, satisfied her every caprice, and with a word the young woman obtained for her creatures favours far beyond their deserts.

The credit she held soon grouped about the minister's favourite a crowd of suppliants seeking audience of her. Jizme, pleased and flattered, presently found that she needed a method of regulating the invasion.

At her request, Mossem cut out of sheets of parchment a number of thin, flexible squares on each of which he finely traced the name : ' Jizme ', further setting out in one corner a diagram of three phases of the moon.

These were in effect visiting cards, which, distributed largely, indicated to interested parties the three reception days selected in each period of four weeks by the all-powerful intermediary.

Jizme thenceforward amused herself with playing the sovereign. Each time one of the fixed dates came round, she put on her finest ornaments and received the crowd of place seekers, promising her support to one and refusing it to another, certain beforehand of seeing her decisions wholly ratified by Mossem.

One thing was nevertheless lacking to Jizme's happiness; beautiful, passionate and full of exuberant youth, she burned with fever and desires.

Now, Mossem, faithful to Rul, had never bestowed so much as a kiss on her who passed in the eyes of all for his idol of love.

Fully aware of being used as a screen, Jizme resolved to yield totally without any scruple to a man who should understand and appreciate her.

At each of her audiences, she had observed, in the front rank of suppliants, a young negro called Naïr, who seemed never to address her but with emotion and timidity.

More than once she fancied she perceived Naïr, concealed behind a bush, watching when she went out in the hope of seeing her for a moment.

Soon she could no longer doubt the passion she had inspired in the lovesick young man. She attached Naïr to her person and gave herself unreservedly to the pleasing suitor whose ardent feelings she had quickly come to share.

A sufficiently plausible excuse justified in Mossem's eyes the new page's assiduity with regard to the favourite.

Ejur, at that moment, was infested by a legion of mosquitoes whose stings produced fever. Now, Naïr knew how to make traps which infallibly caught the dangerous insects.

He had discovered as bait a red flower whose extremely violent scent attracted from afar off the tiny beasts to be captured. The capsules of certain fruits furnished him with filaments of an extreme tenuity out of which he personally wove a tissue finer than spiders' webs, but resistant enough to stop the mosquitoes in flight. This last work required great precision, and Naïr was able to carry it out to perfection only with the help of a long formula of which the text recited by heart indicated one by one the movements to be made and the knots to be tied.

Jizme, like a child, drew ever new pleasure from the spectacle provided by the industrious arrangement of threads delicately interwoven by the fingers of her lover.

Naïr's presence was thus explained by the powerful distraction which this talent full of invention and subtlety afforded Jizme.

An artist in every way, Naïr was able to draw and sought relaxation from his trap-weaving in sketching portraits and landscapes in a bizarre and primitive style. One day, he presented his love with a curious white mat, which he had patiently decorated with little designs representing the most varied subjects. He intended, by means of this gift, to preside over Jizme's sleeping, since henceforward she lay down nightly upon the soft couch whose contact unbrokenly reminded her of the tender and attentive solicitude of her beloved.

The young pair were living thus happily and in peace when an imprudence on the part of Naïr suddenly apprised Mossem of the truth.

Certain of the crates washed up by the sea after the wreck of the *Sylvander* contained articles of clothing which had remained since that time unused. Jizme, with the authorisation of Mossem, took out of this stock all kinds of trinkets which appealed to her light and careless frivolity of disposition.

Gloves particularly amused the laughing child, who, whenever there was any solemnity in the occasion, loved to imprison her hands and arms in sheathes of supple suède.

Searching among all this diversity of objects, Jizme had unearthed a bowler hat which Naïr joyfully adopted. Thereafter, the young negro never appeared without the rigid headgear, which made him easily recognisable at a distance.

To the south-east of Ejur, not far from the right bank of the Tez, stood a large and magnificent garden called the Behuliphruen, kept up in a state of unparalleled luxury by a whole crowd of slaves. A true poet, Talu was fond of flowers and composed the stanzas of his epic beneath the delightful shade of this grandiose park.

In the centre of the Behuliphruen rose a high terrace, admirably set out with greenery. It overlooked the whole vast garden, and the Emperor loved to spend long hours of rest, installed by the leaves and branches of the balustrade surrounding this place of enchanting freshness on all sides. Often, in the evening, he would stand dreaming with Rul at a corner of the terrace from which the view was particularly splendid.

Incapable of appreciating this serene contemplation which seemed to her tedious, Rul one day invited Mossem to come and enliven the imperial *tête-à-tête*. Blind and confident as ever, Talu nowise opposed the realisation of this caprice; Jizme's presence was in itself enough to ward off any untoward suspicion.

Naïr, who had a rendezvous with his love every evening, was annoyed to learn from her of the event which prevented their meeting. Determined to come near Jizme nevertheless, he conceived a daring plan which should allow him to be present as a fifth person at the meeting in the Behuliphruen.

That day, however, Jizme was giving audience to the usual

flood of her petitioners; the reception once having started, Naïr could no longer hold with the young woman the long private discussion needed for the detailed exposition of his project.

Literate as well as artistic, Naïr knew the Ponukelian script, which he had taught Jizme during the course of their frequent and protracted interviews. He took it upon himself to write out for her all the urgent instructions he could not impart to her by word of mouth.

The letter was drawn up on parchment, then, amid the throng, passed furtively from the hands of Naïr to those of Jizme, who tucked it quickly into her waistband.

But Mossem, who was walking among the multitude, had noticed this clandestine manoeuvre. Presently, embracing Jizme, accustomed to receive his public caresses without affront, he possessed himself of the epistle, which he took aside to decipher.

As a heading, Naïr had drawn, in procession, the five personages who were to figure at this evening's occasion; on the right, Talu advanced in splendid isolation; behind his back, Mossem and Rul made mocking gestures, themselves jeered at by Naïr and Jizme, who brought up the rear.

The text contained the following instructions :

Once installed at the corner of the cool terrace, Jizme was to look out for Naïr, who, without making a sound, would approach by a particular path; in the shadows, his silhouette would be easily distinguished from that of any other young negro by the bowler hat he would be at pains to wear. From the spot chosen by Talu for his meditations the ground fell away almost sheer; nevertheless, holding on to roots and brushwood with all ten fingers, Naïr would manage to pull himself cautiously up to the level of the nonchalant group; Jizme was to allow her hand to droop beyond the flowery balustrade, then, having assured herself of the visitor's identity by carefully touching the hat, yield the hand to her lover's kisses, he briefly holding on by the strength of his wrists.

Having engraved upon his memory all the details he had just discovered, Mossem returned to Jizme's side and, under the pretext of fondling her again, succeeded in slipping the letter back into the favourite's loincloth.

Wounded in his self-esteem and furious at the thought that for some time past he had been an object of general derision, Mossem sought means to establish flagrant proof against the two conspirators, whom he proposed to chastise severely.

He worked out a plan and called on Seil Kor, who, at that period, had already been several years in the Emperor's service and, at night, might well be taken for Naïr thanks to an exact conformity in age and build.

This was the project outlined by Mossem :

Wearing the bowler which should transform him, Seil Kor was to appear before Jizme along the path clearly designated in the letter. Before starting his climb, the false Naïr would trace on the hat, in a substance still wet and sticky, certain definite characters. Jizme, according to her usual mania, could not fail to be wearing gloves for her evening with the emperor; in the prudent gesture which according to the instructions in the letter was to precede any kissing, the favourite would incriminate herself by printing on the suede one or another of the revealing characters.

Seil Kor accepted the mission. Refusal was impossible anyway, since the all-powerful Mossem gave order.

In the first place, it was important that Naïr should be prevented from embarking on his nocturnal expedition. And, for fear lest some indiscretion should cause his arrangements to miscarry, Mossem wished to dispense with all outside help.

Forced therefore to act alone, Seil Kor remembered the snares with which huntsmen took game in the Pyrenean forests. With cords salvaged at the time of the wreck of the

*Sylvander*, he placed a trap across the path Naïr was to follow. By means of this ruse, Seil Kor was assured of being able to overcome an adversary whose movements were already hobbled and impeded.

This work done, Seil Kor mixed together chalky soil and water, and heaped it at the foot of the steep slope he proposed to climb at the appropriate moment.

Evening coming on, he placed himself in hiding not far from the snare he had prepared.

Naïr soon appeared and, of a sudden, felt his foot caught in the adroitly set trap. A moment later, the imprudent fellow was gagged and then tied up by Seil Kor, who had leapt on him with a bound.

Satisfied with his discreet and silent victory, Seil Kor put on his victim's hat and approached the place of rendezvous.

Deceived by the silhouette and more particularly by the headgear of the newcomer, Jizme thought she recognised Naïr and stretched her arm beyond the balustrade in anticipation.

Reaching the foot of the slope, Seil Kor dipped his finger in the whitish mixture and, mischievously, traced in capitals on the black hat the French word ' PINCÉE ', which he applied proleptically to the unfortunate Jizme as one who has been pinched or caught; after which, he set himself to climb the wall of earth clutching with difficulty at the smallest boughs capable of sustaining him.

Reaching the level of the terrace, he stopped and felt for the overhanging hand, which, after briefly touching the rigid felt, drooped lower to receive the promised kiss.

Seil Kor silently pressed his lips to the fine leather of the glove with which Jizme, in accordance with Mossem's prediction, had gaily adorned herself.

His task accomplished, he noiselessly descended.

On the terrace, Mossem had all this while watched Jizme's behaviour. He saw her draw back her arm and observed at the same moment as herself a ' C ' which, clearly delineated on the grey glove, extended from the base of her fingers over the whole area of her palm.

Jizme hastily concealed her hand, while Mossem congratulated himself upon the success of his manoeuvre.

An hour later, Mossem finding himself alone with Jizme, tore off the marked glove and took from the unfortunate girl's waist the incriminating letter, which he brusquely placed before her eyes.

Next day, Naïr and Jizme, imprisoned, were placed under the gaze of fierce sentinels.

Talu having demanded to know the explanation of this rigorous measure, Mossem took the opportunity to confirm the Emperor's blind confidence, fearing lest any suspicion should light upon Rul and himself. He presented as the revenge of a jealous lover what in reality was merely the effect of anger at his ruffled self-esteem. Deliberately, he exaggerated the depth of his own resentment and recounted the adventure to his sovereign at great and detailed length, not omitting every particular of the snare, the hat and the glove. He was careful, nevertheless, not to risk allusion to his own intrigue with Rul by any reference to the compromising portraits sketched by Naïr at the beginning of his letter.

Talu approved the punishment inflicted by Mossem on the guilty pair, who were kept in captivity.

Seventeen years had gone by since the disappearance of Sirdah, and Talu lamented his daughter as on the first day.

Having retained in his memory a very precise image of the child so faithfully mourned, he sought to evoke in imagination the daughter he would at that moment have had before his eyes if death had not performed its work.

The little girl's features at an age when she was just weaned, sharply engraved in his mind, formed the basis of his work of meditation. He amplified them without in any way changing their cast, seeming year by year to see them gradually develop, and thus created for himself alone a Sirdah of eighteen whose very definite spirit accompanied him everywhere.

One day, in the course of one of his usual campaigns, Talu discovered a delightful child called Meisdehl, the sight of whom struck him dumb. He had before him the living portrait of Sirdah as she appeared at the age of seven in the unbroken series of images forged by his thought.

It was while inspecting families of prisoners, escaped from the flames of a village burnt by him, that the emperor had first perceived Meisdehl. He at once took the child under his protection and treated her as his own daughter after their return to Ejur.

Among her adoptive brothers, Meisdehl quickly decided that it was Kalj, then aged seven like herself, who was destined to share her hours of play.

Kalj's health was delicate, and had sometimes been despaired of, everything in him seeming caught up in a life of the mind. In subtlety and shrewdness, he surpassed most of those of his brothers who were older than he was, but he was pitiably thin. Aware of his condition, he often gave way to a profound sadness which Meisdehl set herself to overcome. Possessed by a mutual tenderness for each other, the two children formed an inseparable pair, and, from the depths of his grief, seeing the newcomer constantly beside his son, Talu was able to delude himself and at times to believe that he had a daughter.

A short while after the adoption of Meisdehl, natives

arriving from Mihu, a village near the Vorrh, told the inhabitants of Ejur that a fire, started by lightning, had since the previous day been devouring the southerly portion of the immense virgin forest.

Talu, in a closed litter borne by ten stout runners, betook himself to the outskirts of the Vorrh in order to feast his poet's soul upon the dazzling spectacle.

He set foot upon the ground at nightfall. A strong wind from the north-east drove the flames away from him, and he stayed there unmoving to watch the rapidly spreading blaze.

The whole population of Mihu was gathered round about, bent on losing nothing of the grandiose spectacle.

Two hours after the emperor's arrival, hardly more than a dozen trees remained intact, forming a dense copse already licked at by flames.

From this thick woodland suddenly emerged a native girl of eighteen, accompanied by a French soldier in Zouave uniform, armed with his rifle and cartridge pouches.

In the light of the blaze, Talu perceived on the girl's brow a red sign star-patterned with yellow lines which there was no mistaking; before his eyes stood his beloved Sirdah. She differed greatly from the imaginary portrait conceived in grief and so perfectly realised by Meisdehl, but little cared the Emperor for this, and, wild with joy, he rushed forward to embrace his daughter.

He then tried to speak to her, but Sirdah, astonished, did not understand his words.

During the happy father's effusions, a tree whose base was burnt through collapsed suddenly, violently striking the Zouave on the head, so that he lost consciousness. At once Sirdah ran to the soldier manifesting the liveliest concern.

Talu would not leave the wounded man, who evidently inspired in his daughter a pure and affectionate regard; he counted, moreover, upon the revelations of this witness to enlighten the remote mystery of Sirdah's disappearance.

Some moments later, the litter, raised by the bearers, conveyed towards Ejur the Emperor, Sirdah and the still inanimate Zouave.

Next day Talu entered his capital.

Confronted with her daughter, Rul, stricken with terror and threatened with torture, avowed all to the Emperor, who forthwith caused Mossem to be arrested.

Searching his minister's hut for some proof of the base felony, Talu found the love letter written by Naïr to Jizme some months previously. Seeing himself ridiculed in a drawing at the head of the letter, the monarch fell into a fury, then determined to torture both Naïr for his audacity and Jizme for her duplicity in guiltily accepting such a piece of work without denouncing its author.

Carefully tended in a hut where he had been laid, the Zouave recovered consciousness and recounted his Odyssey to Seil Kor, sent to stay at his bedside for this purpose.

Velbar—the wounded man was so named—had been born in Marseilles. His father, a housepainter, had early taught his own trade to the boy, who was very gifted and had perfected himself in his art by following popular courses at which drawing and water-colour were taught free. At eighteen, Velbar had turned out to have a strong baritone voice; for days at a time, occupied on his scaffolding in painting a sign, he would sing at the top of his voice many a romance of the day, and the passers-by stopped to listen, marvelling at the charm and purity of his generous organ.

When he reached the age for active service, Velbar was sent to Bougie to be enlisted in the 5th Zouaves. After a fair crossing, the young man, happy to be seeing a new country, landed on the soil of Africa on a fine November morning, and was immediately directed to the barracks with a large intake of conscripts.

The new Zouave's early days were made unpleasant by a thousand vexations. An evil chance had placed him under the orders of sergeant-major Lécurou, a maniacal and pitiless brute who prided himself on his legendary ferocity.

At this period, in order to meet the needs of a certain Flora Crinis, an exacting and extravagant young woman whose lover he was, Lécurou spent much of his time in a clandestine gambling-den where a roulette wheel turned temptingly day and night. Luck till then having favoured the daring player, Flora, kept in style, showed herself everywhere covered with jewels and sat in state in her coach beside the sergeant-major along the elegant promenade of the town.

During this time Velbar continued his hard apprenticeship to the soldier's trade.

One day, when the regiment on its way back to Bougie after a long march was still in the heart of the countryside, the Zouaves received the order to strike up a cheerful song which should to some extent make them forget their weariness on the way.

Velbar, whose fine voice was known, was appointed to intone the solo couplets of an interminable lament whose unchanging refrain was sung in chorus by the whole regiment.

As the light began to fail they were marching through a small wood in which a solitary dreamer, sitting under a tree, was noting down on a piece of music-paper some melody engendered there in solitude and calm.

Hearing Velbar's voice, alone more resonant than the immense choir which periodically answered it, the inspired idler rose of a sudden and followed the regiment until it entered the town.

This unknown person was no other than the composer Faucillon, whose celebrated opera *Daedalus*, after a highly successful run in France, had recently been played successively in the main towns of Algeria. Accompanied by the singers and orchestra, Faucillon had arrived the previous day in Bougie, one of the stages on this triumphant tour.

Now, since the last performance, the baritone Ardonceau, worn out by the arduous role of Daedalus and afflicted with a lingering hoarseness, no longer found it possible to appear in public; Faucillon, at a loss how to find a replacement for his leading performer, had pricked up his ears at once on hearing the young Zouave singing along the way.

Next day, having picked up the necessary information, Faucillon went looking for Velbar, who jumped for joy at the thought of appearing on the stage. The colonel's authority was easily obtained, and, after some days of hard work under the composer's direction, the youthful beginner felt up to his task.

The performance took place before a packed auditorium; in the first row of a front box, Flora Crinis sat enthroned with sergeant-major Lécurou.

Velbar, magnificent in the part of Daedalus, expressed like a born actor the fears and hopes of an artist obsessed with the grandiose conceptions of his genius. The Greek draperies brought out his fine presence to the full, and the beautiful tone of his powerful voice evoked displays of enthusiasm at the end of every phrase.

Flora did not take her eyes off him, training her opera glasses on him and feeling grow within her irresistible feelings to which the young singer's first appearance had given birth.

In the third act, Velbar triumphed in the work's principal aria, a hymn of joy and pride in which Daedalus, having finished building the labyrinth not without feeling a lively emotion at the sight of his masterpiece, rapturously hails the realisation of his dream.

His admirable interpretation of this stirring passage completed the perturbation in the heart of Flora, who, on the morrow, sketched out a subtle plan for coming near to Velbar.

Before embarking on any project, Flora, who was very
superstitious, always consulted Mother Angelica—a talkative
and familiar old intriguer, at once fortune-teller by cards,
hand-reader, astrologer and money-lender, who, if well-paid,
would further lend herself to almost any other kind of job.

Urgently summoned by letter, Angelica went to see Flora.
The old woman looked every inch a fortune-teller, with her
greasy poke-bag and the ample cloak in which, for ten years,
she had braved the often severe Algerian winters.

Flora avowed her secret and wanted to know, above all
whether her passion had been conceived under lucky auspices
Angelica, thereupon, drew out of her poke-bag a celestial
planisphere which she pinned on the wall; then, taking
yesterday's date as the radix of her horoscope, she plunged
into deep meditation, apparently engrossed in active and
complicated mental reckonings. In the end she pointed her
finger at the constellation of Cancer, whose beneficent influence
would preserve Flora's adventures in love from disappointment.

This first point settled, it was a matter of conducting the
intrigue as secretly as might be, for the suspicious and jealous
warrant officer craftily watched over his mistress's least
doings.

Angelica put the planisphere back in her bag and
from its depths brought out a card pierced with a certain
number of holes irregularly disposed. This apparatus, known
in cartomancy as a *grid* or *grille*, was to allow the two lovers to
correspond without danger. A phrase, traced through the
holes on blank paper, could be rendered unintelligible by
letters added at random to fill up evenly the spaces so left
Velbar alone would be able to make out the sense of the letter
by placing over the text an identical grid.

But this subterfuge required previous explanation and made
it necessary that Velbar and Angelica should meet. The old

creature could hardly go to the barracks without risking a meeting with the sergeant-major, who knew well all about her intimacy with Flora; on the other hand, inviting Velbar to come and see her would arouse the suspicions of the young Zouave, who was bound to construe the appeal as the interested solicitation of a professional interview. Angelica therefore resolved to arrange a meeting in some public place, indicating a sign of recognition which should also obviate their being surprised.

Under Flora's eyes, the old woman drew up an anonymous letter full of alluring promises: Velbar was to install himself the following evening at a table outside the Café Léopold and to order a plate of odds-and-ends at the precise moment at which the bell rang for Benediction at St. James's; at that point a confidential messenger would approach the young soldier and pass him the most flattering revelations.

Next day, at the time stated, Angelica was at her post, at a table outside the Café Léopold, not far from a silent Zouave who was calmly smoking his pipe. The old woman, not knowing Velbar by sight and anxious not to commit a blunder, prudently awaited the agreed signal before broaching her matter.

Suddenly, the bell for a service having shaken the bell-tower close by the church of St. James, the Zouave confirmed the hour and ordered his mixed platter.

Angelica came over and introduced herself speaking of the anonymous letter, while the waiter placed before Velbar the *harlequin* he had ordered, a many-coloured assortment of cold meats and vegetables piled on the same dish.

In a few words the old woman explained the situation, and the delighted Velbar received an exact duplicate of the grill or grid confided to Flora.

Without delay the two lovers started a secret and glowing correspondence. Velbar, having received a substantial fee after the performance of *Daedalus,* devoted part of his earnings to renting and furnishing a pleasant retreat, where he could receive his mistress without fear of being disturbed; with the remainder he wished to give Flora a present and selected, at the leading jeweller's in the town, a silver châtelaine from which hung a charming watch finely engraved.

Flora exclaimed with delight on receiving this delightful souvenir, which she forthwith pinned at her waist; it was agreed that, between herself and Lécurou, she should be understood to have paid for this little extravagance herself.

Nevertheless, despite the constellation of Cancer, the adventure was to have a tragic outcome.

Lécurou had observed certain peculiarities in Flora's conduct, and one day he followed her to the apartment Velbar had rented. Concealing himself at a street corner, he waited two long hours and finally saw the pair of lovers come out and, after a few steps, tenderly take leave of each other.

From the very next day, Lécurou broke off all relations with Flora and swore mortal hatred against Velbar, whom he set himself to persecute cruelly.

He kept ceaseless watch on his rival to catch him out in one fault or another, constantly inflicting upon him the harshest and most unjust punishments. He had a way of jerking back the thumb of his raised right hand and announcing the number of days confinement with the words: ' Four days C.B. !' in a manner which brought the blood to Velbar's face, so that in these moments of rage he came very close to insulting his military superior.

But a terrible example brought to the young Zouave's mind the need for restraining these dangerous impulses to rebellion.

One of his comrades, called Suire, was understood to have led, between the ages of eighteen and twenty, an eventful life. Frequenting the low quarters of Bougie and moving in a world of prostitutes and pimps, Suire, before joining the regiment, had, according to some, been a hired cut-throat with two unsolved murders to his credit.

Suire, untamed and violent by nature, yielded with difficulty to the demands of discipline and found it hard to endure the constant admonishments of Lècurou.

One day, the warrant officer, inspecting billets, ordered Suire to make up his equipment again at once, since it was incorrectly set out.

Suire was in one of his bad moods and made no movement.

The sergeant-major repeated his order, to which Suire replied with one word: 'No!'

Lécurou, in a fury, reviled Suire in a shrill voice, telling him with vicious pleasure of the thirty days in detention likely to follow upon his refusal to obey; then, before withdrawing, as a final insult spat in his face.

At this point Suire lost his head and, seizing his bayonet, struck full in the breast the odious warrant officer, who was at once carried out.

Though bleeding and unconscious, Lécurou had been wounded only slightly by the weapon, which had glanced off one of his ribs.

Suire, nevertheless, went before a court martial and was sentenced to death.

Lécurou, soon recovered, was in charge of the firing squad, of which Velbar was a member.

When the sergeant-major ordered: 'Take aim!' Velbar, thinking that he was about to cause death, felt himself shaken by a great shudder.

Sharply the word 'Fire!' rang out, and Suire fell to the ground, with twelve balls through him.

Velbar would forever retain the memory of that terrible moment.

Flora now openly flaunted her liaison with Velbar; but since her abandonment by Lécurou, the poor girl endlessly contracted new debts. She knew the gaming house which, for some time, had provided the sergeant-major with resources and, bent on tempting fortune in her turn, sat every day before the roulette table.

Persistent ill luck reduced her to her last louis.

She then had recourse to Angelica, and the old woman, scenting business, lent her at a high rate of interest a sufficiently round sum, against the security of her jewels and furniture, which now constituted the borrower's sole assets.

Alas! this new capital did not last long.

One day, installed at the gaming table, Flora, agitated and nervous, risked her last pieces of gold. A few turns sufficed to consummate her ruin. Horror-stricken, seeing in a flash her jewels sold and her furniture seized, the unfortunate woman was haunted by thoughts of suicide.

At that moment a loud noise was heard at the door of this clandestine establishment, and somebody came in shouting: 'The police!'

Those present were seized with panic, and some of them opened windows as though to find a way out. But there were four storeys between the balcony and the street, so that flight was quite impossible.

Presently, the door was forced open, and ten plain-clothes policemen invaded first the entrance hall and then the great room.

The general excitement had raised Flora's perturbation to a point beyond endurance. The prospect of the scandal, added to the spectre of destitution, hastened the accomplishment of her fatal project. With one bound she ran to the balcony and precipitated herself upon the pavement.

Next day, learning at once of the drama at the gaming house and the disappearance of his mistress, Velbar felt a sinister foreboding. He betook himself to the Morgue, where he saw, hanging above the body of a woman, her face crushed and unrecognisable, the famous silver châtelaine he had given to poor Flora. This token served to identify the dead woman, for whose obsequies the young Zouave was able to pay by selling immediately, at a low price, the furnishings recently purchased with the money of his performing fee.

Flora's death did not appease the hatred of Lécurou, who, more than ever, loaded his rival with insults and punishments.

On a May evening, at a halt on a night march performed without moon by starlight alone, Lécurou went up to Velbar and there and then awarded him a week in the guardroom on the pretext that he was improperly dressed. After which the warrant officer coldly poured insults on the young Zouave, who, white with anger, clenched his fists in an effort to retain self-control.

Finally, Lécurou repeated the end of his scene with Suire by spitting in Velbar's face; the latter, in a fit of giddiness and by instinct, without thinking what he was doing, struck the sergeant-major with all his strength. But, in an instant the dreadful consequences of this almost involuntary movement appeared before him with terrifying clarity, while before his eyes he saw the fearful example of Suire falling beneath the firing party's bullets. Pushing aside the warrant officer and the N.C.O.s who came forward to the aid of their leader, he fled straight before him through the countryside and soon found himself safe from pursuit thanks to the darkness of the night.

He reached the harbour at Bougie and succeeded in hiding in the hold of the *St. Irenaeus*, a large steamship bound for South Africa.

The *St. Irenaeus* raised anchor next day; but five days later, crippled after a storm, she ran aground within sight of Mihu. Counting the *Sylvander* and the steamer with the Spanish twins, it was the third time such an event had occurred in these regions since the already distant advent of Suan.

Unexpectedly emerging from his hiding place, Velbar, still in uniform, with his rifle and full cartridge-pouches, now mingled with the other passengers.

The inhabitants of Mihu, well-known cannibals, enclosed their shipwrecked visitors in a pen under a strong guard to feast on their flesh; each day, one of the prisoners, after rapid execution, was forthwith devoured in the presence of all the others. Soon only Velbar was left, having seen his unfortunate companions disappear to the last man.

The day of his own execution, he resolved to attempt the impossible and escape. When the executioners came for him, he cleared a way through the crowd with his rifle-butt, then started running at random, twenty or so natives at his heels.

At the end of an hour of unbridled running, just as his strength began to give out, he saw the verges of the Vorrh and redoubled his efforts in the hope of taking cover beneath the dense foliage of the immense forest.

On their side, the cannibals, shouting to urge themselves on, drew closer to the fugitive, and it was just as they caught up with him that Velbar penetrated the first thickets. The hunt was at once called off, the natives not daring to venture into the dark haunt of evil spirits.

Velbar lived peacefully in the safe retreat offered him by the Vorrh, never venturing outside for fear of being recaptured by the ferocious anthropophagi. He had built himself a little cabin in the branches and fed on berries and roots, keeping his precious rifle and cartridges by him in case of an attack by wild beasts.

At the time of the fatal slap on the sergeant-major's face, Velbar had with him his box of water-colours and a sketch pad. With water from a brook cupped in a hollow stone he was able to dilute his colours and fill his empty days with the charm of work. He meant to set forth in images the sombre drama of Bougie and devoted all his care to this absorbing task.

Long months passed without bringing any change in the situation of the unhappy recluse.

One day, Velbar heard a distant weeping echo where silence normally reigned in his vast domain. Approaching the place from which the sound came, he found Sirdah, not long before left there by Mossem, and took the poor child in his arms, whereupon her cries ceased. Some days before, he had trapped a pair of wild buffalo, which he kept prisoner by strong creepers tied round their horns and affixed to a tree trunk. The milk of the female served him to bring up his foster-child, and his life, till then so solitary, thenceforward possessed its interest and purpose.

As she grew, Sirdah, full of grace and charm, despite her squint, responded with affection to the benefits she received daily from her protector. Velbar taught her French and instructed her never to leave the Vorrh, fearing to see her fall into the hands of the cruel enemies who had so brutally exposed her to death and who could not fail to recognise her because of the sign marked on her forehead.

Years passed, and already the child was becoming a woman when a violent conflagration, consuming the Vorrh, drove out the two recluses who, till the last moment, concealed themselves within the ever-diminishing shelter of the big trees.

Once outside the retreat where he had lived hidden for so long, Velbar expected to fall once more into the hands of the cannibals of Mihu. Fortunately the presence of the Emperor preserved him from this terrible danger.

Talu, when Seil Kor had translated Velbar's recital to him, promised to reward his daughter's saviour worthily.

But, alas! he did not have time to fulfil this generous project.

Velbar, did not, in the outcome, survive the terrible blow he had received when the burning tree fell. A week after his arrival in Ejur, he breathed his last in the arms of his adoptive daughter, who, till the end, bravely and with the most active tenderness watched over her so devoted benefactor, sole prop of her childhood.

Talu, wishing to render a last homage to Velbar, charged Seil Kor to have the Zouave's body gloriously interred midway along the west side of Trophies Square.

With French tombs as a pattern in his mind, Seil Kor, aided by slaves, deposed the body in the place designated, thereafter placing over it a broad tombstone whereupon the uniform, the rifle and the cartridge-pouches were symmetrically ranged. The biographical water-colours found in one of the Zouave's pockets were used to decorate, behind the tomb, a vertical hoarding covered with black material.

After this death, which for some time stupefied her with grief, Sirdah, a sweet and loving nature, bestowed all her affection on the Emperor. Seil Kor had revealed to her in French the secret of her birth, and she hoped, by her constant attentiveness, to compensate her father for the long years of separation which an unjust fate had inflicted upon them both.

With Seil Kor's help she studied the language of her ancestors, so as to be able to converse freely with her future subjects.

Whenever her steps led her near Velbar's tomb, she piously pressed her lips to the stone commemorating the dear departed.

The return of Sirdah gave no umbrage to Meisdehl, still tenderly cherished by the Emperor, who, despite recent happenings, continued to see in her the living image of the unreal phantom he had once so frequently evoked.

In memory of his former love, Talu spared the life of Rul, who, thenceforward counted among the slaves charged with the cultivation of the Behuliphruen, had to stoop all day over the soil, digging and hoeing without respite. The monarch's vengeance had no need to extend itself to the adulterine son, whose resemblance to Mossem had become accentuated with the years. Overcome by Sirdah's arrival and discovery of the plot once concocted on his behalf alone, the unhappy young man, who had believed himself destined to reign one day under the name of Talu VIII, fell into a decline and succumbed after a few weeks.

To Mossem, Naïr and Jizme were reserved fearful tortures, deferred from day to day by the Emperor, who wished to impose on the guilty three by way of expiation the anguish of cruel and protracted waiting.

A negro called Rao, a pupil of Mossem, who had transmitted all his complex knowledge to him, was called to succeed the disgraced minister in the important functions of counsellor and governor.

In the meantime Rul, steeped in humiliations, had sworn to be revenged. Filled with resentment especially against Sirdah, whose return had been the cause of all her troubles, she sought means to slake her hatred of this daughter of hers, whose birth she cursed.

After long reflection, this is what the infamous mother devised.

A certain endemic disease was rife in the country, manifesting itself by the appearance of two highly contagious white scales which covered the eyes and grew thicker daily.

Alone, the witch doctor Bashku, a taciturn and solitary old

man, knew how to cure this dangerous ailment with the help of a secret ointment. But the rapid cure could succeed only at one holy place situated in the very bed of the Tez. Immersed with his patient where a particular eddy formed, Bashku, using his balm, easily detached the two scales, which then floated out to sea, where their dreadful contamination was no longer to be feared. Many victims of the disease, after this operation, recovered their sight at once; but others, less fortunate, remained blind for ever, because of too great an extension of the complaint, which little by little had penetrated the entire eyeball.

Rul was fully acquainted with the contagious nature of this albugo. One evening, escaping from the supervision of the slaves appointed to patrol the Behuliphruen, she reached the sea coast and took a canoe into the mouth of the Tez. She knew that Bashku always performed his operations at nightfall, so that newly opened eyes might first meet a gentle and reposeful light. Protected by the sombre veil of dusk, she waited unnoticed for the arrival of scales removed by the witch doctor, picked one up as it passed by on the stream, then regained the shore at her point of embarkation.

In the middle of the night, she noiselessly entered where Sirdah lay, in the hut adjoining that of the Emperor; then, advancing cautiously, guided by a ray of moonlight, she gently rubbed her sleeping daughter's eyelids with the dangerous scale held between two fingers.

But Talu, awakened by Rul's light steps, had just precipitated himself into Sirdah's hut, in time to see the criminal action. He at once perceived the intention of the unnatural mother, whom he dragged brutally outside and placed in the hands of three slaves ordered to keep her under observation.

The Emperor then returned to Sirdah, whom the noise had roused from a deep sleep; the disease was already at work, and a veil had begun to form over the poor child's eyes.

By the orders of Talu, mad with rage, Rul, destined to an atrocious death, was incarcerated with Mossem, Naïr and Jizme.

By morning, Sirdah's affliction had made lightning progress; two opaque specks, formed in the space of a few hours over her eyes, rendered her totally blind.

Desiring an immediate operation, the Emperor, at nightfall, crossed the Tez with his daughter and approached the sizeable cabin inhabited by Bashku.

But the place consecrated to the magical treatment lay towards the left bank of the river, and, for that reason alone, belonged to Drelshkaf.

Now, King Yaour IX, having learnt of Rul's crime and anticipating the step taken by the father on behalf of his child, had made haste to give Bashku severe and precise instructions.

The witch doctor spoke and refused his aid to Sirdah on the orders of Yaour, who, he added, demanded the young girl's hand in exchange for a cure performed upon his territory.

The result would have been that, thanks to the projected marriage, Yaour, called to share Talu's succession with Sirdah, must in due course unite Ponukele and Drelshkaf under his own dominion.

Sickened by the enunciation of this message and by the idea of seeing his realm pass into the hands of the rival branch, Talu disdained to reply and conducted his daughter back again to Ejur.

Since this episode which went back only a few weeks, the situation had remained unchanged and Sirdah was still blind.

# XII

ALL this while stretched out on the sand in the shade of the high cliff, we had followed, without interruption, the ups and downs of the lengthy drama recounted to us by Seil Kor.

In the meantime, the negroes had extracted from the depths of the *Lynceus* a mass of objects and boxes which they suddenly raised to their shoulders, obeying an order from Seil Kor, whose clear voice, once his narration was at an end, had just given the signal for departure. Several further journeys would be needed to discharge the whole cargo of the ship, which by degrees would be transported in its entirety to Ejur.

A few moments later, formed into a column amid the negroes bowed beneath the multiplicity of their burdens, our group, led by Seil Kor, set out by a direct route for the capital. The dwarf Philippo was carried like a child by his showman Jenn, while Tancred Bucharessas sat, with his family of performing cats, on a legless cripple's trolley pushed by his son Hector. At our head, Olga Chervonenkova, followed by Sladky and Milenkaya, marched beside the circus rider Urbain, who, mounted on his horse Romulus, proudly dominated the whole procession.

Half an hour sufficed for us to reach Ejur, where presently we saw the Emperor, who in order to greet us had grouped about him, in Trophies Square, his daughter, his ten wives and all his sons, then numbering thirty-six.

Seil Kor exchanged some words with Talu and at once translated to us the decree promulgated by the sovereign will : each of us must write a letter to his family, with the purpose of obtaining a ransom whose size would be proportionate to the external appearance of the signatory; this done, Seil Kor, marching to the north with a large detachment of natives, would go to Porto Novo where he would dispatch the precious correspondence to Europe; once in possession of the sums demanded the faithful mandatory would purchase various articles of trade which his men, still led by him, would bear back to Ejur. After which, the same Seil Kor would be our guide to Porto Novo, where every facility for our repatriation would await us.

Each letter had to contain a specific warning to its recipient that the least attempt to secure our rescue would be the signal for our immediate death. In any case, prompt capital punishment awaited those who went unransomed.

By a curious scruple, Talu, not wishing to appear a robber, left us in full possession of the money in our pockets. True, such a cash deduction in advance would have added but little to the gross proceeds of our ransom money.

A voluminous supply of writing paper was unpacked, and each of us made haste to compose his letter, indicating the redemptive sum fixed in each case by Seil Kor at the Emperor's instigation.


A week later, Seil Kor set off for Porto Novo, accompanied by the same blacks who, appearing before our eyes at the time of our running aground, had in less than a week, by continual hithering and thithering, transported to Ejur the total plunder of our unfortunate ship, frequently revisited by its numerous former passengers.

For us, his departure marked the beginning of a monotonous and wearisome life. We cried out upon the hour of our deliverance, sleeping at night in the shelter of the huts reserved to our use and spending our days reading or speaking French with Sirdah, delighted to make the acquaintance of compatriots of Velbar's.

To give us a source of occupation and amusement, Juillard then put up the idea of founding, about a picked body of us, a curious sort of club each of whose members should be required to distinguish himself either by an original work or by some kind of sensational performance.

Applications poured in, and Juillard, to whom we owed the original idea, was made to accept the presidency of the new association, which took the high-sounding title of ' Incomparables Club '. Each accepted member would have to make ready for a great gala performance designed to celebrate the liberating return of Seil Kor.

The club could hardly do without some form of head-quarters, and so Chènevillot offered his services in erecting a structure which should at least emblemise our organisation. Juillard accepted the offer, suggesting that, in view of the proposed display, this monument should be given the form of a raised stage.

But the Emperor's authority was needed before a space could be laid out for the purpose in Trophies Square.

Sirdah, wholly devoted to our cause, undertook to approach Talu, who, delighted that we should wish to embellish his capital, welcomed our request while nevertheless wishing to know the purpose of the edifice. Sirdah told him briefly about the gala, and the Emperor, rejoicing at the prospect of this unexpected festival, freely authorised us to select among the booty taken from the *Lynceus* everything that we might need for the organisation of the spectacle.

When the girl had told us of the happy outcome of her

mission, Chènevillot, aided by his workmen, who were not short of tools, cut down a certain number of trees in the Behuliphruen. Their trunks were cut up into planks, and the outlines of his construction became visible on that side of Trophies Square farthest from the sea.

Desirous of creating a spirit of emulation among the members of the Club, Juillard resolved to invent a new decoration for the most meritorious. Having long sought a form of badge at once novel and easy to make, his choice fell upon a Greek capital *delta*, which seemed to him to combine the two essential conditions. Taking to pieces an old container found among the stock in the *Lynceus*, he provided himself with a piece of sheet-metal from which he was able to cut out six triangles surmounted by a ring; hung from a short length of blue ribbon, each *delta* thus formed was meant to hang on the breast of a *knight* of the order.

Wishing in addition to institute a different and superlative distinction, Juillard, without changing the pattern, cut out a single giant *delta* made to be worn at the left side.

The decorations were to be given back at the end of the gala performance.

Meanwhile everyone made advance preparations for the great day.

Olga Chervonenkova, proposing to execute the ' Nymph's Dance ', her most resounding success of former times, practised frequently by herself in the hope of recovering her original litheness.

Juillard drafted on the history of the ' Electors of Brandenburg' a brilliant lecture with illustrations in the form of portraits.

Having promised to figure in the programme, Balbet, whose baggage contained weapons and ammunition, found all his cartridges spoilt by damp, the sea, at high tide, having taken advantage of a breach made at the time of our running aground to invade part of the hold of the *Lynceus*. Informed of this mishap, Sirdah generously offered him Velbar's weapon and cartridge-pouches. The offer was accepted, and Balbet entered into possession of an excellent Gras rifle and twenty-four cartridges in perfect condition as a result of the dryness of the African climate. Leaving all in its place on the Zouave's tomb, the champion announced for the day of the gala a wondrous exhibition of marksmanship, followed by a sensational match with La Billaudière-Maisonnial's mechanical foil.

Luxo's cases of goods had suffered even more than Balbet's from the flooding of the hold, and all his fireworks, happily insured, were irrevocably lost. Only the final set-piece, packed separately and with special care, had escaped; Luxo therefore meant to embellish our elaborate festival with the group of dazzling portraits which could not now arrive in time for the marriage of Baron Ballesteros.

The ichthyologist Martignon spent his time at sea in a dug-out canoe procured by Sirdah. Armed with an immense trawl and long lines extracted from one of his trunks, he made perpetual soundings, in the hope of some interesting discovery with which to enrich the gala programme.

All the other members of the Club, inventors, artistes, animal trainers, freaks or acrobats, practised their varied specialities, determined to be in good form on the day of the solemnities.

In a part of the *Lynceus* which had suffered particularly, were found twelve two-wheeled vehicles, rather like Roman chariots garishly painted. On their tours, the Bucharessas and Alcott families, combining forces, used all this coachwork for a curious musical exercise.

Each chariot, once set in motion, gave out a pure and vibrant note produced by the action of the wheels.

During their displays, Stephen Alcott and his six sons with the four Bucharessas brothers and their sister would suddenly appear in the circus ring and each step into one of the chariots, drawn by a trained horse.

The twelve resonant vehicles, ranged side by side along a radius of the circular track, gave out the diatonic scale of *C* major, from a low tonic to *G* in the octave above.

At a sign from Stephen Alcott, the slow and melodious promenade began. The chariots, advancing one after the other according to an order and rhythm determined beforehand, executed a variety of popular airs, carefully chosen among those which lacked any harmonic modulation. The alignment was soon broken by the intensity and frequency of the notes; one chariot, in the course of a round, would be four or five yards in front of another, which, having to give out only a semiquaver, barely progressed. Soon dispersed about the whole area of the ring, the horses, expertly touched with the whip, moved sharply on the beat.

Eleven chariots had been damaged in the wreck. The only one left intact was confiscated by Talu for the use of the young Kalj, who, growing weaker every day, had need of long, healthy outings without fatigue.

A wicker armchair from the *Lynceus* was fastened by its four legs to the floor of the vehicle, whose turning wheels produced the upper *C*.

A slave placed between the shafts completed the equipage,

with which Kalj seemed enchanted. Thereafter the young invalid was frequently to be seen, installed in his wicker chair and valiantly accompanied by Meisdehl, who walked or ran beside him.

# XIII

IN three weeks Chènevillot completed a small stage of very smart appearance. Among the workmen, who had all displayed indefatigable zeal, the decorator Toresse and the upholsterer Beaucreau merited special praise. Toresse, who, mistrustful of American materials, had provided himself with drums of various colours, had painted the whole structure a magnificent red; across the proscenium arch, the words: *Incomparables Club* were surrounded with bright rays to symbolise the fame of this brilliant association. Beaucreau having, for his part, brought a stock of frabrics destined for Ballesteros, had used a fine scarlet damask to make a pair of big curtains which could be drawn close or flung wide to the wings. A white chintz with fine arabesques in gold served to mask a wall of planks at the back.

Chènevillot's work was thought highly successful, and Carmichael was called upon to inaugurate the new stage by singing in his marvellous head-voice a few ballads from his repertoire.

That very day, at about four o'clock, Carmichael having unpacked his female accoutrements withdrew to his hut and an hour later reappeared completely transformed.

He wore a robe of blue silk ornamented with a sweeping train upon which the number 472 might be seen in black; a lady's wig of thick flaxen hair, in perfect harmony with the yet-beardless face, completed the strange transformation.

Interrogated about the curious cipher embroidered on his skirt, Carmichael told us the following story.

Towards the end of winter, pressed to go to America where a brilliant engagement awaited him, but detained in Marseilles until the 14th of March, the date of his service ballot, Carmichael, among the various passenger boats, had picked on the *Lynceus*, due to sail on the 15th of the same month.

At that time, the young man was singing every evening with stunning success at the *Folies Marseillaises*. On the morning of the 14th of March, when he appeared at the town hall, the assembled conscripts recognised without difficulty their well-known compatriot and with one accord, after the draw, gathered about him on the way out.

Carmichael, following their example, was made to pin on his hat a brightly embroidered number, and, for an hour or so, they all paraded joyously and fraternally about the streets of the town gambolling and singing.

When they separated, Carmichael distributed free tickets among his new friends, who, in the evening, burst into the corridors of the *Folies Marseillaises* waving in tipsy hands their hats still adorned with the gaily embroidered numerals. The drunkest of them all, son of one of the leading tailors in the town, seeing Carmichael made up and ready to go on, drew from his pocket a pair of scissors and a needle and thread wrapped up in a large piece of black silk, then, with drunken persistence, demanded to be allowed to sew on the elegant blue gown the number 472 which his illustrious comrade had drawn that morning.

Carmichael, laughing, lent himself with a good grace to this comical notion, and, after ten minutes' work, three figures artistically cut out and stitched were set out in black on the long train.

A few moments later, the conscripts, settled in the auditorium, loudly acclaimed Carmichael, encoring all his ballads and shouting: 'Long live *472*!' to the great amusement of the audience who could not make head or tail of the number visible on the young singer's skirt.

Embarking next day, Carmichael had not had time to unpick the stitches and now wished to keep the curious ornament as a precious souvenir of his native town, from which the merest caprice on Talu's part might yet keep him severed for all time.

His story at an end, Carmichael appeared upon the stage of the Incomparables and sang in dazzling fashion the *Aubade* of Darricelli. His head voice, soaring with unparalleled flexibility to the topmost limit of the soprano range, executed the most disconcerting *vocalises* as if they had been child's play; the chromatic scales went off like rockets, and the trills, of fabulous rapidity, seemed to go on for ever.

A prolonged ovation greeted the final cadence, presently followed by five other ballads, no less stupefying than the first. Carmichael, as he went off stage was greeted enthusiastically by all the spectators, excited and grateful.

Talu and Sirdah, present from the beginning of the performance, visibly shared our enthusiasm. The Emperor, dumbfounded, positively gaped at Carmichael, whose eccentric costume and make-up clearly fascinated him.

Then certain imperious words, promptly translated by Sirdah, informed us that Talu, wishing to sing like Carmichael, demanded from the young artist a course of lessons, the first of which was to start forthwith.

Sirdah had not finished her translation when the Emperor stalked on to the stage, where Carmichael followed him with perfect docility.

There, for half an hour, Talu, producing a falsetto voice

of no little purity, strove humbly to copy the examples given by Carmichael, who, extremely surprised to discover the monarch's unexpected facility, displayed a zeal both indefatigable and sincere.

After this unexpected session, the tragic actress Adinolfa wished to try out the acoustics of Trophies Square from the point of view of declamation. Clothed in a magnificent jade gown hurriedly donned for the occasion, she climbed up on to the stage and recited Italian poems with impressive mimic accompaniment.

Meisdehl, the Emperor's adopted daughter, had just joined us and seemed petrified by the celebrated performer's inspired gesticulations.

Next day, Adinolfa received a great surprise as she strolled beneath the odorous vaults of the Behuliphruen, whose luxurious vegetation daily attracted her vibrant soul, forever in search of natural or artistic splendours.

The tragic actress had not long set foot in a woodland region carpeted with bright flowers. She became aware of a clearing in the middle of which Meisdehl, improvising in her own tongue words of high-soaring lyricism, reproduced before Kalj the prodigious mimicry which, the previous afternoon, after Talu's lesson, had drawn all eyes to the stage of the Incomparables.

Twenty yards away stood the chariot, guarded by the slave who lay stretched out on a bed of moss.

Adinolfa, without making a noise, waited for some time, watching Meisdehl, whose gestures astonished her by their graceful aptness. Interested in the revelation of this dramatic instinct, she approached the little girl to teach her the fundamental principles of stage movement and bearing.

This first lesson produced immediate results. Meisdehl had no difficulty in understanding the subtlest indications and spontaneously exhibited a play of physiognomy essentially tragic and wholly personal.

During the days which followed, a number of sessions were devoted to the same study, and Meisdehl quickly became an accomplished actress.

Encouraged by this wonderful progress, Adinolfa wished to teach her pupil a whole scene, to be performed on the day of the gala.

Seeking to bring out her *protégée's* first appearance in the strongest possible relief, the tragedienne conceived an ingenious idea which perforce led her to tell us something of her past.

All the peoples of the world acclaimed Adinolfa, but the English in particular made a fanatically devoted cult of her. The ovations she received from the London public were like no others, and her photographs were sold in thousands all over Great Britain, which became a second home to her.

Desirous of owning a fixed residence for the prolonged visits she made every year to the city of mists, the tragic actress bought, on the banks of the Thames, a sumptuous country house of great antiquity; the owner, a certain Lord Dewsbury, ruined by wild speculations, sold her in a lump, at a low price, the building and everything it contained.

From this dwelling one communicated easily with London, while preserving the advantage of open space and clean air.

Among the various reception rooms on the ground floor, the tragedienne was particularly fond of a vast library, whose walls were wholly lined with old books in precious bindings. A long shelf filled with theatrical works attracted the great artist's attention more often than any other, and, knowing English well, she passed many hours turning the pages of the national masterpieces of her land of adoption.

Adinolfa, one day, had taken down, and set out on her table, ten volumes of Shakespeare at a time, in order to look for a particular note of whose existence she knew, without specifically recalling the title of the play to which it formed part of the commentary.

The note duly found and transcribed, the tragic actress neatly assembled the volumes to restore them to their place; but, again, standing before the appropriate shelf, she noticed a thick layer of dust in the empty space. Placing her burden for the time being on a chair, she was impelled to dust the smooth surface with her handkerchief, going so far as to rub with this improvised pad the back of the piece of furniture, of which the vertical part also called out for its share of cleaning.

All of a sudden, there sounded a sharp click, produced by a secret spring which Adinolfa had just set in action by pressing involuntarily upon a determinate spot.

A thin, narrow piece of wood swung out suddenly and revealed a hiding-place from which the tragic actress, greatly excited, took out, not without infinite precautions, a very old and barely legible manuscript.

She immediately took her discovery to London to the great expert Creighton, who, after rapidly examining it under a magnifying glass, allowed a cry of stupefaction to escape him.

There could be no doubt that before their eyes was the manuscript of *Romeo and Juliet,* in Shakespeare's own hand!

Dazzled by this revelation, Adinolfa engaged Creighton to deliver to her a clear and faithful copy of the precious document, which might contain some unknown scene of prodigious interest. Then, having informed herself of the value of the voluminous autograph, which the expert put at a fabulous price, she set off, reflectively, to her new dwelling.

According to the precise and formal contract of sale, the entire contents of the house belonged by right to the tragic actress. But Adinolfa was too scrupulous to profit from a fortuitous circumstance which made the bargain shamefully advantageous. She therefore wrote to Lord Dewsbury and told him what had happened, sending him a cheque for the amount which according to the expert the impressive relic was worth.

Lord Dewsbury gave evidence of his warm gratitude in a long letter of thanks, in which he also provided a likely explanation of the mysterious discovery. Only an ancestor of his, Albert Dewsbury, a great collector of autographs and rare books, could have devised such a hiding-place to preserve from theft a manuscript of so great importance. Now, Albert Dewsbury, who had died suddenly when in full health, his skull shattered by a terrible riding accident, had not had leisure to reveal to his son, as no doubt he had meant to do during his last moments, the existence of the treasure so carefully set apart, which had remained in the same place ever since.

A fortnight later, Creighton himself brought the manuscript back to the tragedienne, accompanied by two copies, the first conforming scrupulously to the text with all its archaisms and obscurities, the second perfectly clear and comprehensible, a veritable translation modernised as to language and spelling.

When the expert had gone, Adinolfa took the second copy and began to read it attentively.

Each page plunged her into fresh amazement.

She had many times played the part of Juliet and knew the whole drama by heart. Now, in the course of her reading, she constantly discovered lines and speeches, stage business, details of gesture and costume wholly new and unsuspected.

From beginning to end, the play was thus enriched with countless embellishments which, without fundamentally altering its nature, studded it with unexpected pictorial effects.

Certain of holding in her hands the true version of the celebrated tragedy of Verona, the actress made haste to announce her discovery in *The Times,* which devoted a whole page to quotations from the manuscript itself.

The insertion created an immense stir. Artists and scholars flocked to the ancient dwelling of the Dewsburys to see the extraordinary holograph, whose pages Adinolfa allowed to be freely turned under, however, her discreetly exercised constant supervision.

Two camps at once formed, and a violent controversy developed between the famous document's supporters and the opponents who declared it apocryphal. The columns of the newspapers were filled with heated argument, the contradictory proofs and details of which made a topic of conversation in England and throughout the world.

Adinolfa would have liked to profit from this public excitement to put the play on in its new version, with herself in the part of Juliet, a sensational creation which might place an indelible halo about her name.

But no manager accepted the task offered. The boundless expense involved in all the new settings required by page after page of the manuscript frightened the most daring of them, and the great actress knocked on all doors in vain.

Discouraged, Adinolfa ceased to interest herself in the matter, and the polemics soon came to an end, dethroned in public interest by the reports of a sensational crime.

Now, it was the final scene of Shakespeare's drama that Adinolfa wanted to make Meisdehl play, in conformity with the celebrated holograph. The tragedienne had at her disposal the modernised copy, brought at whatever peril with a view to some approach being made to American managements. Kalj, sensitive and highly gifted, would make a charming Romeo, and mime, fully elaborated, would suffice without the dialogue inaccessible to the two children; the subject was, indeed, of so popular a nature that it could not fail to be easily understood without text.

In the absence of full stage costume, some bits of apparel or ornament had to be found to make the two characters recognisable. A form of head-dress might be comparatively simple and easily made. But, according to the manuscript, the two lovers were dressed in red-ornamented materials, with head-dresses of different styles and *richly embroidered*.

This last indication worried Adinolfa, and she was haunted by it, one day, on her customary walk among the verdure in the Behuliphruen. Suddenly, as she was walking along with her eyes cast down, absorbed in her reflections, she started at the sound of a sort of slow, interrupted monologue. She turned her head and perceived Juillard, who, sitting cross-legged on the turf, held an exercise book in his hand and was making notes which he spoke aloud. A large illustrated volume, lying open on the ground, attracted the tragic actress's attention by reason of certain reddish tones which harmonised closely with her innermost thoughts. She approached Juillard, who expatiated upon the charms of his chosen retreat. There, since latterly completing his lecture for the gala, he came each day to prepare, in silence and tranquillity, a long work on the war of 1870. With a gesture he indicated, spread around him, several books which had appeared during the terrible struggle and, among them, the large volume open at two pages, observed by the tragic actress, which depicted, with considerable liveliness, one the charge at Reichshoffen, the other an episode under the Commune; the red tones, on the left-hand page those of the uniforms and plumes, on the right of a conflagration, might indeed at a distance give an illusion of the embroideries called for by the Shakespearian autograph.

Wishing to use as a fabric this paper coloured according to the scenes it represented, Adinolfa made her request to Juillard, who without further ado detached the coveted sheets.

With scissors and pins, the tragedienne made up for Kalj

and Meisdehl two classical head-dresses for the lovers of Verona.

This first point settled, Adinolfa took up Shakespeare's work again, and carefully studied the smallest details of stage presentation.

Certain episodes in the final fragment found their explanation in an extended prologue comprising two scenes devoted to the childhood of Romeo and Juliet, then strangers to each other.

It was with this prologue that Adinolfa's mind was most preoccupied.

In the first scene, Romeo as a child listened to the lessons of his preceptor, Father Valdivieso, a learned monk who inculcated in his pupil the purest and most religious principles of morality.

For many years past, Valdivieso spent all his nights at work, surrounding himself with folios in which he delighted and with ancient parchments whose secrets never eluded his infallible sagacity. Endowed with immense powers of memory and a voice and delivery of great persuasiveness, he charmed his disciple with vivid tales, whose sense almost invariably concealed some profitable teaching. The opening scene was taken up wholly by him, apart from the young Romeo's occasional questioning interruptions.

Biblical instances crowded upon the monk's lips. He minutely conjured up the temptation of Eve, then recounted the story of the debauched Thisias, who, in the heart of Sion, amid an orgy, saw appear before him the spectre of God the Father, terrible in anger.

Then came the following details about the legend of Pheior of Alexandria, a young libertine contemporary with Thisias.

In despair at the defection of a beloved mistress who had signified the rupture to him by voluntarily forgetting a lovers' meeting, Pheior, renouncing his life of pleasure and seeking consolation in faith, had retired to the desert to live as an anchorite, occasionally returning to preach the holy word in those places which had witnessed his past errors.

In consequence of long privations, Pheior had grown extremely emaciated; his head, naturally large, now seemed immense by contrast with his wasted frame, and above all his temples stood out conspicuously to either side of his sunken visage.

One day, Pheior appeared in the public square at a moment when the assembled citizens were debating affairs of state. At that epoch two separate assemblies, that of the young people and that of the elders, met on a fixed day in this forum, the former putting forward bold projects in law-making which the latter moderated and rectified. Each of the two groups disposed itself in rectangular formation over the space of approximately an acre.

The appearance of Pheior, famous for his sudden conversion, caused a halt in the deliberations.

The neophyte, according to his custom, at once began to preach fervently on the scorn of riches and pleasure, addressing himself more especially to the younger clan whom he seemed to reproach with every form of vice and turpitude.

Angered by so much direct provocation, those who he thus challenged flung themselves upon him in rage and cast him down upon the ground. Too weak to defend himself, Pheior picked himself up with difficulty and withdrew, black and blue all over, cursing his assailants. All at once, at a turning of the street, he fell to his knees, in ecstasy, at the sight of his former lover, who passed without recognising him, richly adorned and followed by a crowd of slaves. Pheior, for a moment, was overcome by his old passion; but, once the vision had faded, he managed to regain possession of himself and made his way back to the desert, where, after several years of continual penance, he died a victor over his inclinations and pardoned.

After the legend of Pheior, the monk Valdivieso recounted two famous martyrdoms, that of Jeremiah stoned to death by his countrymen with edged and pointed flints, then that of St. Ignatius cast to the wild beasts, who tore his body while, by antithesis, his soul rose up to Paradise, presented under the fairy guise of a marvellous island.

Taken together, these speeches displayed a close unity. Their subjects strikingly chosen, had as their aim to entice Romeo's spirit towards the good, thereby explaining the ease with which Juliet, the image of pure and conjugal love, triumphantly took possession of the young man at first given over to trivial and debasing intrigues.

The second scene of the prologue, a touching parallel to the first, showed Juliet as a child sitting with her nurse, who charmed her with pleasing and with frightening tales; among the characters of fable depicted by the story-teller was the good fairy Urgela shaking out her tresses to scatter pieces of gold wherever she passed, then the ogress Pergovedula who, hideous, with yellow face and green lips, ate two heifers for supper when she lacked children with which to satisfy her appetite.

In the final scene which Adinolfa meant to present, numerous images from the prologue reappeared before the eyes of the two lovers, who, after drinking the poison draught, became a prey to successive hallucinations.

From the indications in the manuscript, these many phantoms composed a sequence of *tableaux vivants* succeeding each other with a rapidity which could not fail to raise insurmountable difficulties there in Ejur.

Adinolfa then thought of Fuxier, whose pastilles might provide a pictorial effect replacing costumes and accessories.

Acceding to the desire of the tragic actress and promising

to put all the expected visions in hand, Fuxier, thoroughly acquainted with the finer points of the English language, glanced at the prologue and final scene and found in them ample material for a job that would interest him.

One thing specially mentioned in the manuscript was a greenish fire, near Juliet's tomb, casting its tragic light over the poignant scene played by the two lovers. The brazier, whose flames could be coloured with sea-salt, would also serve very well for the evocative pastilles. Adinolfa, who would make herself up to appear at the end as the ogress Pergovedula, could lie down behind the tomb, and, hidden, from all eyes, throw upon the fire, at the appropriate moment, such and such a pastille or lozenge productive of such and such an image.

The procedure did not obviate all need for suppers. Two apparitions, that of Capulet draped in a garment with gold reflections and that of Christ motionless on the ass, were to be made by Soreau, who had all the necessary elements in the wardrobe of his company. He could change out of sight in a few seconds, and the docile Milenkaya would be used to good purpose. Chènevillot promised to incorporate in the backcloth two lattice-work screens cleverly painted, which a lamp with a reflector would make transparent in turn at the right moment; behind these, two recesses of appropriate size would be set at the desired height.

The spectre of Romeo needing, at the end, to descend from above in the presence of the corpse itself, one of Kalj's brothers, close enough to him in age and looks, would be called into service as his double. A second head-dress like the first was cut out of what remained of the page devoted to the cuirassiers of Reichshoffen, and Chènevillot would have no difficulty in arranging with a rope and pulley from the *Lynceus*, a system of suspension to be operated by hand.

To conjure up the figure of Urgela, among the ship's cargo

a dummy was found intact at the bottom of a packing-case addressed to a hairdresser in Buenos Aires. A wheeled pedestal could easily be made for the pink and white bust with its big blue eyes. Not far from the box, a great many gilt counters, not unlike twenty-france louis, had fallen out of a burst parcel full of toys; a little gum attached them very lightly to the dummy's magnificent golden hair, let down and spread in tresses on all sides; the least jolt would shake off this glittering money thus profusely scattered by the generous fairy.

All the rest of the setting would be seen to by Chènevillot, including the tomb and brazier.

According to a brief passage in the manscript, Romeo put around Juliet's neck on her awakening from her sleep of lethargy a rich necklace of rubies, at first intended, in the bridegroom's mind, to adorn only the cold corpse of his beloved.

This detail furnished Bex with an occasion for using one of his special balms, always successfully employed in his learned triturations.

This was an anaesthetic sufficiently powerful to render the skin indifferent to burns; rubbing this protective ointment on his hands, Bex was able to handle at no matter what temperature a metal first isolated by him and called *bexium*. But for the previous discovery of the precious ingredient, the chemist would never have discovered bexium, whose special properties precisely required extreme variations of temperature.

To replace the necklace of rubies of which not even an imitation was to be found in Ejur, Bex proposed hot coals fastened to an asbestos thread which he undertook to furnish. Kalj would simply have to take the curious red and sparkling jewellery from the brazier to adorn Meisdehl, whose breast and shoulders would be immunised beforehand with the infallible balm.

The tragedienne accepted Bex's offer, after assuring herself of the agreement of Meisdehl, who proved trusting and brave.

The entire scene was to have been played without dialogue. But, in their studies of mime, Kalj and Meisdehl displayed so much intelligence and goodwill that Adinolfa, encouraged by her success, tried to teach her pupils one or two phrases translated into French and explanatory of the different apparitions. The attempt yielded immediate results, and thereafter it only remained to perfect, up to the date of the gala, the stage business so well understood by the two children.

# XIV

STIMULATED by the success of the Incomparables theatre, Juillard proposed another foundation which might increase excitement about the great day and provide Chènevillot with a further occasion to exercise his gifts as a constructor. The idea was to issue shares in respect of each member of the club and to institute a game of chance in which the first prize should be represented by the future holder of the chief decoration of the new order. This proposal once adopted, it was put into execution without delay.

Fifty passengers began by setting up a kitty of ten thousand francs, each contributing two hundred francs; for each member of the Club a hundred shares were then issued, mere slips of paper bearing his signature.

All the shares were put together and shuffled like playing cards, then grouped in fifty equal packets fairly distributed among the fifty passengers.

At the conclusion of the gala, the ten thousand francs would be shared among those who held shares in the person fortunate enough to be elected wearer of the supreme emblem of the *delta*; between now and then, the shares had time to undergo every sort of fluctuation, according to the chances each of the competitors seemed to offer.

The members of the Club were not themselves allowed to speculate, for the same reason as betting is forbidden to jockeys.

Intermediaries were needed to regulate the flow of scrip among the different players. Hounsfield, Cerjat and their three clerks, having all five agreed to act as stockbrokers, the pool money was deposited with them, and Chènevillot was to erect a new building at which transactions could be made.

At the end of a fortnight, a small stock exchange, exactly reproducing in miniature the Paris Bourse, had been set up facing the Incomparables stage; this monument, constructed in wood, looked very like stone once Toresse had given it a coat of white paint.

To make room for this useful building, the mortal remains of the Zouave, together with the tombstone and the black panel with its bright water-colours, had been moved some yards to the south.

The very originality of a market based on the Incomparables membership itself called for a distinctive language, and it was decided that only orders placed in alexandrines would be accepted.

At six o'clock, on the very day of its completion, the Bourse opened for the first time, and the five stockbrokers sat at five tables set out for them behind the small colonnade. Soon they were reading aloud the numerous bills put into their hands by the speculators grouped around them, buying and selling orders couched in halting alexandrines full of padding and misplaced hiatuses. A price was quoted according to the scale of the offer or demand, and the shares, at once paid and delivered, passed from hand to hand. New bills ceaselessly showered upon the tables, and for an hour there was noisy and fantastic dealing. Each name stood for one or another of the securities. At the close of the session *Carmichaels* stood at fifty-two francs and *Tancred Bucharessases* at two louis, whereas *Martignons* could be acquired for twenty-eight sous and *Olga Chervonenkovas* for sixty centimes. *Balbets,* because of the shooting exhibition which was considered very promising, found buyers at forty francs, and *Luxos* realised eighteen francs ninety, on account of the astonishing set-piece for which great expectations were entertained.

The stock exchange closed at seven sharp, but from that date onwards it opened for twenty minutes every day, to the joy of the speculators, many of whom, unconcerned with the final result, thought only of making a killing on daily movements, to this end causing rumours of every kind to circulate. On one day *Carmichaels* dropped nine points because the young singer was said to be hoarse; next day the news was recognised as false, and the security rose sharply by twelve francs. *Balbets* were also markedly subject to fluctuation, due to endless conflicting reports on the working order of the Gras rifle and the state of preservation of the cartridges.

Thanks to his daily lessons, Talu had succeeded in singing Darricelli's *Aubade,* repeating it bar by bar after Carmichael standing beside him, the Emperor now wished to put on the female costume which had first aroused his cupidity, and to complete his education by cultivating the art of bearing and gesture. Sirdah translated her father's wishes, and he, helped by the young Marseillais, carefully and with all a child's pleasure dressed himself in the blue gown and flaxen wig, whose dual strangeness enraptured the soul of a poet-monarch somewhat histrionically inclined.

The Emperor, thus costumed as a female singer, walked on to the stage, and this time Carmichael, in the course of his lesson, instructed his pupil piecemeal in the arm-movements he used, also teaching him to move easily and to kick the train adroitly behind him at each turn. Thereafter Talu always studied in full dress and in the end acquitted himself perfectly of his self-imposed task.

A series of *tableaux vivants* were to be performed on gala day by the company of operetta singers, sufficiently well provided with costumes and accessories.

Soreau, who had inaugurated and taken charge of this project, meant to begin with a *Banquet of the Gods of Olympus,* easily put on with the available sets and costumes for *Orpheus in the Underworld.*

For the other presentations, Soreau took as his inspiration five stories collected by him in the course of tours in North America, England, Russia, Greece and Italy.

The first was a Canadian tale heard in Quebec, a children's story which may be summarised as follows :

On the banks of Lake Ontario there lived a rich planter of French origin whose name was Jouandon.

His wife had recently died, and Jouandon bestowed all his affection upon his daughter, Ursula, a pretty child of eight, entrusted to the care of the devoted Maffa, a gentle, pleasing Huron who had suckled her.

Jouandon became a target for the manoeuvres of a scheming woman called Gervaise, who, so poor and ugly that at twenty-five she was still a spinster, had taken it into her head to marry the rich planter.

By nature a weak man, Jouandon was so ensnared by the amorous farce skilfully enacted by the shrew, that presently she became his second wife.

From that moment, life was unbearable in the house which had once been so tranquil and full of sunshine. Gervaise had brought her sister Agatha and her two brothers Claude and Justin with her, all three of them as covetous as herself; this infernal brood ruled the household, shrieking and gesticulating from morning to night. Ursula was the principal butt of the raillery of Gervaise and her acolytes, and it was with great difficulty that Maffa managed to protect the little girl from the ill-treatment with which they threatened her.

229

Two years later Jouandon, a prey to sorrow and remorse, died of a consumption, blaming himself for the unhappiness he had brought on his daughter as well as himself by a disastrous union which he lacked the strength to break.

Gervaise and her three accomplices redoubled their attacks on the unfortunate Ursula, hoping that she would die like her father and leave them to take possession of his wealth.

Maffa, outraged, one day visited the warriors of her tribe and explained the situation to the old medicine man Nô, who was renowned for the extent of his powers.

Nô promised to punish the miscreants, and followed Maffa back to the ill-fated house.

As they walked along the edge of Lake Ontario, they saw Gervaise and Agatha in the distance, coming down to the shore escorted by their two brothers, who were carrying Ursula, silent and motionless, in their arms.

The four monsters, taking advantage of her nurse's absence, had gagged the child and were about to throw her into the deep waters of the lake.

Maffa and Nô hid behind a clump of trees, and the party reached the bank without noticing them.

Just as the brothers were lifting Ursula's body to fling it into the water, Nô uttered a magic incantation in a resounding voice, and at once four metamorphoses took place.

Gervaise was changed into a she-ass and made to stand before a trough of appetising bran : but no sooner did she approach this abundant provision than a kind of rowel caught at her jaw and prevented her from satisfying her pangs of hunger.

When she wearied of this torture and tried to escape the tempting delusion, a gold grating appeared before her, an unexpected obstacle barring her path, ready to rise up at any point within a strictly limited circle.

Agatha, turned into a goose, ran wildly off, pursued by

Boreas, who blew on her with all his might, at the same time lashing her with a thorny rose.

Claude retained his human body, but his head took on the appearance of a boar's snout. Three objects of various weight, an egg, a glove and a wisp of straw, skipped from his hands which, in spite of themselves, threw them up continuously into the air and skilfully caught them again.

Like a juggler who, instead of controlling the balls, let himself be dragged along by them, the wretched fellow rushed off in a straight line, under the influence of some dizzying magnetic pull.

Justin, transformed into a pike, was cast into the lake and compelled to swim round it endlessly at great speed, like a horse loosed on a gigantic racecourse.

Maffa and Nô went up to Ursula and removed her gag.

Filled with compassion and forgetting all her resentment, the little girl, who had watched the fourfold phenomenon, interceded on behalf of her tormentors.

She asked the medicine man how the spell could be broken, earnestly pleading the cause of the miscreants, who to her mind did not deserve eternal punishment.

Moved by such kindness, Nô gave her this precious information: once a year, on the anniversary of the incantation and at the very moment at which it had been uttered, the three other victims of the spell would return to that part of the bank where the she-ass, the only one to remain in place during the aimless wanderings of the three others, would be found. Their reunion would last only a second, for no pause was allowed to the miserable fugitives. If, during this barely perceptible moment, some generous hand, equipped with the appropriate device, contrived to fish the pike out of the water and land it on the bank, the charm would immediately be broken and the four accursed creatures restored to their human form; but the least clumsiness in the movement intended to liberate them would postpone the possibility of a further attempt until the following year.

Ursula, the details of this revelation engraved on her memory, thanked Nô, who returned alone to the warriors of his tribe.

A year later, a few minutes before the appointed hour, Ursula stepped into the boat with Maffa and kept watch for the pike, near the spot where the she-ass still sniffed in vain at her manger, itself as full as ever.

Suddenly the little girl saw in the distance, through the transparent water, the swift-moving fish she was waiting for; at the same moment, from opposite points on the horizon, appeared the juggler with the boar's head and the goose lashed on by the cruel Boreas.

Ursula at once lowered a large net vertically into the water, across the path of the pike, which sped like an arrow into the middle of the snare.

With a brisk jerk the young fisher-girl tried to cast the fish on to the shore. But no doubt expiation was not yet accomplished, for the mesh, though fine and strong, let its catch through, so that it fell back into the water and continued on its wild course. The juggler and the goose, reunited for a second near the she-ass, passed each other without slowing down and soon vanished on their separate ways.

Everything seemed to indicate that Ursula's disappointment was due to a supernatural influence, for after the event there was no tear in the net. Three further attempts, separated each time by the interval of a year, ended in the same negative result.

Finally, in the fifth year, Ursula acted with such accuracy and skill that the pike reached the very edge of the bank without having time to slip away through the cords which held it captive.

Immediately the four kinsfolk resumed their human form

and, terrified by the possibility of some further spell, left the region without delay and were never seen there again.

In England, Soreau had learnt the following fact, reported in his *Memories of Handel* by Lord Corfield, an intimate friend of the great composer.

In 1756, Handel, who was then an old man and had already been blind for more than four years, rarely went out of his London house, where crowds of his admirers visited him.

One evening the eminent musician was in his study on the first floor, a huge, luxurious room which he preferred to the ground-floor apartments because of a magnificent organ, set against one of the panels.

Under the bright lights, a number of guests were chatting noisily, enlivened by a sumptuous meal with which the master, a great lover of delicate food and good wine, had entertained them.

Lord Corfield, who was among those present, turned the conversation on to the genius of their host and praised his masterpieces with the sincerest enthusiasm. The others chorused their agreement, and each expressed his admiration for the force of that inborn creative gift which no ordinary man could acquire even at the cost of the most assiduous labour.

Corfield maintained that a phrase sprung from a brow illuminated by the divine spark, developed by a mere technician in however mediocre a fashion could breathe life into many pages of music. On the other hand, added the speaker, an ordinary theme treated by the most inspired mind must inevitably remain heavy and clumsy and never lose the indelible mark of its origin.

Handel protested at these words, claiming that he would undertake to write a whole oratorio worthy to be included in the list of his works, on a theme which had been mechanically constructed by accidental procedure.

As there were murmurs of doubt at this claim, Handel, animated by the evening's libations, rose suddenly, declaring that he wished, at that very moment and before witnesses, to establish in a forthright manner the basis of the work in question. Feeling his way, the famous composer walked over to the fireplace and took from a vase a number of sprigs of holly left over from the previous Christmas. He arranged these in a row on the marble, drawing attention to the fact that there were seven sprigs. Each was to represent a note in the scale and to bear some distinguishing mark.

Madge, the master's old housekeeper, an accomplished needlewoman, was immediately sent for and called on to produce seven narrow ribbons of different shades.

The resourceful woman found no difficulty in so trivial a request and retired for a moment to fetch seven silk bows, one of each of the colours of the prism. Corfield, at the request of the great musician, tied a bow round each stem without disarranging the row.

This task completed, Handel asked everyone there to look for a moment at the scale represented before their eyes, and to concentrate on remembering the connection between the colours and the notes.

Next, the master, whose sense of touch was remarkably heightened by blindness, proceeded to his own minute examination of the sprigs, carefully noting any peculiarities in the pattern of the leaves or the arrangement of the prickles.

As soon as he was sure of himself, Handel put all the branches together in his left hand and, pointing to his writing desk, asked Corfield to bring his pen and inkwell.

The great man went out of the room, guided by one of his faithful disciples and was led to the staircase, where a flat, white balustrade lent itself admirably to his purpose.

Handel shuffled the branches of holly for a long time so that they kept no trace of their original order, and then called Corfield, who handed him the pen dipped in ink. Brushing them lightly with the free fingers of his right hand, the blind man picked out one of the prickly sprays, which for him had no individual character except to the touch, and, going up to the balustrade, wrote easily in ordinary letters, the note which this momentary contact had indicated.

Going one step down, Handel reshuffled the thick bunch and by the same unguided tactile means, picked out a second note, which he wrote a little further down the balustrade.

The great man continued his descent in this way, slowly and methodically. At each step he conscientiously shuffled the bundle thoroughly before selecting, with the tips of his fingers, the arbitrary indication of a given note, which he at once inscribed in perfectly legible writing.

The guests followed their host, step by step, establishing with ease the accuracy of his work by the different coloured ribbons. From time to time, Corfield took the pen and dipped it in the ink before returning it to the blind man.

Ten minutes later Handel wrote down his twenty-third note, and, from the last step, reached ground level. He went to a third seat and sat down for a moment to rest from his efforts, explaining to his friends the reason why he had chosen so unusual a method of inscription.

Feeling that his end was near, Handel had bequeathed his house to the city of London to be made into a museum. A great number of manuscripts, curiosities and *memorabilia* of every kind must already have made a visit to the illustrious abode attractive. Nevertheless, the great man was still haunted by the idea of continually adding to the attractions of a future pilgrimage. That was why, seizing a favourable opportunity, he had that evening made an imperishable monument of the balustrade by writing on it the strange and disconnected theme whose length was determined only by the number of stairs, of which he had till then taken no precise account, thus adding a further peculiarity to the mechanical and deliberate part of the composition.

Refreshed by a few moments' rest, Handel was escorted by his friends back to the room on the first floor, where the evening ended merrily. Corfield undertook to make a musical transcript of the phrase which had been worked out by no direction but that of chance, and the master promised to adhere rigidly to the indications of the outline, only reserving the right to use his own discretion in two matters: first, that of the values of the notes, and secondly, that of register, which must be allowed to change without restriction from one octave to another.

Next day Handel set to work, with the help of a secretary who was accustomed to writing at his dictation. Blindness had never diminished the famous musician's intellectual activity.

In his hands the weirdly-shaped theme assumed a beautiful and interesting form, due to ingenious combinations of harmony and rhythm.

The same phrase of twenty-three notes recurred throughout, each time differently presented, and alone constituted the famous *Vesper* oratorio, a work of unmistakable power and serenity, still universally admired.


Soreau, on his travels in Russia, had taken these historical notes on Czar Alexis Mihailovitch.

Towards the end of 1648, Alexis, still a child but already Emperor for three years, left the government in the hands of his two favourites, Plehtcheiev and Morosov, whose injustice and cruelty aroused discontent everywhere.

Plehtcheiev especially, despised by all who approached him, left implacable rancour wherever he went.

One December morning, a rumour spread through the palace: Plehtcheiev, howling with pain in his private apartment, was racked by frightful convulsions, blood in his eyes and his mouth foaming.

When the czar, accompanied by his doctor, came to the place, a horrifying spectacle met him. Stretched out on the carpet, Plehtcheiev, his limbs contracted, his face and hands totally blue, had just breathed his last.

On a table could be seen the remains of the morning meal of which the dead man had partaken. The doctor approached and recognised by the smell, in a few drops of liquid at the bottom of a cup, traces of an extremely violent poison.

The czar, at once instituting inquiries, summoned all Plehtcheiev's servants. But no avowal was elicited, nor, subsequently, did the most thorough search yield any result.

Alexis then put into operation means calculated to lead the guilty person to betray himself unwittingly. In the sight and knowledge of all, he shut himself up alone in his chapel to pray God to inspire him. An hour later he opened the door and summoned about him the servants who were under suspicion and who filed silently into the holy place.

Turning towards one wall, Alexis pointed out to the newcomers a precious window whose admirable stained glass mosaic showed Christ's agony on the cross at sundown. Almost on the horizon, the sun, about to vanish, was represented by a perfectly regular red-gold disc.

On the orders of Alexis, two servants detached from the group stepped up on the stonework and reached the window. With their knives they detached the strips of lead soldered about the circumference of the glorious star, then took in their fingers the round piece of glass and bore it brilliant and intact to the czar.

Before making use of this curious object, Alexis recounted in these terms a vision he had just had, in this very place, in solitary meditation.

Shut in for some minutes, Alexis had been praying God to reveal to him the name of the guilty man, when a sudden brightness caused him to raise his eyes. He thereupon saw in the window now incomplete the figure of Jesus move. The eyes of the Crucified burned upon him, and then the lips moving and living articulated the following sentence: ' Remove from the glasswork that sun which illuminates my torment; through this prism sanctified by my agony, your eyes will strike down the guilty one, who, for punishment, will suffer the effects of the poison administered by his hand.' Having spoken these words, the image of Christ became immobile as before, and dazed by the miracle, the czar remained for a long time in prayer to render thanks to the Lord.

The group of servants had listened to this account without making any movement.

Alexis, without thereafter speaking, slowly raised the reddening sun to the level of his eyes and fixed one by one, through the diaphanous disc, the suspects aligned before him.

The czar rightly counted upon the consequences of religious exaltation to achieve his end, for his words had profoundly affected his listeners. Of a sudden, stricken by the questing look which shone through the coloured glass, a man reeled, uttering a cry, and fell into the arms of his comrades, his limbs contorted, face and hands turned blue, like Plehtcheiev at the moment of his death. The czar approached the unfortunate man, who confessed his crime before expiring with the most frightful sufferings.

Greece had provided Soreau with a poetical anecdote, when during a stay in Athens, he had profited by his hours of liberty to visit, in the company of a guide, the sights of the town and the surrounding countryside.

One day, in the depths of the wood of Argyros, the guide led Soreau to the point at which two shady paths crossed and begged him to try an echo celebrated for its extraordinary purity.

Soreau obeyed and uttered a sequence of words and other sounds which were at once reproduced with perfect accuracy.

The guide then told him the following story, which gave the place an unexpected interest.

In 1827, the idol of all Greece, who owed its independence to him, Canaris had recently taken his seat in the Hellenic Parliament.

One summer evening, the famous sailor, accompanied by a few close friends, was strolling in the wood of Argyros, savouring the charm of a glorious sunset, speaking of the future of the country whose happiness constituted his sole preoccupation.

When they reached the echoing crossroads, Canaris, who had never visited the neighbourhood before, received from one of his companions the customary revelation of the acoustical phenomenon put to the proof by all who walked that way.

Wishing himself to hear the mysterious voice, the hero stood on the spot pointed out to him, then at random called out the word ' Rose.'

The echo faithfully repeated this vocable, but, to everyone's great surprise, an exquisite and penetrating scent of roses at the same moment filled the air.

Canaris repeated the experiment, naming in succession the most odoriferous flowers; each time the clear and prompt reply came enveloped in an intoxicating breeze of the corresponding aroma.

Next day, the news, spread abroad from mouth to mouth, inflamed the enthusiasm of the Greeks for their saviour. According to them, nature itself had wished to honour the victor by sprinkling in his path the subtle, delicate soul of the rarest petals.

A more recent item of news reminded Soreau of his stay in Italy.

It concerned Prince Savellini, an incorrigible kleptomaniac who, despite his immense fortune, frequented railway stations and overcrowded places in general, gathering each day, with miraculous skill, an abundant harvest of watches and purses.

The prince's madness drove him above all to rob the poor. Dressed with supreme elegance and wearing jewels of inestimable worth, he would repair to the lowest slums in Rome, seeking out with the utmost refinement the greasiest pockets into which he might plunge his ring-laden hands.

Arriving one day in an ill-famed street, haunt of prostitutes and pimps, he espied from afar a gathering which at once made him quicken his steps.

Approaching, he distinguished thirty or forty loafers of the worst kind, forming an attentive circle about two of their own kind who were fighting with knives.

A cloud seemed to pass before the prince's eyes; never before had such an occasion of satisfying his vice been offered him.

Mad with joy, clenching his jaws to prevent his teeth chattering, he walked forward reeling on trembling legs, his breast hammered by heavy heart-beats which interfered with his breathing.

Favoured by the interest of the bloody spectacle which

captivated all minds, the kleptomaniac was able to exercise his art in all freedom, exploring with unequalled touch pockets cut from blue calico or rough corduroy.

Small change, cheap watches, tobacco pouches and baubles of every kind were engulfed in the depths of the enormous cavities the prince had caused to be sewn inside his luxurious fur coat.

A number of police, observing the brawl, suddenly swooped on the group and seized the two combatants, whom they led off to the station, together with the prince whose little game had not escaped them.

A search made at the Savellini palace brought to light the poor maniac's innumerable acts of petty theft.

Next day a frightful scandal broke out in the newspapers, and the noble kleptomaniac became a laughing-stock throughout Italy.


Helped by Chènevillot, who promised his collaboration in arranging all the stage properties and accessories, Soreau devoted himself feverishly to putting on the six projected *tableaux*.

For the Banquet of the Gods, a black rope, impossible to distinguish against a background of the same colour, was needed for Mercury's aerial entry; the ship's cook would undertake to set out a richly provided table.

The Lake Ontario legend called for more complicated efforts. On loan from Olga Chervonenkova, the she-ass Milenkaya, wearing on its jaws the two visible ends of an imaginary suture, would play her part before a trough of imitation bran which, made out of brown paper in tiny fragments, would offer her no dangerous temptation likely to show up the impediment as a falsehood. Soreau had chosen to represent the precise moment of one of the fruitless attempts to put an end to the bewitchment. Stella Bucharessas would be the charitable Ursula vainly trying to catch the fugitive pike; beside her, Jeanne Souze, her face and hands darkly made up, would appear in the part of the faithful Maffa. Downstage from the she-ass, Soreau as Boreas would be whipping on a goose out of the ship's cook's poultry supplies; the bird's wings would be kept apart by an invisible framework, and its feet, glued to the boards, would maintain an attitude of rapid flight. Among the company's accessories was found, for the juggler, a pasteboard boar's head of perfect execution; it had been habitually used in the third act of an operetta in which all the characters attended the masked ball of a South American millionaire.

For the scene of Handel writing, Chènevillot was given very precise indications by Soreau, who had seen with his own eyes, in London, the famous balustrade, piously preserved in the museum at South Kensington.

The Czar Alexis and Canaris scenes offered few difficulties, apart from that of diffusing a variety of scents in the latter.

Only Darriand could solve this problem. Pursuing his studies in sea plants, he had undertaken more general research into vegetable odours.

Meaning to pass his time profitably at sea, this brilliant scientist had provided himself with essences of all kinds, which, mixed with delicacy, were capable of yielding the most diverse aromas.

Hidden in the wings, Darriand himself would repeat, like an echo, the flower names called, each time uncorking a few seconds in advance a flask filled with an extremely volatile compound, the emanations from which should then from all sides assail the nostrils of the spectators.

In the kleptomania scene, Soreau, portraying Prince Savellini, would simply wear a comfortable fur coat, which during the crossing had allowed him to brave on the bridge the winds always blowing freshly on the high seas.


Carmichael, cast in the part of narrator, would in a few words explain the subject of each of the six groupings.

# XV

E JUR contained a specimen of quite captivating originality, namely Fogar, the Emperor's eldest son.

Barely fifteen years old, this adolescent astonished us all by his sometimes frightening oddities.

Attracted to the supernatural, Fogar had heard from the mouth of the witch doctor Bashku a variety of magical formulae which he turned to uses of his own.

A born poet like his father, the young man was passionately fond of nature. The ocean particularly exerted on his mind an irresistible spell. He would sit on the beach for hours watching the ebb and flow, dreaming of the secret marvels concealed in those liquid abysses. An excellent swimmer, he bathed with delight in the element so fascinating to him, diving and staying under as long as he could in stealthy exploration of the mysterious spaces which haunted his precocious imagination.

Among other dark practices, Bashku had taught Fogar means to put himself, without help, into a state of lethargy near death.

Lying on his primitive cot, the young man, immobilising himself in a kind of hypnotical ecstasy, contrived little by little to suspend his heartbeats while completely stopping the respiratory oscillations of his thorax.

Sometimes, when the experiment was over, Fogar felt certain passages of his veins obstructed by blood already coagulated.

But this was foreseen and, to remedy his condition, the adolescent always had within reach a special flower Bashku had told him of.

With a thorn from its stalk he opened the swollen vein and took out the hard clot. A single petal, crushed in his fingers, then yielded a violet fluid a few drops of which sufficed to close up the mortally dangerous fissure.

Driven by his obsessive desire to visit the submarine depths, which his mind peopled with bewildering fantasms, Fogar determined to cultivate this strange art which permitted him temporarily to annul his vital functions.

His shining purpose was to submerge for a long while under the water, taking advantage of the state of hypnosis which so totally checked the play of his lungs.

Training progressively, he could now stay half an hour in this state of artificial death needed to fulfil his aims.

He began by lying down on his cot, thus imposing on his circulation a beneficent calm which facilitated the task.

After some minutes, heart and lungs motionless, Fogar still retained a dream-like half-consciousness accompanied by almost mechanical activity.

He then attempted to stand upright, but after taking a few steps like an automaton fell to the ground without all sense of balance.

Scorning all hindrances and dangers, Fogar wished without delay to attempt the aquatic expedition so long projected.

He went down to the beach, provided with a thorny violet flower which he placed in a hollow in the rocks.

Next, lying down on the sand, he abandoned himself, successfully to the hypnotic sleep.

Presently his breathing stopped and his heart ceased to beat. Then, like a sleepwalker, Fogar arose and went into the sea.

Held upright by the denser element, he easily kept his

balance and without tottering descended the abrupt slopes which formed a continuation of the shore.

A cleft in the rock suddenly gave him access to a deep and involved labyrinth which he explored at random, still descending.

Free and unburdened, he passed through narrowly winding galleries, where no diver would have dared to risk his air pipe.

After countless turnings he came out into a vast cavern, whose walls, smeared with some phosphorescent substance, shone with the most gorgeous brilliancy.

Strange creatures of the sea peopled on all sides this fairyland, whose magnificence surpassed all that the adolescent had created in imagination beforehand.

It was enough for him to stretch out a hand to take possession of the most astonishing marvels.

Fogar took several steps towards a living sponge which remained motionless on a rocky ledge. The phosphorescent emanations, passing through the animal's body, showed, at the centre of its saturated tissue, a miniature human heart attached to a network of blood vessels.

With great caution Fogar took up the curious specimen, which, not belonging to the vegetable kingdom, had no root to keep it in place.

Just above this, three samples no less peculiar clung to the cavern wall.

The first, elongated in form, bore a row of fine tentacles like the fringe of some article of furniture or clothing.

The second, thin, soft and pliant like a closely woven fabric, formed a triangle adhering to the wall by its base; it was striped all over with salient arteries, which, duly completed by two round eyes that were mere black spots, gave the whole waving object the appearance of a pennant or flag belonging to some unknown nation.

The last sample, smaller than its two neighbours, bore on its back a carapace of extreme whiteness, which, like solidified soap lather, was remarkable for its delicacy and lightness.

Adding this threefold booty to his sponge, Fogar was about to retrace his steps.

At the last moment he picked up in a corner of the grotto a large gelatinous block. Finding no particular interest in the object, he put it carelessly down on a neighbouring rock whose surface bristled with rough patches and jagged points.

Seeming to be awakened by contact with these painful asperities, the block quivered and raised, like a distress signal, a tentacle like an elephant's trunk, but divided at the end into three divergent branches.

Each of these branches terminated in a sucker reminiscent of the terrible arms of an octopus.

As the prickles penetrated deeper into the flesh, the animal suffered increasingly.

Its exasperation presently manifested itself in unexpected fashion. The branches with their suckers began to turn like the spokes of a wheel, at first slowly but then with growing speed.

Changing his mind at the sight of this strange phenomenon, Fogar once again took up the block, now judged worthy of attention. Leaving the spiny surface which caused it so much hurt, the animal's roundabout motion abruptly stopped, and it subsided into its former torpid state.

The young man reached the way out of the grotto.

There, a floating form barred his way, placed at eye-level.

It might have been some round, light plate of metal, descending slowly, kept up by the density of the water.

With a movement of his arm, Fogar tried to brush the obstacle away.

But at the first touch the timid, sensitive sheet folded up, changing shape and even colour.

247

Avidly taking possession of this new specimen, to which in the first place he had attached no price, Fogar began his ascent along the winding corridor already once traversed.

Sustained by the liquid pressure, he walked uphill without fatigue to the beach, where he was able to take some further steps before allowing himself to fall to the ground.

Bit by bit, his heart and lungs resumed their normal functioning, and lethargic sleep gave way to complete lucidity.

Fogar looked about him, only half recalling the details of his solitary journey.

The experiment, more prolonged than was customary, had multiplied in his veins the swellings due to coagulation of the blood.

Fogar stood up and hurried to where he had prudently laid the violet flower.

The usual operation, followed by immediate sealing, delivered him of the long clots, which he threw down carelessly on the sand.

Immediately there were signs of movement among the group of sea creatures, which, since the adolescent fell to the ground, had themselves remained limply there.

Accustomed no doubt to feed by suction on the blood of their prey, the three specimens taken from the vertical wall, obedient to some irresistible instinct, seized ravenously upon the dull, thin, coagulated cylinders.

This unexpected meal was accompanied by the sound of gluttonous little hiccups from the strange mollusc with the white shell.

During this time, the block with the three rotating branches, the sponge and the flat, greyish disc remained motionless on the fine sand.

Entirely recovered, Fogar ran to Ejur and brought back to the beach a receptacle which he filled with sea-water before placing in it the denizens of the submarine grotto.

In the days which followed, Fogar, very proud of the results of his underwater adventure, considered how best to display his curious finds on gala day.

He had closely studied his six exhibits, which, once removed from their element, continued to live, though remaining completely without motion.

Now, this inertia did not please Fogar, who, rejecting the trite motion of a mere aquarium display, wanted to show his creatures to advantage like a showman exhibiting animals in a fairground.

Remembering the speed with which half his troupe had seized on the clots of blood he had thrown on the beach, he determined to use the same means of stimulating them again.

The experiment would thus have to be framed within a lethargic-sleep session, conducted in public by the young black, lazily extended upon his cot in the centre of his various animals symmetrically disposed.

For the sponge, a useful method was discovered by accident.

During the first attempts to accustom his pupils to the open air, Fogar, proceeding by trial and error, had made a point of pouring sea-water from time to time on the living tissues, which might have perished from an extreme of dryness.

One day, concerned to use his supply of sea-water sparingly, the young man used fresh water and began by pouring it on the sponge, which at once contracted itself energetically to expel with horror a liquid ill-adapted to its vital functions.

Dousing it in the same way on the important day could not fail to induce the same effects and to provoke the behaviour advertised.

The gelatinous block appeared totally apathetic.

Fortunately, thinking about the grotto, Fogar remembered

the asperities of the rock which, grievously penetrating the animal's fleshy parts, had provoked the gyratory movement of its three diverging stalks.

He sought a way of imitating with elegance the crooked and irregular prickles of the stone.

A swish and rustling haunted his memory, and there came to his mind the gown chosen by Adinolfa to inaugurate the Incomparables' performance.

He engaged Sirdah to ask the tragic actress for some of the longer jet bugle-beads sewn to the silk.

Adinolfa kindly placed the whole costume at his disposal, and it was easy for him to garner what he needed from the abundantly decorated skirt and bodice.

A small quantity of cement, borrowed from one of Chènevillot's workmen, formed a thin layer spread evenly over a piece of cloth.

Presently a hundred jet bugles, planted in ten equal rows in the substance at first soft but quick to harden, raised up vertically their small, menacing points.

In order to add to the interest of his presentation of the gelatinous block, Fogar wanted some prey to be attached to each of the suckers in which the three revolving stalks terminated, thus emphasising their muscular force and speed.

At his request, the Bucharessas family promised the help of three performing cats, which would soon recover from their momentary giddiness.

The grey-coloured plate, once out of water, became rigid like zinc.

But Fogar discovered that, by blowing on it, he could make it warp and cockle in a variety of graceful and subtle ways of which he meant to make use on the day of the gala.

Wishing to achieve continuous and protracted transformations without pulmonary fatigue, the young man, again translated by his sister, had recourse to Bex himself, who, with a spare battery destined eventually for a thermo-mechanical orchestra devised in the course of his all-night research, made a light and practical electric fan.

This piece of apparatus had the advantage over simple blowing that its gentle, uninterrupted breath was perfectly regular.

Fogar, ceaselessly at Bex's side, had studied with passion the working of the different components of the artful breeze-generating instrument.

With his marked faculty for assimilation, he had understood all the finer points of the mechanism, expressing in gesture his admiration for such and such a piece of fine gearing or cleverly placed ratchet tooth.

Interested by this unusual nature, hardly to be expected in such a region, Bex instructed Fogar in certain of his chemical secrets and went so far as to put on for him a performance by the automatic orchestra.

Fogar stood dumbfounded as one instrument after another was started off to produce a flow of sustained and varied harmony.

One detail, however, surprised him by its comparative weakness, and, through the intermediary of Sirdah, who was present, he was able to put his questions to Bex.

What troubled him was to see the strings powerless to produce more than one note each at a time. According to him, certain rodents, to be found in a particular part of the Behuliphruen, had a mane, each hair of which, if stretched and subjected to friction, gave out two distinct notes simultaneously.

Bex refused to admit this as a possibility and, shrugging his shoulders, allowed himself to be led off by Fogar, who, sure of his facts, insisted on taking him to the haunt of the rodents in question.

Together with his guide, the chemist ventured into the

251

depths of the Behuliphruen and came to a place riddled with the holes of burrows.

Fogar halted, then suddenly offered Bex an astonishing piece of mimicry, with his finger tracing zig-zags of lightning on the air and with his throat imitating the rumbling of thunder.

Bex signified understanding and approbation; the young man had explained to him, clearly enough, that the rodents, at that moment scattered about the woodland, were much afraid of storms and would creep timorously back to their holes at the first sound of thunder.

Looking upward Bex observed the untroubled purity of the sky and wondered what Fogar proposed to do about it; but the latter divined his thought and motioned him to be patient.

The shallow depression in which they stood was shaded by large trees of a curious formation, whose fruits, like gigantic bananas, littered the ground about them.

With his fingers, Fogar peeled one of these fruits, then moulded its easily malleable whitish inside in such a way as to straighten out its slightly curved form.

In this way he obtained a perfectly regular cylinder of the stuff, which he pierced lengthwise with a thin, straight piece of twig.

Through the empty, luminous hole he passed a length of creeper detached from the tree trunks, then consolidated the whole thing by rapid further kneading.

Little by little the fruit had been transformed into a veritable candle, whose highly inflammable wick caught fire suddenly from flying sparks struck by Fogar from two stones selected with care.

Presently Bex saw the purpose of this complicated stratagem.

The candle, placed upright on a flat stone, produced, as it burned, a resonant and continuous sputtering extraordinarily like the sound of thunder.

The chemist approached, intrigued by the strange properties of the combustible fruit, which parodied the fury of a violent storm so closely that the one could have been mistaken for the other.

All of a sudden there was a positive stampede among the trees, and Bex saw approach a horde of black animals, which, deceived by the false thunder, were hastening back to their burrows.

When the pack was within reach, Fogar, throwing a stone into their midst, killed one rodent outright. It remained stretched out on the ground while its congeners plunged into their innumerable holes.

Snuffing out the vegetable wick, whose noisy carbonisation lacked further utility, the adolescent picked up the rodent and placed it before the eyes of Bex.

The animal, which bore a remote resemblance to a squirrel, had a thick, tough mane running along the full length of its spine.

Examining the hairs, the chemist noted certain remarkable nodosities, capable doubtless of producing the double sounds which so strongly aroused his curiosity.

As they left the place, Fogar, on the advice of his companion, picked up the extinguished candle, of which only a small portion had been consumed.

Returning to Ejur, Bex wished at once to verify his young guide's assertions.

From the rodent's back he picked out a number of threads in which the nodules were differently spaced.

Next, in the absence of any proper sounding-board, he clamped together two pieces of thin wood and bored small, regularly spaced holes through the two.

Thereupon, each solid hair was passed through the two boards. Each end was thickly knotted upon itself to secure firm attachment. The two pieces of wood were then drawn as far apart as possible and vertically wedged in such a way as to maintain the necessary tension in hairs suddenly transformed into sounding strings.

Fogar himself provided a narrow, flexible branch which, cut in the heart of the Behuliphruen and split along its full length, offered an inner surface at once smooth and resinously clinging.

Carefully trimmed by Bex, part of the twig became a fragile bow, which presently and effortlessly attacked the strings of the miniature lute so quickly put together.

As Fogar had predicted, each string, vibrating alone, produced two notes of equal resonance at the same time.

Bex enthusiastically persuaded the young man, on gala day, to display this previously unimagined instrument together with the vegetable candle easily lighted again.


Encouraged by his success, Fogar sought new marvels with which to augment still further the interest of his performance.

Seeing, one evening, a sailor from the *Lynceus* washing linen in the stream of the Tez, he was struck by the similarity between one of his marine animals and the soapsuds on the surface of the water.

Having done the wash, the sailor, as a joke, gave his piece of soap to Fogar, accompanying the gift with a rough but well-intentioned and friendly joke on the colour of the young negro's skin.

The adolescent, clumsily, felt the wet lump shoot out of his fingers, but, finding it and picking it up again more cautiously, thought of a double use to which he could put it at the gala.

In the first place Fogar intended to place on the piece of soap the creature with the white carapace, which, taken thus

254

for inert lather, would impress the spectators with its sudden revelation of activity.

Then, taking advantage of the extraordinary slipperiness of a substance new to him, Fogar proposed to aim the piece of soap, its instability heightened by sufficient moisture, at a specific target.

In this connection, the young man remembered an ingot of gold perceived by Bashku at the bottom of the Tez, one day when the river was exceptionally limpid. Diving sharply, the witch-doctor had seized the bright object, which he had since kept by him with jealous watchfulness.

Given its cylindrical form rounded at the ends, the ingot would lend itself admirably to the difficult experiment conceived by Fogar.

But the witch-doctor attached too great a price to his find to deign to be separated from it even for a moment.

Thinking that the Tez must certainly conceal in its depths other ingots like the first, Fogar planned a fresh-water dive from which he expected fruitful results. Like a gambler whose luck is in, he could only imagine success and saw himself already in possession of a number of precious cylinders which, by their very brilliance together with the interest of their origin, would stimulate his reflections at the same time as they added lustre to his sleeping-place, already so richly furnished with animal treasures.

Once more providing himself with a violet flower, Fogar lay down on the banks of the Tez to await the onset of lethargic sleep.

Attaining the curious state of half-consciousness favourable to his designs, he rolled down to the river and disappeared into its depths at the very point at which Bashku had discovered his ingot.

Kneeling on the bottom, Fogar felt in the sand with his fingers and, after a prolonged search, found three bright cylinders of gold which, no doubt washed down from distant regions, had acquired a high polish by rubbing.

The young man had just risen to his feet, ready to rise again to the surface of the water, when suddenly he stopped, rooted to the spot by surprise.

An enormous plant, whitish in colour, opening widely from top to bottom of its stem, rose vertically beside him like a giant reed.

Upon the screen thus deployed, Fogar saw himself kneeling in the sand, his body leaning forward. Presently the picture changed, showing the same person in a different position.

Further changes took place, and the astonished youth saw his principal movements reproduced by the strange sensitive plate, which had been acting unknown to him since his slow arrival at the bottom of the water.

One by one the three ingots extracted from the sand shone on the living panel, which faithfully reproduced all their colour with a degree of attenuation due to the partial opacity of the liquid medium.

Barely once terminated, the sequence of reproductions began all over again, just as before and in the same order.

Without waiting for the end of this new cycle, Fogar scooped mud away from the immense white reed, which he was then able to remove from the soil with its root intact.

Several plants of the same species, but not so well-grown, were to be found nearby. The skilful diver uprooted several, then went back into the open air with his ingots and little harvest.

Brought back to full consciousness and freed of his blood clots by the use of the violet flower, Fogar hastened to shut himself up in his hut and examine his remarkable plants at leisure.

The first of them endlessly repeated the same succession of images in an invariable order.

But the others, though exactly similar in all the distinguishing marks of the species, offered no obvious intake to impressions of light.

The evidence was that only in a particular phase of their giant maturation did the snowy reeds register the coloured forms impinging upon their tissue.

The young man determined to watch out for this moment in order to turn it to advantage.

The views imprinted on the first plant could not be expected to satisfy him, given their disturbed and cloudy appearance.

He wanted to produce sharp, distinct proofs, worth setting to full advantage before the public gaze.

Without seeking help, Fogar went to the Behuliphruen and dug up a supply of earth and leaf-mould which he spread out in a thick layer against one wall of his hut.

There he transplanted his monster reeds, which, like certain amphibious sea-weeds, accommodated themselves without difficulty to this new and wholly terrestrial cultivation.

From that moment the youthful black did not stir out of his hut, jealously watching his flower-bed, which he tended with unceasing care.

One day, inspecting it, he saw that one of the plants, already well-grown, seemed to have reached a certain point in its blossoming.

Suddenly there was further movement in the vegetable tissue, and Fogar examined it even more closely.

The whitish, vertical surface was changing at regular intervals in consequence of a curious molecular action.

A series of transformations of this kind took place during a considerable lapse of time; then the nature of the phenomenon changed, and Fogar, this time less surprised, saw his own features strongly reproduced by the plant, avid of pictorial assimilation.

Different poses and expressions of the single model passed in turn over the screen inwardly disturbed by continuous agitation, and the adolescent received confirmation of the enigma which he had more or less divined : his arrival at the bottom of the Tez had coincided with the recording stage reached in the evolution of the first plant, which at once had eagerly seized upon the images then at hand.

Unfortunately the new sequence of pictures, perfect in respect of their clarity, altogether lacked beauty and interest. Fogar, not having been warned, had taken up every kind of ungainly attitude, and grimacing portraits of him succeeded each other with the most tedious monotony.

Observing a nearby plant which looked as though it were about to enter upon its period of light-receptiveness, the young man busied himself with preparing in advance some visual arrangement worthy of attention.

A few days before, returning through the Behuliphruen with his provision of leaf-mould, Fogar had noticed Juillard installed in a thickly shaded spot.

It was his favourite place for working—where indeed Adinolfa had already once surprised him poring over old illustrated papers.

This time, taking up a new line of research, Juillard was turning the pages of a precious folio, sumptuously illustrated with Oriental engravings in colour.

After idly admiring the dazzling pages for a few minutes, Fogar had gone on his way without even arousing the attention of the profoundly absorbed thinker.

Now the book, haunting his memory, seemed to him made for the purpose he had in mind.

Unknown to Juillard he laid hold of the luxurious work. The illuminations contemplated at leisure, having aroused his curiosity, he went looking for Sirdah to know what the story was about.

The girl got Carmichael to read the not very abstruse text to her and was then able to give her brother the following summary of an Arabian tale entitled: *The Poet and the Morisco*.

Once upon a time, there lived in Baghdad a rich merchant named Shahnijar.

A man of refined taste, Shahnijar cultivated all the pleasures of life and was especially fond of art, women and good cheer.

It was the mission of the poet Ghiriz, whom the merchant had attached to his person, to compose many a gay or plaintive strophe and then sing what he had written to airs which he would improvise with the greatest charm.

Determined that life should seem rosy from the very moment of his awakening, Shahnijar insisted on Ghiriz singing him each day a morning serenade which should sweetly clear his brain of the pale shapes conjured up by even the fairest dreams.

Punctually at daybreak, the obedient poet each day went down into the splendid garden which surrounded his master's palace on all sides. Beneath the rich sleeper's windows, he took up his station near the marble basin of a fountain, from whose jade spout emerged a slender jet of water.

Raising to his lips a kind of speaking tube in dull metal, Ghiriz would then start to sing some elegy newly unfolded in his fertile imagination. The strange acoustical properties of the light trumpet were such that it sounded a lower third to each note of the song.

Thus the poet truly performed as it were a duet with himself and further increased the effect of his already impressive voice and words.

Soon Shahnijar, fully awake, would appear at the window with his favourite concubine, Neddu, the fair Morisco with whom he was madly infatuated.

259

Upon the instant, Ghiriz felt his heart beat with a violent agitation. He gazed with intoxication upon the divine Neddu, who, for her part, cast lingering looks of ardent love upon him.

The morning serenade over, the window closed, and, as he wandered beneath the blue sky, the poet's soul was filled with the dazzling but, alas, too fleeting vision. Ghiriz loved Neddu passionately and knew himself to be loved by her.

Each evening, Shahnijar, firm in his dilettantism and desirous of watching the sunset, set out with his favourite to climb a sandy mound with a magnificent view to the west.

From the top of this barren eminence, the affable merchant feasted his happy eyes upon the enchanting spectacle offered by the blood-red horizon.

Once the opulent ball of fire had quite vanished, Shahnijar and his companion went down again arm in arm, he eagerly anticipating the cunningly contrived dishes and carefully prepared drinks which should before long contribute to his jubilant sense of well-being.

Ghiriz awaited the moment of their retirement, then, finding himself alone, hastened to kiss with fervour the clearly defined imprints of Neddu's little feet in the soft sand.

Those were the poet's most intense moments of happiness, since he had no other means of communicating with the Morisco woman so jealously guarded by Shahnijar.

Weary at last of loving from afar without hope of closer meeting, Ghiriz went to consult Ku Ngan, a Chinaman who followed in Baghdad the dual profession of prophet and sorcerer.

Interrogated on the outcome of an affair hitherto so frustrated, Ku Ngan led Ghiriz into his garden, then released a great bird of prey which thereupon in its flight described increasingly large and majestical curves upon the air.

The Chinaman studied the evolutions of the powerful

winged creature and to the poet announced that his desires would not long go unfulfilled.

Called in, the bird came and perched on its master's shoulder. He, followed by Ghiriz, returned to his laboratory.

The Chinaman spread out before him a number of documents and, from what he read there, drew up certain instructions which the poet must follow to attain his goal.

In exchange for this work and as fee for consultation, Ghiriz paid the Chinaman in gold pieces.

Once outside, the poet made hopeful haste to decipher the wizard's screed.

What he found in it was the recipe for a culinary preparation, whose good smell itself should send Shahnijar into a deep and lasting sleep.

In addition, a magical formula had been clearly traced at the foot of the page.

Spoken aloud three times, this apparently incoherent succession of syllables would give to the dish itself, upon which the soporific comestibles were served, a crystalline sonority directly connected with the state of drowsiness in which the potentially embarrassing witness lay.

While the reverberation was strong and rapid, the two lovers could freely abandon themselves to their transports, without fear of a man deeply sunk in slumber.

A gradual *decrescendo*, the sign that he would presently awake, would give them adequate warning of the danger they ran.

That same evening, Ghiriz prepared the food in question and placed it on a chafing dish in the middle of the table copiously laid for his master.

At the sight of a new speciality set before him in unaccustomed fashion, the delighted Shahnijar raised up the dish in both hands to sniff voluptuously at the strange scents it gave off.

But, at once stricken with torpidity, he slid heavily to the floor, his head hanging and his eyes shut.

Ghiriz clearly enunciated his threefold incantation, and the dish, fallen back on to the table, gave out a powerful and quickly repeated ringing tone.

Hearing from her poet how effective the Chinaman's intervention had been, the fair Neddu trembled with pleasure and proposed a nocturnal outing in Shahnijar's immense garden.

The Morisco's faithful black slave Stingo was stationed beside the merchant, with instructions to warn the two lovers at the first sign of weakening resonance in the dish.

Confident in their sentinel's perfect devotion, Ghiriz and Neddu hastened away, without a care.

They spent a long night of intoxication in a very Eden of enchantment, amid flowers of the utmost rarity, then peacefully went to sleep at dawn, cradled by the murmuring of a waterfall.

The sun stood high in the heavens when Stingo came to alert them to the fact that the magical ringing had begun to grow weaker and must presently cease.

Startled to wakefulness and still full of voluptuous memories, the two lovers fearfully confronted the prospect of being separated again.

Neddu now thought only of shaking off Shahnijar's yoke and fleeing with Ghiriz.

A zebra suddenly appeared before the two, drawn by chance to this place in the course of its wanderings.

Frightened by the presence of unexpected creatures barring its way, the animal was about to retrace its steps.

But, upon an order from his mistress, the negro gave a leap and, seizing it by the nostrils, promptly mastered the courser.

Ghiriz had apprehended Neddu's thought, he quickly and

262

lightly bestrode the zebra, then helped his companion to climb up behind him.

Within a moment, the two fugitives, with a sign of farewell to Stingo, were galloping far away on their speedy mount. The Morisco, laughing at their poverty, waved before Ghiriz a purse containing one or two pieces of gold, sole provision against the cost of their venture. He, having only yesterday given his all to Ku Ngan, could add nothing to so modest a store.

Towards evening, at the end of its mad, unbroken course, the exhausted zebra collapsed in the midst of a dark forest.

Sure of having for the moment baffled pursuit, Ghiriz and Neddu sought means to appease a hunger made sharp by fatigue and whipping wind.

The two lovers divided the task between them. Ghiriz was to gather sweet fruits, whilst Neddu would look for some clear spring at which they might quench their thirst.

As a meeting place, they selected an ancient tree whose gigantic trunk was easily recognisable, and in the deepening twilight they departed severally on their foraging expedition.

After long search, now in one direction, now in another, Neddu found the wished-for stream.

The young woman meant to go back immediately, but, night having rapidly fallen, she more and more lost her way and, in a growing panic, wandered for hours without finding the huge tree for which she was looking.

Mad with grief, Neddu started to pray, vowing that she would fast ten days on end if she succeeded in meeting with Ghiriz.

Confronted and heartened by this impulse of feeling towards the Supreme Power, she walked on.

Not long afterwards, without knowing by what mysterious roundabout way, she suddenly found herself in the presence of Ghiriz, who, with haggard eye, not daring to leave the agreed meeting place, called and shouted repeatedly as he waited.

Neddu flung herself into the poet's arms, thanking Allah for his so prompt intervention.

Ghiriz showed her his harvest of fruits, but Neddu refused her share, explaining by what efficacious vow they had been restored to each other.

Next day, the two fugitives went their way on foot; in the night the zebra had broken loose from its bonds and made off.

For several days, the pair wandered without aim from village to village.

Neddu began to feel the tortures of hunger. Though in despair, Ghiriz dared not urge her to infringe her promise, afraid of bringing down upon her the wrath of Heaven.

On the tenth day, the young woman was so weak that she could barely walk even leaning upon the arm of her lover.

She suddenly reeled and fell inanimate to the ground.

At Ghiriz' cries for help, a woman who sold victuals from a roadside stall hurried towards them.

Feeling that death was about to remove his mistress from him, the poet took a rapid decision.

At his request, the eager market-woman brought a variety of foodstuffs, and Neddu, finally opening her eyes, delightedly ate her fill of this restoring food.

Endowed with new strength, the young woman set off once more on her way, to avoid the numerous emissaries whom the rich Shahnijar, whose passionate ardour she knew, had doubtless set forth on her tracks.

But she was a prey to constant uneasiness, troubled by remorse at having broken her fast before its intended term.

An encounter the following day augmented her fears, which of a sudden became more sharply defined in her mind.

She was accosted in open country by an evident madman who, gesticulating wildly, prophesied her impending fall from a dizzy height as a punishment for her perjury.

For some hours Ghiriz and Neddu remained unspeaking, painfully disturbed by this strange prophecy.

Towards evening, at a turn in the road, the young woman uttered a cry of terror, waving off with her hand some horrible vision. In front of her, innumerable eyes without body or face appeared two by two, staring at her with reproach and condemnation.

Moreover, beneath the fascination of their gaze, she was being drawn gradually toward the edge of the road, which overhung a bottomless abyss from which jagged rocks jutted.

Ghiriz remained unaware of the nature of his dear love's hallucination and could not understand her state of dread.

Then, without any possibility of him stretching out a hand to hold her, he saw Neddu dragged to the precipice's edge by some invisible power.

In her fall, the unhappy creature's body was flung from one rock to another, still threatened by those eyes which seemed to judge her for the insult to Divinity.

Ghiriz peered down into the gulf and, wishing to share the destiny of his beloved, with a great leap flung himself into the void.

Their two bodies fell dead side by side, united eternally in depths beyond human reach.


Fogar had listened attentively to Sirdah's narration.

The illuminated designs now took on for him a clear and unified significance, which decided him to use them as he had planned.

At the time of his inoffensive theft, the adolescent had, by way of precaution, removed, as well as the folio, an album for schoolboys each page of which showed the portrait of an animal with the Latin designation of the species underneath.

The coloured scenes from the Arabian tale being perhaps insufficiently numerous, this second work, in which each view was self-sufficient, offered a copious supplement capable of sustaining to the very end the spectacle needed by the plant.

Armed with the folio and the reserve album, Fogar waited for the propitious moment, now a conscious and forewarned observer.

When the moment came, he successively placed before the enormous white reed, whose atomic transformations he duly noted, all the Oriental prints disposed according to their order in the narrative.

This sequence completed, he opened the album, of which only a single page was recorded at the last moment.

The receptive phase being now over, the young man was able to conclude that his experiment had been perfectly successful, when he saw the images pass over the vegetable screen in sharp and delicate impression.

All that remained was to take care of the plant, destined to reproduce indefinitely the rare pictures which now formed part of itself.

Fogar secretly restored the two volumes to their places; Juillard engrossed in some new study, had not so much as suspected their momentary disappearance.

Possessing all the elements of his display, the lad found an ingenious method of co-ordinating them.

He decided to place everything together on his cot, so convenient to him for achieving the lethargic sleep which generated the blood clots.

Chènevillot endowed the bunk with the necessary appendages, carefully adapted to the special form of each particular animal or object.

The automatic variegation of the giant reed seemed designed to distract the spectators during the voluntary syncope, which had to be prolonged to the point of monotony.

Nevertheless, the first phase of the swoon offering a real attraction due to the gradual disappearance of life and breath, it would be a good thing to leave Fogar alone in the limelight up to the moment of total prostration at which he was like a corpse.

To this end, Chènevillot arranged the plant as a tester over the bed and placed over it an electric bulb with a powerful reflector.

The hour of approaching darkness being chosen for the experiment, the changing views could be made alternately dazzling or obscure at the obedient caprice of a current turned on or off.

Fogar, bent on doing everything himself, must alone control the lighting. But, during the lethargic somnolence, a complete rigidity of the limbs was necessary to bring on sanguine condensation. Chènevillot therefore submitted the electric current to the action of a horizontal spindle, ending in a sort of crutch-handle fitted to the sleeper's left armpit. Still lucid enough to perceive the onset of the first image, the youth could thus, with an imperceptible movement of his body, turn on the spotlight at the required moment.

A little alcove, provided with its own lighting, would serve to exhibit in all its details the inner structure of the bizarre and animated sponge.

When Chènevillot had finished his work, Fogar practised making his wet soap bounce on to the three ingots of gold clamped into firm supports at the foot of his bed.

He quickly acquired a marvellous skill at this difficult game, bringing off real feats of precision and balance.

Betweenwhiles he solicitously tended his plant.

Its root, treated with every care, now rested in an earthenware vessel attached to his cot. Regular watering maintained the vitality of its tissues, on which the unceasingly reborn imprints preserved all their sharpness.

# XVI

SINCE our arrival in Ejur, the Hungarian Skariofszky had been practising every day on his zither with its pure and disturbing sounds.

Buttoned up in his gipsy uniform which he never left off, the skilful virtuoso performed the most staggering pieces, which always filled the natives with admiration.

Each of his performances was followed by a numerous and attentive group of Ponukelians.

Irritated by this persistent audience, the great artist would have liked to find, for his work, a solitary and attractive retreat, where he might be free from importunate visitors.

Carrying his zither and the folding support on which it commonly stood, he reached the Behuliphruen, beneath whose lofty trees he penetrated at a lively pace without seeming to hesitate about the direction to be taken.

After marching no small distance, he stopped beside a spring in a picturesque and charming spot.

Skariofszky already knew this haunt of solitude and mystery; one day he had even attempted to bathe in the limpid stream, which flowed with a thousand reflections over bright micaceous rocks; but, to his surprise, he had not been able to overcome the resistance of the water, whose prodigious density forbade all penetration to any depth; getting down on his hands and knees, he had managed to cross the weighty river in all directions without wetting his body held above the surface.

This time paying no attention to the strange water-course, Skariofszky made haste to set up zither and support before a low rock on which he proposed to sit.

Installed before his instrument, the virtuoso began to play a slow Hungarian tune full of tenderness and languor.

After a few bars, though much occupied with the hither-and-thither of his light drumsticks, Skariofszky had the distinct visual impression of a slight movement being performed towards the river.

A rapid look showed him an enormous worm, which, rising from the water, began to creep along the verge.

Without breaking off, the *Tzigane,* with a series of furtive glances, watched the newcomer which gently approached the zither.

Coming to a halt beneath the stand, the worm coiled up without fear between the feet of the Hungarian, who, looking down, saw it motionless, flat on the ground.

Quickly forgetting the incident, Skariofszky went on with his practising, and for three long hours floods of harmony poured without respite from his poetical instrument.

When the evening came, the performer stood up at last; looking up at the clear sky free from all threat of rain, he decided to leave the zither where it was until the next session.

At the moment of leaving his retreat he noticed that the worm, returning on its tracks, was making for the edge of the bank to disappear presently into the depths of the river.

Next day, Skariofszky installed himself anew beside the extraordinary spring and began with a *valse-caprice* in slow time.

While he was going over the first repeat, the virtuoso's attention was somewhat distracted by the colossal worm, which, rising from the current, went straight to its post of the previous day and there remained gracefully coiled until the end of the musical performance.

On this occasion also, before withdrawing, Skariofszky was able to see that the inoffensive reptile, saturated with melody, had noiselessly slipped into the tranquil brook.

The same routine was followed on succeeding days. After the fashion of a snake-charmer, the Hungarian, by his talent, unfailingly attracted the melomaniacal worm, which once caught could no longer escape from its ecstasy.

The *Tzigane* took a lively interest in the reptile, whose confidence astonished him; one evening, when he had finished practising, he barred its way with his hand, meaning to make some attempt at taming it.

The worm, quite without signs of apprehensiveness, climbed up the fingers placed before it, then coiled itself several times round the Hungarian's wrist, while he progressively rolled up his sleeve.

Skariofszky was surprised by the formidable burden he now had to bear.

Adapted to the river water's dense environment, the worm, despite its pliancy, was enormously heavy.

This first experiment was followed by many others. The worm soon knew its master and obeyed his least call.

Such docility gave rise in the *Tzigane's* mind to a training scheme which might yield precious results.

It was a matter of leading the reptile itself to elicit sounds from the zither, by patiently developing its mysterious passion for the vibration of sound-waves in the air.

After much reflection, Skariofszky thought of a means of utilising the specific weight of the water inhabited by the worm.

The rocks in the river provided him with four sheets of solid yet transparent mica, which, trimmed and squared, then cemented together with clay, formed a receptacle adapted to the ends he envisaged. Two stout branches, vertically planted in the ground to either side of the zither, held between their forked extremities what was in effect a long, narrow trough, buddle, sluice-box or flume.

Skariofszky trained the worm to slip into this mica receptacle then, as it stretched out, to block up a groove cut along the lower groin.

Equipped with a gourd, it did not take him long to draw a few quarts of water from the spring and pour them into the transparent sluice.

Subsequently, with the end of a twig, he lifted, for a quarter of a second, a minute portion of the extended body.

A drop of water escaped and struck a zither string which gave out a clear note.

The experiment, further conducted a number of times at points nearby, produced a succession of notes in the form of a *ritornello*.

Suddenly the same musical phrase was repeated by the worm, which itself made way for the liquid drops by a series of twitches executed without fault at the points required.

Never would Skariofszky have dared to count on such immediate understanding. His task now seemed at once easy and profitable.

Bar by bar he taught the worm various lively or melancholy Hungarian tunes.

The gipsy began by using his twig to teach the reptile, which then without help reproduced the piece called for.

Seeing water drip inside the zither by two sound-holes, Skariofszky, with a pin, made an imperceptible hole in the base of the instrument, to let out the excess liquid in a fine cascade.

It was replaced occasionally from the river close by, and the work proceeded without hindrance.

In due course, as his ambition grew, the Hungarian, a twig in each hand, wanted to obtain two notes at a time.

The worm at once lending itself to this further demand, the pieces for zither, invariably based on the often simultaneous striking of two hammers, could all be undertaken.

Determined to appear at the gala no longer as a performer but as an animal-trainer, the *Tzigane*, for several days, settled down with enthusiasm to his work of education.

In the end, multiplying the difficulties, he tied a long twig to each of his ten fingers and taught the worm polyphonic acrobatics normally excluded from his own repertory.

Thenceforth assured of worthily exhibiting the astounding reptile, Skariofszky sought diverse means of perfecting his apparatus in other ways.

At his request, Chènevillot replaced with a double fitting in metal, attached to the zither stand itself, the two forked branches which had till then held the mica receptacle in place.

Felts were also placed on the instrument in such a way as to exercise a partially muting effect on the resounding shock of the heavy drops of water.

To avoid inundating Trophies Square, an earthenware pot with a padded spout was to collect the slight overflow from the base of the zither.

These preparations completed, Skariofszky put the final touches to the worm's education, as, daily, at the first note of the zither, it emerged from the dense river, to be expeditiously thrust back into it by the Hungarian himself at the close of the day's work.

# XVII

OF all the Emperor's sons, Rhejed, aged twelve, was the most boisterous and full of mischief.

He spent his time inventing countless fantastic games, often wild enough to endanger his life.

The Behuliphruen, habitual scene of his exploits, provided him with many ways of satisfying his high-spirited moods.

Sometimes the agile piccaninny would climb a huge tree to collect birds' nests from its topmost branches; sometimes he would throw stones at birds or quadrupeds, for which he also set ingenious snares.

One day, as he came to a small clearing, Rhejed noticed a rodent with red fur, sniffing the wind as though uncertain of its way.

The child had in his hand a stout stick recently cut from a bush. With one stroke of this primitive weapon he felled the rodent, which lay on its side in the middle of the clearing.

Approaching, Rhejed observed an abundant spittle running from the jaws of the dead creature and giving off an unusual, prodigiously strong odour; sickened by the spectacle, he crossed the open space and went on his way.

Hearing a sudden, violent beating of wings, he looked round and saw a formidable bird of prey with long, wader's legs, which, after circling, swooped down beside the rodent.

Rhejed turned back with the idea of killing the winged creature, already pecking at the dead rodent.

Meaning to take careful aim at the vulnerable head, he approached silently from in front while the bird's neck was lowered.

To his surprise the child noticed above the beak two olfactory orifices, which, doubtless struck at a distance by the smell of the curious slaver, had apprised the bird impatient for food and of, then guided it to, the promised feast.

Still armed with his long stick, Rhejed leaped forward and struck the bird sharply on the back of the head, so that it fell without a cry.

But, seeking to inspect his new victim at closer quarters, the child felt as though riveted to the ground by an invincible force.

His right foot rested on a flat, heavy stone covered by the rodent's slobber.

This substance, already half dry, formed an irresistibly powerful glue, and Rhejed was able to disengage his bare foot only by violent effort and at the cost of deep and painful sores. Fearing to be caught again, the young rascal, once free, thought only of getting away quickly from the dangerous spot.

A moment later, the sound of quivering wings made him turn his head, and he observed in the air a second winged creature of the same species, which, advised by the ever more penetrating smell, sped to the tempting quarry.

Rhejed thereupon conceived a bold plan, based at once on the adhesive properties of the extraordinary spittle and on the evident perturbation caused by the smell it exhaled to the members of a powerfully winged clan.

Recently trodden grasses showed him the way the doomed rodent had come.

At a point on this track, likely to be followed before long by animals of the same race, Rhejed dug a small trench which light branches hid completely.

Next day, delighted with the success of his trap, the child drew out of the narrow excavation, and carried away living to his hut, a rodent with reddish fleece exactly like the first.

Fired to emulation by Fogar's projects, the venturesome Rhejed wished to add drama to the gala by causing himself to be lifted up into the air by one of the birds with distended nostrils in the Behuliphruen.

The rodent, killed at the last moment, would provide a copious slaver which, attracting the winged creature by its emanations, would further serve in quickly putting together a form of aerial harness.

To this end, a flat object was needed, suitable for collecting the animal glue, which, merely spilt on the ground, would have remained unusable.

Rhejed, exploring the wreckage of the *Lynceus,* found a light cupboard door very well adapted to his intentions.

The child explained his plan only in part, keeping to himself, for fear of the inevitable paternal *veto,* all that related to his journey into the azure.

# XVIII

I T was two months since Seil Kor had departed, and we awaited his return with some impatience, for, the gala preparations being complete, we felt that boredom, till then kept at bay by work or speculation, would soon assail us again.

Fortunately, a quite unexpected happening came to offer us distraction enough.

One evening, Sirdah recounted to us a serious incident which had taken place that very day.

Towards three o'clock, an ambassador from King Yaour, crossing the Tez in a dug-out, had been admitted to the hut of Talu, to whom he brought good tidings : the sovereign of Drelshkaf, informed about what was afoot in Ejur, was obsessed by a fervent wish to hear the Emperor sing falsetto clad in his magnificent costume; he agreed unconditionally to Sirdah's cure if the blind girl's father would in his presence appear on the Incomparables stage and sing Darricelli's *Aubade* in a woman's voice.

Flattered by this request and delighted at the thought of restoring sight to his daughter at such little cost, Talu had already begun to answer in the affirmative, when Gaïz Duh— that was the negro ambassador's name—came a few steps closer and offered secret revelations in a low voice. The pretended desire so ardently professed was merely a ruse whereby Yaour hoped to penetrate freely into Ejur at the head of a numerous retinue. Familiar with Talu's vanity and

277

knowing beforehand that his redoubtable neighbour would want to impress him by receiving him in the midst of his troops, the king intended to trap the enemy forces in the relatively confined space of Trophies Square. While the Ejurian populace, drawn there by the ceremony, crowded about the outskirts of the parade, the Drelshkaffian army would cross the Tez by a rapidly improvised bridge of canoes, then spread out to form a human girdle about the capital, thereafter invading the square from all sides at once during the performance. At the same moment, Yaour would give his retinue the order to attack, and the Ponukelian warriors, pressed together as in a vice, would be massacred by their fiery aggressors, among whose many advantages would be that of surprise. Master of the situation, Yaour would be proclaimed Emperor, having reduced Talu and all his line to slavery.

Thus without remorse did Gaïz Duh betray his master, who rewarded his services poorly and sometimes brutally. In the matter of recompense for his information, he relied on Talu's generosity.

Determined to profit by the warning, the Emperor dismissed Gaïz Duh with the mission of inviting King Yaour the following day at sunset. Scenting in advance a splendid reward, the ambassador went away full of hope, while Talu revolved in his head a scheme of defence and attack.

Next day, by order of the Emperor, half the Ponukelian troops concealed themselves among the trees and shrubs in the Behuliphruen, while the rest disposed themselves in small groups among huts in the more southerly parts of Ejur.

At the appointed hour, Yaour and his escort led by Gaïz Duh, standing upright in ten or more dug-out canoes, crossed the Tez.

Positioned on the right bank, Rao, Mossem's successor, watched them disembark; he conducted the king to Trophies Square, where Talu awaited him without weapons, tricked out in his feminine rig and surrounded only by a handful of defenders.

As he arrived, Yaour glanced about him and seemed disturbed by the absence of the warriors he counted on trapping. Talu marched before him, and the two monarchs exchanged some few observations, which Sirdah, remaining with us, translated in a whisper.

In the first place, Yaour, vainly bent on dissimulating his uneasiness, enquired whether he should not enjoy the good fortune of seeing the fine Ponukelian troops, whose pride and daring were so vaunted abroad. Talu replied that his guest was a few moments early and that the warriors, at present still adorning themselves for the occasion, would soon appear on parade to heighten its importance by their presence. Reassured by this announcement, but fearful of having aroused the Emperor's suspicions by an imprudent question, Yaour then affected a concern with various trivialities. He displayed extravagant admiration for Talu's accoutrements, expressing a passionate desire to possess some costume of the same kind.

At these words, the Emperor, seeking a way to gain time until the arrival of the enemy forces, turned abruptly to our party and, through the intermediary of Sirdah, ordered us to find in our baggage a costume analogous to his own.

Accustomed to playing Goethe's *Faust* on her tours, Adinolfa speedily ran off and before long returned, bearing her Marguerite robe and wig over her arm.

At the sight of the gift he was offered, Yaour beamed and exclaimed. Casting his weapons on the ground, he was able, without difficulty, being extremely thin, to get into the dress, which was hooked up over his loin-cloth; then, placing the flaxen wig with its two long plaits on his head, he strutted majestically, appearing truly overjoyed at the effect of his fantastic disguise.

But a great clamour was suddenly heard outside, and Yaour, scenting some betrayal, hurriedly picked up his arms and ran off with his retainers. Gaïz Duh alone, prepared to fight in the ranks of his enemies, joined the Ponukelian warriors, who, behind Talu and Rao, hastened after the king. Immediately, drawn by the stirring spectacle in preparation, our party set off at a run in the same direction and before long reached the southern tip of Ejur.

We quickly saw what had taken place. The Drelshkaffian army, in accordance with the royal decision, had crossed the Tez by canoe bridge; as the last man set foot on the right bank, Talu's bands, signalling to each other with cries, had emerged from the huts of Ejur and the thickets of the Behuliphruen and closed in on the enemy from all sides, profitably employing the tactics imagined by Yaour. Already the ground was strewn with Drelshkaffian dead and wounded, and the Emperor's troops seemed assured of victory.

Yaour, still rigged out in his gown and wig, had bravely flung himself into the thick of the fighting beside his forces. Armed with a spear, Talu, his train over his left arm, rushed at him and a strange duel ensued between the two monarchs in carnival dress. The King at first succeeded in warding off a series of blows, but presently the Emperor, following up a cunning feint, pierced his opponent deeply to her heart.

At once discouraged by the death of their chief, the decimated Drelshkaffians gave themselves up and were led off to Ejur as prisoners.

Apart from that of Yaour, all the dead bodies were cast into the Tez, which occupied itself with carrying them out to sea.

# XIX

SHORTLY before Talu's victory, an astonishing item of news had spread to Ejur; it concerned the presence in Yaour's company of a European couple consisting of a young woman and her brother brought to the far side of the Tez by chance during a piece of exploration.

The brother seemed to be rather a background figure, but the woman traveller, beautiful and captivating, boldly proclaimed her liaison with Yaour upon whom her charm and allure had at once produced their full impression.

After the battle, Talu caused the two strangers to be brought before him, granting them freedom of movement until such time as their fate should be firmly decided.

The woman explorer—a Frenchwoman called Louise Montalescot—quickly established relations with us and, happy to find herself among countrymen of hers, recounted to us the chain of events which had led her with her brother to this remote African territory.

Of humble origins, Louise had been born in the suburbs of Paris. Her father, employed in a pottery works, earned his living by modelling vases and other receptacles; his work showed a true sculptor's talent, about which the worthy man displayed no trace of vanity.

Louise had a younger brother, the object of her warmest affection. Norbert—that was the youngster's name—practised from earliest childhood under his father's instruction and achieved a remarkable facility in modelling fine statuettes in the form of flasks and candlesticks.

Sent out early to school, Louise displayed a remarkable capacity for study; doing very well in examinations, she won a scholarship to a girls' high school and was thus able to pass on to greater things. At twenty, equipped with all her certificates, she made a good living by giving lessons and was able to perfect herself in all branches of science and letters. Consumed by a passion for fruitful toil, she regretted the time she had to spend in sleeping and eating.

Particularly fanatical in her devotion to chemistry, she keenly pursued, during the long night watches, an important discovery long germinating in her mind. The problem was to generate, by purely photographic means, a motor force sufficiently precise to guide a pencil or brush with certainty. Already Louise was within sight of her goal; but she still lacked a particular essential oil till then undiscovered. On Sundays she went out botanising in the woods around Paris, vainly searching for the unknown plant which should complete her mixture.

Reading in the accounts of exploration wonderful descriptions of tropical flora, the girl dreamed of wandering through the burning regions of central Africa, certain that, amid that unparalleled vegetation, her slender chances of success must be a hundred times greater.

In order to divert her mind from this fixed idea, Louise worked day by day on a short, illustrated botanical treatise, a popular work designed to show the astonishing variety of the vegetable kingdom. She quickly finished this little work, of which a great many copies were printed and sold, thus giving her a small fortune.

Finding herself in possession of this unexpected sum, the girl now thought only of undertaking the expedition so ardently desired.

But, for some time past, she had been feeling discomfort in her right lung—a painful and persistent tightness and a sensation of being unable to drive out an accumulation of air. Wishing to take authoritative advice before setting out on her travels, she went to see Dr. Renesme, whose famous works on diseases of the chest she had read and admired.

The great specialist was struck by the peculiarity of the case. An internal tumour had formed in Louise's lung, and the poor physical condition of the affected part prevented full expulsion of the air she breathed in.

According to Renesme, the infection was undoubtedly due to certain harmful gases the girl had absorbed during the course of her chemical experiments.

It became urgently necessary to create an artificial escape for the air, since, without such a precaution, the tumour was bound to grow indefinitely. Moreover, the respiratory system must be provided with some kind of sounding apparatus whereby its healthy functioning might be in evidence at all times—the least obstruction at any point being likely to cause irreparable progress of the extumescence.

Admirably endowed from a physical point of view, Louise, despite the seriousness of her character, was not wholly exempt from a certain coquetry. In despair at Renesme's revelation, she sought means to make the surgical instrument, hence-forward to form part of her person, as aesthetically pleasing as might be.

Taking as a pretext her imminent departure for perilous regions, she resolved to adopt male attire, as more convenient and comfortable during the hardships of an explorer's life.

She decided on an officer's uniform; she could then make the sounding tubes look like the aglets of a shoulder-knot, imitating the subterfuge by which the ear trumpets of deaf persons may be concealed in umbrella frames or the handles of fans.

Renesme lent himself gladly to the gratification of this whim and constructed his apparatus accordingly.

The operation was a complete success; the tumour, situated in the lower part of the lung, was made to communicate with the air outside by means of a narrow aperture, to which was fitted a rigid tube subdivided into several hollow, resonant tagged points.

Thanks to the beneficent action of this valve, Louise was thenceforward able to lead without fear a life of toil and fatigue. Each night she had to close the aperture with a metal plug, after having removed the apparatus, which lost its utility during the calm, regular breathing of sleep.

When she first saw herself in her officer's uniform, the girl was somewhat consoled for her sad misadventure. She found the new costume very becoming and was able to admire the effect of her splendid fair hair, which she allowed to fall in natural curls below the small forage cap worn jauntily over one ear.

Even at times when she was most actively engrossed in her studies, Louise had never neglected her brother Norbert.

She had become yet more tenderly attentive to him after the demise of their parents, who had both died during the course of a terrible winter productive of fatal epidemics.

Norbert now occupied his father's position at the pottery works and turned his hand wonderfully to the rapid execution of all kinds of figurines full of life and grace. Apart from this very real talent, the young man lacked intelligence and was altogether under the admirable influence of his sister.

Louise wanted to share her sudden affluence with Norbert; she therefore resolved that he should accompany her on her grand voyage.

The girl had recently taken an interest in a tame magpie found in curious circumstances. Her first sight of the bird had been one Sunday, out in the woods at Charville. Noon had just struck distantly, and Louise, after a tiring botanical ramble, had sat down at the foot of a tree for a frugal meal. Suddenly a bold and greedy magpie hopped towards her, as if looking for bread crumbs, which were at once thrown to it in abundance. The bird, filled with gratitude, approached yet closer without fear, allowing the lady bountiful to stroke it and pick it up. Touched by this confiding sympathy, she took the bird home and began its education. Presently the magpie came at her least call to perch on its mistress's shoulder and carried its obedience so far as to fetch in its beak whatever small object she pointed to.

Louise was now too attached to her winged comrade to accept the idea of abandoning it to the care of a paid keeper She therefore had the bird with her the day when, full of exuberant optimism, she took the express to Marseilles in company with her brother.

Brought to Porto Novo by a rapid steamship, brother and sister quickly recruited a small white escort and set off southward. Louise's plan was to reach the Vorrh, mentioned in several volumes of exploration; it was there in particular that her imagination discovered beforehand every kind of vegetable prodigy.

Her hope was not deceived when after long hardships she came to the imposing virgin forest. At once she began her researches, overjoyed on seeing almost at every step, in the form of flower or plant, some new and unknown treasure.

Before her departure, Louise had compounded a corrosive liquid able to facilitate her task. A drop of this chemical solution, poured on any vegetable matter, was bound to reveal, by partial combustion accompanied by a light smoke, the undoubted presence of the desired essential oil.

Despite the infinite variety of specimens accumulated in the Vorrh, continually repeated trials proved vain. For many days Louise courageously pursued her labour, pushing ever farther beneath the magnificent foliage. Sometimes, perceiving on a tree some curious and enticing leaf, she would point it out to the magpie, who picked it with his beak and brought it to her.

The whole Vorrh was thus crossed from north to south without result. Louise, in despair, was making her usual experiment only in the most purely mechanical way when suddenly a drop of her preparation, poured on a new plant only to salve her conscience, induced the brief combustion so long vainly sought.

The girl experienced a minute's intoxication which compensated her for all her past disappointments. She made an abundant picking of the precious small, reddish plant, whose seeds, cultivated under heat, were to yield her future supplies.

It was at nightfall that the traveller had made her memorable discovery; they made camp where they had halted, and everyone lay down to sleep, after a solid meal during which all was decided for a prompt return to Porto Novo.

But the following day, on awakening, Louise and Norbert found themselves alone. Their companions had betrayed them, taking away, after cutting through its straps, a satchel, always carried across her back by the girl, whose many compartments contained a considerable weight of gold and notes. Planning to avoid prosecution, the wretches had waited until they reached the farthest point, thus removing all chance of return from the two left without provisions.

Louise did not propose to attempt the impossible by seeking to regain Porto Novo; she marched, on the contrary, to the south, hoping to reach some native village from which she might get herself repatriated on the promise of a ransom.

She gathered an abundant supply of fruits and presently emerged from the Vorrh, having crossed the huge forest without encountering any sign of Velbar or Sirdah, soon to be driven from their retreat by the great fire.

After some hours on the march, Louise was stopped by the Tez, whose course, some way from Ejur, turned sharply towards the north. At that moment, the trunk of a tree appeared floating downstream. At a sign from his sister, Norbert grabbed at the long piece of wreckage, and, using a stout branch as a stern-oar, the two exiles succeeded in crossing the river, installed in reasonable comfort on the wet bark. The girl had gladly seized this opportunity of putting a barrier between her and her guides, who, perhaps regretting that they had spared their victims, might yet return to kill them.

From this point onward, brother and sister kept to the left bank of the Tez and thus fell into the hands of Yaour, whom the beauty of Louise disturbed profoundly.

In the course of her studies, the girl had mixed in a world of men and women students whose advanced views had left their mark on her; she freely advertised her scorn for certain social conventions and even went so far as to preach free love. Yaour, young and of imposing countenance, exercised a powerful attraction on a mind so given to the unknown. Now, according to her ideas, two people drawn to each other by a reciprocal impulse ought not to be restrained by any prejudice. Proud and happy at the romantic side of the adventure, she gave herself unreservedly to the alien king whose passion had been kindled at the first glance.

All plans for repatriation were adjourned by this unexpected event.

At the time of their treacherous desertion in the heart of the Vorrh, the guides had left a further bag whose contents, useless to them but infinitely precious to Louise, consisted of numerous objects and ingredients connected with the great photographic discovery till then incomplete.

The young woman took up her work again with ardour, no longer doubtful of success now that she possessed the formerly unavailable essential oil extracted from the red plants in the virgin forest.

As she finished her story, Louise freely avowed to us the violent grief caused her by the death of the unfortunate Yaour, of whom the glowing remembrance could not fail to remain with her for life.

# XX

THE day after his victory, the Emperor sent Sirdah to us charged with a complicated mission.

Talu, who to the functions of a sovereign joined those of a religious leader, had to crown himself king of Drelshkaf, a title to which his recent success gave him the right.

Now, the monarch meant to raise the prestige of this signal proclamation by making it coincide with the gala of the Incomparables.

Wishing to impress his subjects, he further requested us to suggest to him some grandiose tradition in use among white people.

Juillard at once called to mind the holy *ampulla* and offered his services in drawing up in advance all the necessary details on the manner of administering the consecrated oil. At the same time, Chènevillot spoke of setting up a small altar on the north side of Trophies Square.

This first question settled, Sirdah continued with the statement of her petition.

Yaour IX, having no kin descended from Yaour I, his death marked the final extinction of his race.

To embellish the crowning ceremony and affirm the incontestable rights of the Talus, the emperor wished to exhibit some form of genealogical document upon which, taking Suan as its point of departure, the annihilation of the rival branch might be strikingly emphasised.

Very proud of his European origins, the Emperor insisted on the inclusion in the projected document of the ancient portrait, piously transmitted from father to son in the Talu line, representing the two Spanish sisters, wives of Suan.

Juillard gladly undertook to draw up this dynastic instrument, destined to figure upon the altar which Chènevillot had already erected in his mind.

Apart from these various details, a curious extra part was to be played by the unfortunate Yaour's body itself.

The spear with which the Emperor had struck the dead king had been smeared at the point, like many Ponukelian weapons, with a violent poison which, while ensuring immediate death, also possessed the remarkable property of keeping the tissues from immediate putrefaction.

Thus the body of the conquered leader could, even after a considerable delay, be placed on the occasion of the solemnities beneath the decayed rubber tree formerly dedicated to the race of the Yaours.

To the Emperor's mind, this humiliation of the accursed plant called, by contrast, for a proud badge of honour to be placed on the palm later planted by Talu IV.

The sign-painter Toresse was picked to compose a commemorative inscription recalling the already remote restoration, whose date coincided exactly with that of the tree's genesis.

Sirdah informed us at the same time that coronation day would be marked by the punishment of all the guilty, whose executioner was to be Rao.

Gaïz Duh, whose demand for a handsome reward had elicited from the Emperor only the reply: ' You are a traitor, and you will be punished as a traitor,' was to have his head cut off with the edge of an axe made of a special wood as resistant as iron and calculated to avoid all effusion of blood.

Rul would perish by the long gold pins which she had worn for so many years in her hair; their points would pierce her flesh through the eyelets of the red corset, now reduced to a rag by long use.

For Jizme, the Emperor, whose imagination had reached the end of its resources, asked us to suggest some penalty in use in our own lands. Chènevillot then had an idea which, while sparing the condemned all suffering, had the further advantage of putting off her death to a date perhaps remote. Among his supplies, the architect possessed a lightning conductor of the latest model, which he had destined for Baron Ballesteros. It would be easy, when the next storm approached, to connect Jizme to the apparatus's conducting rod and so cause her to be electrocuted by the clouds. Now, bad weather was uncommon in Ejur, and some unexpected happening, capable of setting the victim free, might very well precede the earliest flash of lightning to come.

The industrious Naïr's life was to be spared because of the useful traps he made for destroying mosquitoes. However, for the author of the illustrated letter addressed to Jizme, mere captivity without further torment, constituting, it seemed, too mild a chastisement, Talu wished to have erected, at the side of Trophies Square, a plinth on which could be fixed the snare set one evening by Seil Kor. Doomed to perpetual immobility and with barely room to lie down and sleep, Naïr, his foot caught in the loop which had already once proved fatal to him, would toil without respite at the putting together of his frail contrivances. To add mental suffering to the crippling physical constraint, the bowler hat, the suede glove and the letter with its little drawings, the instruments of his ridiculous misadventure, would be permanently set before his eyes.

So that the minor parts should all be filled at his coronation,

Talu further demanded a small prison, from which the condemned, living proofs of his absolute power, should be made to witness his triumph.

After her account of this baleful news, Sirdah imparted to us a happy event equally appointed for gala day. This was to be her own cure effected by the witch-doctor Bashku, now under the authority of Talu. In his impatience, the Emperor had wanted to take his daughter to the skilful operating surgeon on the very evening of the battle of the Tez. But Sirdah had not wished to recover her sight on a day sullied by the shedding of so much blood. She preferred to keep this supplementary joy for the date of the coronation, already marked by the signal glorification of her father.

A few words concerning the Montalescots ended Sirdah's commission.

In the eyes of the Emperor, Louise had deserved the ultimate penalty by the sole fact of her amorous liaison with the mortal enemy of whom all memory was to be destroyed. Talu even went as far as to include the inoffensive Norbert in the hatred inspired in him by anything which, near or far, had met with favour from Yaour. But Sirdah, opportunely, had whetted her father's curiosity by telling him about the great discovery on which the young woman was bent; desirous of seeing the projected apparatus at work, Talu had agreed to postpone judgement on the student, who might freely pursue her work.

A week sufficed Chènevillot to complete his new contract. On the north side of Trophies Square rose a small altar, approached by several broad steps; facing it, to the south, extended a prison for the condemned, and, not far from the Incomparables stage, stood a wooden plinth, fitted with all the required accessories, upon which Naïr was immediately installed.

Particularly delighted with the idea of causing Jizme to perish by a spark from heaven, Talu had concurred heartily in Chènevillot's plan. Informed of the end which awaited her, the unfortunate girl had obtained from the Emperor two last favours; that of dying upon the white mat covered with drawings which her lover had formerly given her, and that of wearing about her neck, at the fatal instant, a card showing three phases of the moon, which, evoking the days of her brilliant receptions, would remind her in her distress of that period of all-powerful splendour.

Chènevillot had made use of the mat in question in arranging an electrocutionary contrivance which only lightning should activate.

# XXI

T HE Montalescots quickly became accustomed to their new abode. Louise zealously occupied herself with her extraordinary discovery, while Norbert eagerly explored the Behuliphruen or the right bank of the Tez.

The tame magpie, still faithful, roused everyone's admiration by its devotion and intelligence; the bird, making further progress every day, carried out with marvellous exactitude the most various orders issued by its mistress.

One day, wandering beside the Tez, Norbert's attention was caught by the extreme malleability of a moist yellow earth, of which he at once laid in a supply. The young man was thenceforward able to occupy his leisure in modelling, with his habitual facility, charming statuettes deliciously posed, which, once dried in the sun, took on the consistency and the appearance of terracotta. Talu, manifestly interested in these artistic labours, seemed to be turning over in his mind some project which a fortuitous circumstance was indeed about to bring to fruition.

During our sojourn in Ejur, we had not gone altogether short of butcher's meat, a stock of animals having been embarked on the *Lynceus* to be slaughtered in the course of our journey. Thanks to the parsimony of the ship's cook, who had been careful of his precious supplies, a few calves still remained to undergo the fate of their companions. The provident fellow finally decided to break into this group of

294

survivors and one evening served up for dinner, together with appetising slices of the first victim, a dish of calf's lights delicately seasoned. Talu, who out of instinctive curiosity had always shown himself partial to our European dishes, carefully tasted this last concoction, of which he at once begged to know the source and the natural appearance.

Next day, Sirdah, in great distress, came to us from her father, upon whose painful instructions she offered us no little commentary of her own.

As she saw it, Talu execrated Louise, whose image was always associated in his mind with that of Yaour. Brother and sister were confused in the same feeling of mad aversion, and the Emperor would grant them a double *exeat* only in exchange for impracticable marvels, whose details he had laboriously worked out with every refinement of cruelty and malice.

Among the crates and bales disgorged by the *Lynceus* when it was wrecked, there was a consignment of toys addressed to a merchant in Buenos Aires. Talu had had every item, all new to him, shown to him in detail, taking a particular interest in the mechanical toys, which he loved to wind up himself. He had taken a special fancy to a model railway which delighted him by the marvellous way in which its rolling stock could be made to run this way or that about a complicated network of rails easily taken to pieces. It was this amusing invention which had in part suggested to him the idea whose details Sirdah now recounted to us.

Inspired by his dinner the previous evening, Talu demanded from poor Norbert a life-sized statue, engaging in subject and light enough to travel, without damaging them, on two plain rails made of that same insubstantial matter so well prepared by the ship's cook last night. It addition, without this time mentioning their weight, the emperor required three works of sculpture, more or less elaborately jointed, whose mechanism could be set in motion only by the magpie with its beak or claws.

If these conditions were met, and if the apparatus which Louise hoped to complete worked satisfactorily, brother and sister were then assured of their freedom and might thereafter join the rest of us on our way to Porto Novo.

Despite the extreme rigour of what was exacted, Louise, without yielding to despondency, saw that it was her duty to guide and encourage Norbert.

The problem was, in the first place, to find a material at once light, flexible and resistant, from which a statue could be made almost without weight.

A search was made among the baggage taken from our ship, and Louise soon uttered a cry of joy on discovering several large packages stuffed with corset whalebones of a uniform black. Inspecting the labels, we saw that dispatch had been made by a firm in liquidation, which had doubtless parted with much reserve stock at a reduction to some American manufacturer.

Too much being at stake to allow room for any scruple, Louise took possession of the merchandise, ready to indemnify the consignee later.

To select an engaging subject, as demanded by the emperor, the young woman had only to dip into a memory copiously furnished by much reading. She recalled an anecdote told by Thucydides in his *History of the Peloponnesian War*, when in a preliminary sketch the illustrious chronicler is comparing the Athenian with the Spartan character.

This is in substance the classical tale so often translated by succeeding generations of schoolboys.

A rich Lacedaemonian called Ktenas had in his service a large number of helots.

Instead of despising these slaves reduced by his fellow citizens to beasts of burden, Ktenas thought only how to raise their moral and intellectual level by education. His noble and humanitarian purpose was to make them his equals, and, in order to compel the laziest of them to study with zeal, he had recourse to the severest punishments, not fearing on occasion to exercise his right of life and death.

The most recalcitrant of the group was unquestionably a certain Saridakis, who, as ill-endowed as he was apathetic, allowed all his comrades to out-distance him without shame.

Despite the harshest chastisement, Saridakis made no progress, vainly spending hour after hour over the simple conjugation of auxiliary verbs.

Ktenas saw in this manifestation of total incapacity an occasion for bringing home a terrible lesson to his pupils.

He gave Saridakis three days to commit the verb

$$\mathring{\eta}\delta\tau o\nu$$
$$\mathring{\eta}\delta\tau\eta\nu$$

finally to memory. At the end of this period, the helot, in front of all his schoolfellows, would recite his lesson to Ktenas, whose hand armed with a dagger would at the slightest fault strike the guilty one to the heart.

Knowing for certain that his master would keep his terrible promise, Saridakis, racking his brains, made heroic efforts to prepare himself for the final test.

On the appointed day, Ktenas, calling his slaves together, stood close to Saridakis, directing the point of his blade at the unfortunate man's breast. The scene was short; the pupil made a gross mistake in the dual of the aorist, and a heavy blow sounded at once amid the anguished silence. The helot, pierced through the heart, turned a moment upon himself and fell dead at the feet of his inexorable judge.

Without hesitation, Louise adopted this moving story as her model.

Following his sister's indications, Norbert succeeded in building up, with the horny, flexible baleens, a light statue mounted on wheels. The nails and tools necessary to this work were provided by Chènevillot, who himself constructed a carefully balanced tipping platform on which the delicate, fragile rails could be laid at the last moment. To finish off the work, full of impressive vigour, Louise traced on the black plinth in large white letters, an explanatory title, above the famous dual murmured by the expiring lips of the helot.

The mobile effigies ordered by the emperor now required three further subjects.

The enthusiastic Louise was a great admirer of Kant, the portraits of whom remained distinct in her mind. Under her eyes Norbert modelled a bust of the celebrated philosopher, being careful to hollow out the interior and so leave at the top of the head only a thin layer of clay. Chènevillot placed inside the skull an arrangement of electric bulbs with powerful reflectors, whose light should represent the genial warmth of some luminous thought.

Louise's next inspiration was an old and touching Breton legend about the celebrated and heroic lie told by the nun Perpetua, who fearlessly risked her life in refusing to hand over to the myrmidons of the law two fugitives who had taken refuge in her convent.

In this case Norbert had to model a whole group with art and patience.

Finally, the young man, docile instrument of his sister's instructions, evoked the regent d'Orléans bowing low before Louis XV; the studious girl loved the antithesis implied by this humble mark of respect paid to a child by the most powerful figure in the realm.

Each of these works was provided with a simple mechanism, specifically adapted to the beak and claws of the magpie, which required more training in this matter than had been expected.

These new tasks were indeed far more complicated than the insignificant parlour tricks so far acquired by the bird. The movements had to be performed in sequence without signals or other guidance, and the winged creature did not find it easy to commit to memory so varied and precise a series of manoeuvres. Norbert helped his sister with this piece of training, upon which so much hung.

Meanwhile Louise actively pursued her work in chemistry, whose final operations called for premises fitted up in a very special manner from the point of view of lighting.

At her request, Chènevillot built a tiny cabinet whose walls did not admit the slightest chink of light.

A highly attenuated yellowish light alone could be admitted to the centre of the laboratory; any sort of tinted glass, however much darkened and opaque, could not fail to produce disastrous reflections on the strange sensitive plate in preparation.

The solution of the problem was provided by Juillard, who had been present at Louise's discussions with the architect.

Among the volumes in his large trunks, the scholar possessed a rare copy of *The Fair Maid of Perth,* a first edition of this famous work. Its pages more than a century old were completely yellow and would serve to filter and dull the blinding light of the African sun.

Despite the inestimable price of this extremely rare volume, Juillard did not hesitate to offer it to the student, who, finding it perfectly adapted to her needs, warmly thanked its donator.

Chènevillot cut out the pages in the form of tiles, which, overlapping and imbricated in thickness and held in place by thin woodwork, formed the upper part of the little cell. A sliding panel contrived in this light roofing would allow the prisoner to take a breath of fresh air from time to time after carefully covering her various implements and ingredients. Prudence being, because of the gravity of the circumstances, far more important than comfort, it was through this solitary opening that Louise would effect her entries and exits, by means of two small step-ladders made by the architect for this purpose. The least infiltration of light would jeopardise the work's success, and a panel in the roof would lend itself better than any lateral doorway to an hermetical closure guaranteed by its own weight.

The cabinet had been built in Trophies Square, not far from the stock exchange, from which it was separated by Norbert's statues carefully aligned. Before putting the roof in place, Chènevillot had arranged the interior, which contained one of the step-ladders, a light chair and a table bearing the equipment necessary to the marvellous discovery.

Louise thereafter spent the greater part of her time shut up in her laboratory, among her chemicals, her dishes and her plants; her moments of leisure were employed in perfecting the training of the magpie, which often stayed with her in the heart of her flimsy dungeon.

When the young woman was interrogated on the outcome of her chemical triturations, she appeared to be full of joy and hope.

# XXII

IN the midst of all this, Seil Kor reappeared at the head of his black bearers, bending beneath the weight of the merchandise bought with the ransom money. Each tributary had paid in the measure of his means, and the poorest sailors' families, putting all their savings together, had resignedly added their quota to the total.

After a long conference with the Emperor, Seil Kor came to us to communicate the news. The letters we had written having produced a large enough sum, our liberation, from that point of view, would not be delayed. But an unforeseen condition still had to be met.

Since his sanguinary engagement with the Drelshkaffian troops, Talu, seeking out solitude among the trees in the Behuliphruen, had spent many hours in composing a large number of resounding strophes which, taking as their subject the victory gained over Yaour, were to enrich the *Jeruka* with a supplementary canto entitled *The Battle of the Tez*.

At his coronation, the Emperor would have the whole epic sung by his troops; but the new canto, finished only that morning, was yet unknown to the black warriors, and much hard work would be needed to teach it to so numerous an assembly.

Consequently, Talu imposed on Carmichael the task of performing on the appointed day, in a ringing head-voice, the more recent portions of his work. This decision would have the further advantage of giving prominence to the unpublished stanzas of the vast poem and making its first performance a *sensation*.

In singing *The Battle of the Tez,* the young man from Marseilles would retain his male attire, for Talu wanted to anoint himself king of Drelshkaf in the very garb he had worn on the day of his victory, a form of costume he considered both highly effective and full of majesty. The Emperor intended moreover to figure in the programme singing the *Aubade* by Darricelli.

Concluding his explanation, Seil Kor handed Carmichael a large sheet of paper covered by him with strange but perfectly legible words, whose peculiarities of pronunciation were faithfully indicated in French characters; it was *The Battle of the Tez,* transcribed there and then by the young black from the Emperor's dictation.

The melodic line consisted of a single short motive endlessly repeated, and Carmichael easily picked it up from Seil Kor.

Counting on fear to ensure perfect interpretation, Talu made it clear at the outset that the smallest lapse of memory would be punished with three hours' detention during which, in preparation for a further lyric recital under the same rules, Carmichael, immobile and on his feet, his face turned towards one of the sycamores in Trophies Square, would repeat his lesson under the close supervision of a black guard.

The young singer having signified his compulsory acquiescence, Seil Kor, still acting on behalf of Talu, demanded from us our advice on the part Sirdah's thirty-six brothers might play in the coronation ceremonies.

It seemed to us that children of their age would best

be employed as pages and that they would add pictorial detail to the scene by bearing their father's long train at the moment when he should advance majestically towards the altar. But six at the most would find room in this employment, and so lots had to be drawn. Chènevillot therefore undertook to make a big dice which would serve to nominate the chosen among the numerous little boys divided into six rows.

As to the emperor's ten wives, they were to perform the *Luen' Shetuz,* an hieratical dance intimately bound up with the more important ritual occasions.

In conclusion, Seil Kor showed us a long roll of parchment covered with warring groups crudely drawn by Talu.

In the course of his campaigns, the Emperor, without writing anything down, took daily notes in the form of pictures, recording in this way, while the memory was fresh and clear in his mind, the various operations accomplished by his troops.

On his return to the capital, he would then make use of this strategic guide when composing his verses, so that in effect we had before our eyes the original canvas for the *Jeruka.*

Having found in our baggage a recording barometer whose workings he had had explained to him, Talu dreamed of seeing his drawings file past automatically on the moving roller of the precious instrument.

La Billaudière-Maisonnial, accustomed to delicate work of this kind, undertook to fulfil the imperial desire; he removed the fragile mechanism from the barograph and accelerated its movement, so that presently an ingenious apparatus, faced with the parchment roll, turned ceaselessly near the Incomparables stage.

303

# XXIII

SEVERAL more days passed, during which Carmichael parrot-fashion learned the barbaric text of *The Battle of the Tez*. Guided by Seil Kor, he had effortlessly memorised the strange air adapted to the verses and felt himself ready to sing the new fragment of the *Jeruka* with mastery.

On the exchange market, *Carmichaels* had risen further since a Ponukelian song, a monstrous and outlandish work from the point of view both of its words and music, had been substituted for the young Marseillais's habitual repertory.

As the great day approached, speculation soared again, and a final session, which promised to be brisk, was to be held just before the performance opened.

Desirous of contributing to the gala's magnificence by weaving a rich coronation robe for the emperor, Bedu installed his famous loom, which had suffered no damage in the shipwreck, on the Tez.

His design showed a map of Africa surrounded by a wide expanse of sea and marked all the territory under Talu's sway in bright red.

The southern limit of Drelshkaf, being imperfectly known, allowed scope to the artist, and by way of flattery he extended the kingdom as far as the Cape of Good Hope, whose name he set out in full.

The paddle-blades being regulated, the machine was set in motion, and presently a heavy state robe was ready to fall, at the most solemn moment, upon the sovereign's shoulders.

Encouraged by his success, Bedu wanted to arrange a surprise for Sirdah, who had always shown us so much kindness and devotion.

He designed her a sumptuous model cloak, whose ornamentation was to show many moving scenes from the Flood.

The inventor proposed to set his apparatus to execute this on the very morning of the coronation and to let it be carried out before Sirdah, who, after her cure, could not fail to view with a keen pleasure the spectacle afforded by the prodigious mechanism's entrancing play.

Bashku's operation being due to take place at nightfall, an acetylene lamp, found among the equipment of the *Lynceus* and installed at the water's edge, would project upon the machine itself the reflector's dazzle.

To amplify the spectacle on the river's bank, Fuxier meant to prepare a number of his blue pastilles, which, dropped into the stream, would set up on the surface all sorts of distinct if fugitive images.

Before setting to work, he consulted us collectively about subjects to be treated and was offered a great variety of ideas, from which he selected the following:

1. Perseus bearing aloft the head of Medusa.
2. A Spanish fiesta with wild dancing.
3. The legend of the Provençal poet Giapalu, who, going one day to seek inspiration on the picturesque site where Var springs from the earth, allowed his secrets to be discovered by the ancient river, which came and read over his shoulder. Next day, its murmuring waters recited from source to mouth the new verses, which struck with the hallmark of genius,

305

were known at once throughout the land without any author's name being attached to them. Giapalu, dumbfounded, vainly strove to establish his paternity; he was treated as an impostor, and the poor poet died of grief without having known renown.

4. A peculiarity of the land of Cockaigne concerning the regularity of the wind, which provided its inhabitants with the exact time, without any need to look after or wind up clocks.

5. A love affair of the Prince de Conti, recounted by himself in his correspondence in the following discreet terms :

In the spring of the year 1695, François-Louis de Bourbon, Prince de Conti, was the guest of an octogenarian, the Marquis de ***, whose country house lay amid vast, shady parkland.

The previous year, the marquis had married a young wife of whom he was extremely jealous, although his relations with her were those of a father.

Each night, the Prince de Conti visited the marquise, whose twenty years were hardly to be accommodated by eternal solitude.

These visits called for infinite precautions. To provide him with a pretext for flight in case of an alert being raised, the prince, before each meeting, turned loose in the park a tame jay which had for a long time accompanied him on his travels.

One night, having conceived a suspicion, the marquis knocked at his guest's door; obtaining no response, he went into the empty room and saw the absent man's clothes scattered about the furniture.

The octogenarian immediately proceeded to his wife's quarters and demanded to be received forthwith. The marquise opened her window and again closed it noiselessly, while her lover let himself down to the ground. This manoeuvre had taken a few seconds at most, and the door was unlocked as quickly as seemed reasonable.

The jealous old man entered without speaking and searched vainly about his wife's room. After which, the idea of an escape by way of the window having entered his mind, he left the house and began to ferret around the park.

Presently he came upon Conti half-dressed, who explained to him the trouble to which he had been put by the escape of his jay.

The marquis went along with his guest to see if he was speaking the truth. After some few steps, the prince cried: 'Here it is!' and pointed out, perched in a tree, the tame bird, which at the first call flew down and perched on his finger.

The old man's suspicions were at once dissipated, and the honour of the marquise was saved.

Provided with these five subjects, Fuxier once more took up his lump of blue material and embarked on the same kind of minute labour as had already produced the interior modelling needed in a variety of red pastilles for his representations of Shakespeare.

# XXIV

ONE morning, Seil Kor came near to perishing as a result of his devotion to the Emperor. At about ten o'clock, he was carried bleeding into Trophies Square and put in the hands of Dr. Leflaive.

A rapid and unexpected event had caused the accident.

A few minutes before, the traitor Gaïz Duh had succeeded in escaping. Seil Kor, a witness of this daring feat, had flung himself in pursuit of the fugitive, whom he soon caught and seized by the left arm.

Gaïz Duh, whose right hand was holding a weapon, had turned in anger and struck Seil Kor on the head; the slight delay due to this scene of violence had given the guards time to run up and to lead away both the prisoner and his victim.

Dr. Leflaive bandaged the wound and undertook that the invalid should survive.

Next day, all danger of death had been averted, but physical disturbances presently manifested themselves, determined by a cerebral lesion of some gravity. Seil Kor had lost his memory and no longer recognised any of the faces around him.

Darriand, visiting the invalid, saw in this a marvellous opportunity for performing a miracle by the aid of his hypnotic plants. Possessing several rolls of film free of all colouring, he asked Bedu to paint on one of these long, flexible and transparent strips a number of scenes drawn from the most significant period of Seil Kor's life.

The idyll with Nina must incontestably hold preference. Brought into the company of his little friend, whom he would believe really present before his eyes, the young negro might experience a salutary emotion capable of suddenly restoring all his faculties to him.

Among the poor lunatic's treasures was found a large photograph, which, showing Nina in full face, provided Bedu with the necessary indications.


Having finished the preparation of his lozenges, Fuxier, at our request, thought to conclude his sequence of experiments with the swift ripening of a bunch of grapes each of which should enclose a different subject.

New inspirations were sought from one to another of us.

Free to decide for himself how many grapes there should be, Fuxier stopped at ten and cast his choice on the following themes:

1. A glimpse of Celtic Gaul.

2. The famous vision of Count Valtguire, who in a dream saw a demon sawing through the body of his mortal enemy, Odo, son of Robert the Strong. Encouraged by this sign, which appeared to promise him Heaven's support in consigning his adversary to death and damnation, Valtguire, putting all prudence aside, redoubled his zeal in the bloody campaign he was waging against Odo and his followers. This enthusiasm proved fatal to him and resulted in his capture and immediate decollation.

3. An evocation of ancient Rome at the time of its greatest splendour, symbolised by games in the Forum.

4. Napoleon victorious in Spain but cursed by the population always on the point of revolt.

5. A gospel story of St. Luke's recounting three miracles performed by Jesus upon the offspring of Gadaliel and his wife, whose modest hut, illuminated by the divine Master's presence, was suddenly filled with radiant echoes after sheltering the bitterest grief. Two days before the celestial visit, the oldest of the children, a pale, sickly boy of fifteen, had died suddenly while plying his trade as a basket-maker. Stretched out upon his couch, he still held in his stiff fingers the twin osiers with which he was working at the fatal moment. Of two sisters dearly loved by the dead boy, the first had lost her speech as the result of a seizure caused by the sight of his corpse; as to the younger, she was but a plain, hunch-backed cripple, who could not console her parents for their double misfortune. Entering, Jesus stretched out a hand towards the impressionable dumb girl, who, healed immediately, emitted a loud, rapid, endless trill seeming to announce the return of joy and hope. A second movement of the all-powerful hand, this time in the direction of the funeral couch, restored life to the dead youth, who, taking up his interrupted task, bent and knotted the supple, docile withies in his practised fingers. At the same moment, a new marvel was shown forth beneath the dazzled eyes of the parents: Jesus had just touched with his finger the gentle cripple, abruptly beautiful and erect.

6. The ballad of Hans the Lusty, legendary woodcutter of the Black Forest, who in spite of his great age bore on his shoulders more logs and faggots than all his six sons together.

7. A passage from *Émile*, in which Jean-Jacques Rousseau describes at some length his hero's first sensation of virility at the sight of an unknown young woman in poppy-red robe seated at her door.

310

8. A reproduction of Raphael's picture entitled *Satan Wounded by the Angel's Sword*.

Provided with all these materials, Fuxier set to work, affording us the captivating spectacle of his strange, patient labour.

Seated before his vine-stock, he undercut the germ of the future bunch of grapes with steel instruments of extreme delicacy, those which served also for the inner construction of his lozenges or pastilles.

Now and then he dipped into a tiny box for colouring matters suitable for amalgamating with the various figures at the time of their expansion.

For hours at a stretch he pursued his miraculous toil, specifically attacking the precise spot at which the individual grapes should develop, deprived in advance of their stones by this fearful trituration.

# XXV

WHEN everybody had declared himself ready, Talu fixed the date of the coronation and chose the equivalent in the Ponukelian calendar of the 25th of June.

On the 24th, the ichthyologist Martignon, who had never interrupted his canoe excursions along the coast, returned in a state of agitation about a surprising discovery he had just made in the course of deep soundings.

He was carefully carrying in both arms an aquarium entirely hidden beneath a light plaid carriage-rug and refused to display its contents with the purpose of saving up its effects till the following day.

This event made a significant fluctuation in *Martignons* foreseeable for the last session on the market.

On June 25th, from two o'clock in the afternoon, everyone prepared himself for the solemnities.

A cruet called upon to represent the holy *ampulla* was selected from among the oil and vinegar bottles of the *Lynceus*, then placed on the altar to be used by Talu, whom Juillard had instructed in the art of greasing his forehead.

Near this stoppered flagon was propped a large sheet of parchment, a solemn proclamation or bull dictated by the Emperor to Rao.

Balbet, having devised a previously unseen display of marksmanship, stuck in the ground, to the right of the altar, a stout post cut by one of Chènevillot's workmen; behind it, aligned in the desired axis, the trunk of a sycamore presented a limited surface which, flattened vertically on the architect's instructions, should stop the bullets without risk of troublesome rebound.

At the top of the post the celebrated marksman placed an egg coddled by the ship's cook to just such a point that the white was solid and the yolk soft.

This egg, perfectly fresh, had just been laid by one of the hens taken on board the *Lynceus* at Marseilles.


Olga Chervonenkova, her hair and bosom ornamented with foliage picked in the Behuliphruen, had got herself up in a dancer's costume put together by herself with much difficulty. Hector Bucharessas had made her a present of one of his spare pairs of fleshings, which, patiently unpicked and re-sewn, now imprisoned the legs and thighs of the imposing matron; several window curtains, selected from the stock of the upholsterer Beaucreau, had provided muslin for the skirt, and the *ensemble* was completed with a low-necked, sky-blue bodice detached by the Latvian from an evening gown she had brought with her to wear on evenings at the great theatres of Buenos Aires.

Once upon a time, to begin her stage performances in the *Pas de la Nymphe*, Olga, trim and slender, had appeared riding upon a doe, in a wild, deep forest scene. Anxious now to effect a similar entry, the former ballerina meant to be borne in by Sladky, for a trial the previous day had established that the graceful animal was strong enough to support for a few seconds the enormous weight of his mistress.

Awaiting the moment of its appearance, the docile and faithful elk went peacefully about at the Latvian's side.

Bedu had that very morning finished the painted film designed to re-awaken Seil Kor's sleeping memory. Bent on achieving the very sharpest projections, Darriand meant to try the experiment when night had quite fallen, using the cap, mask and ruff Nina had once cut out; the collocation of these three objects, piously preserved by the precocious lover, might indeed contribute largely to the sudden revivification of his old memories.

By working very hard, Louise Montalescot had found the long-sought solution of her problem. Spending all night in her laboratory, sufficiently lighted by a moon then full and at its brightest, the young woman was certain of completing her apparatus, which would be ready to function at daybreak. The poetical first light of dawn would lend itself perfectly to a first attempt at automatic reproduction, and Talu, full of curiosity, gave his approbation to Sirdah, charged with the task of submitting to him this plan for an early morning experiment.

As to the magpie, it had now learnt its part with flawless certainty, and the Emperor only had to choose his moment to put it to the proof. The helot himself was to be set in movement by the bird upon two lines which Norbert had just made out of veal lung provided by the ship's cook.

As four o'clock approached, Mossem, Rul, Gaïz Duh and Jizme were shut into the prison constructed by Chènevillot.

Rao kept the key, then set about recruiting a handful of

slaves to help him in the task of organisation which the Emperor had long since confided to him.

Presently, Talu appeared in full dress.

All the extras and supers were in place, including the Ponukelian troops who were to sing the *Jeruka*.

As the great hour approached, Juillard gave his last instructions to our group, already gathered on the south of the public place.

In the matter of awarding decorations, the historian would go by the instinctive reactions of the black public, which seemed likely to offer a just and sincere judgement.

Since our applause was likely to influence the native audience and above all to affect the distributor of insignia, we were asked to preserve a mute immobility after each display.

At the last moment, wishing to make as sensational an entry as possible, the Emperor told Rao to draw up outside Trophies Square a procession to move forward slowly in a determined order.

Silence fell among us all, and the reader knows how the ceremony of the coronation, then the gala performance, completed after a peaceful night by Louise Montalescot's experiment, were followed by the aggravating detention which Carmichael had to endure in my company under the eyes of a native sentinel.

# XXVI

For three hours past, the young man from Marseilles, afraid of a second punishment, had been practising *The Battle of the Tez*, which he now quietly sang through without me being able to detect a single fault on the text in the sycamore shade.

Suddenly Talu, appearing in the distance, approached us accompanied by Sirdah.

The Emperor himself had come to release his brilliant interpreter, whom he wished to submit without delay to a further trial.

Delighted to be put to the test at a moment when his freshly exercised memory made him sure of himself, Carmichael, singing out now in full soprano register, this time articulated every word of the incomprehensible song through to the end without the least error.

Dazzled by this faultless execution, Talu set off on his way back to the imperial hut, charging Sirdah to express his entire contentment to the interested party.

Liberated by so agreeable an expression of opinion, Carmichael took from my hands, and tore up with joyful haste, the infernal text which reminded him of so many hours of nerve-racking and tedious labour.

This gesture of harmless revenge meeting with my full inward approbation, I left Trophies Square in his company to see to my packing, which there was nothing now to delay.

Our departure took place that very day, in the early afternoon. The Montalescots were attached to the procession, which, led by Seil Kor now wholly cured, comprised all those who had sailed with the *Lynceus*.

Talu had placed at our disposition a certain number of natives ordered to carry our provisions and such baggage as we had left.

A litter borne by four blacks was reserved to Olga Chervonenkova, still suffering from her torn ligament.

Ten days' march took us to Porto Novo; there, loaded with well-deserved thanks for his loyal services, Seil Kor bade us farewell and with his escort set off again on the road to Ejur.

The captain of a liner bound for Marseilles agreed to see to our repatriation. It was to France that everybody was anxious to return, for, after so many disturbing adventures, there was no longer any question of proceeding directly to America.

We made an uneventful crossing, and on the 19th of July we took leave of each other on the quayside at La Joliette, after a cordial exchange of handshakes, in which only Tancred Bucharessas could take no part.